"Fun yet serious, this no-holds-barred novel tackles peri-menopause brilliantly. I loved reading how Nika came into her own. I finished it in one sitting and am recommending it to everyone!"
—Barbara Bos, founder of *Women Writers, Women's Books*

"*The Marriage Debt* highlights the lasting strength of love and friendship when experiencing life's inevitable transformations. Consolino's insightful writing makes this book a must-read for anyone who values novels that explore the intricacies of daily life and the resilience of the human spirit."
—Carol Thompson for Reader's Favorite

"*The Marriage Debt* is an unbridled glimpse into a middle-aged perimenopausal woman's life, one that's astoundingly important as well as often overlooked. Christina Consolino writes complex, realistic family stories with grace, honesty, and wisdom that allows the reader to empathize and root for her female-identified main characters with fervor. This impactful story of expectations when married—between parents, children, and husbands—is beautifully told and will stick with you long after you read the last page. Read it, let it resonate, then share it with your loved ones so that they can feel heard and seen, which is always a gift in Consolino's novels."

—C. D'Angelo, award-winning author of *The Gift*

"At long last, an absolutely absorbing, heartfelt novel that brilliantly fences with the taboos of aging, sexual dysfunction, and faltering family dynamics! *The Marriage Debt*'s engaging, authentic characters will resonate with readers of all ages."

—*New York Times* bestselling author Parris Afton Bonds

"In *The Marriage Debt*, Consolino bravely tackles issues of women's bodily changes and how that can impact intimacy and relationships of all stripes. Too often, these issues are trivialized, overlooked, or swept aside in stories—and in society. Consolino's engaging and page-turning novel approaches these issues with compassion and sensitivity--never lecturing or stopping the action to pontificate, but instead showing how one woman might handle these issues in a way that's both true to herself and compassionate to her partner. Heartfelt, relevant, and timely!"

—Sharon Short, author of *Trouble Island*

the marriage debt

CHRISTINA CONSOLINO

Text copyright © 2025 by Christina Consolino
All Rights Reserved. Printed in the United States of America
Published by Motina Books, LLC, Highlands Ranch, Colorado
www.MotinaBooks.com

Library of Congress Cataloguing-in-Publication Data:
Names: Consolino, Christina
Title: The Marriage Debt
Description: First Edition. | Highlands Ranch:
Motina Books, 2025

Identifiers:
LCCN: 2024953100

ISBN-13: 979-8-88784-054-3 (e-book)
ISBN-13: 979-8-88784-055-0 (paperback)

Subjects: BISAC:
FICTION / Women
FICTION / Friendship
FICTION / Family Life / General

Cover Art and Design
Kim Wilson, Kiwi Cover Design Co.
Sarah Kil, Sarah Kil Creative Studio

To Kelsey and Jane,
two extraordinary librarians and friends.
You have made an enormous difference in many people's
lives.

And to Timmy,
whose humor, patience, and love
have made a difference in mine.

Your task is not to seek for love,
but merely to seek and find all the barriers within yourself
that you have built against it.
~Rumi

prologue

The clock ticks away as Nika Stewart lies awake, eyes wide open. The room is awash in dull grays and browns and blacks, and Nika blinks to make out the numbers on the clock. Four fifty-six.

Next to her on the mattress, her husband fidgets, and the covers slide away from her legs. Goosebumps follow as a cool breeze whispers past her. Without the covers completely shielding her body, there's no hope of going back to sleep.

She pulls on the coverlet and rolls to her side, dragging much of the fabric with her. Then, Ethan's warm hand settles on her hip. Within seconds, his fingers migrate across her belly and below. Always a morning person, Nika won't mind the early start to her day, but she's not in the mood for sex at this moment. Though she's cold now, within the blink of an eye, her body will likely become a raging inferno, her skin full of brambles. So far, menopause has been a bitch to deal with, the symptoms holding onto her with the tenacity of the wild violets littering the flower beds. Nika squirms against Ethan's solid chest, but he pulls the elastic of her pajamas away from her body, sliding them down her legs with his feet. Then, he gets to work on her panties.

"Now?" she says.

"Yes, why not?" He nuzzles his nose against Nika's neck and inhales.

"Because . . ." Thoughts invade Nika's mind. *Because I'm tired. Because this week has been difficult. Because I don't want to.* But once the sun throws back its own covers, any intimacy will be left behind. And who knows what the day might bring?

Ethan inhales once more. "You know what? It's okay. It's early, and you like a slow slide into your day. Maybe tomorrow." He burrows his head into her hair and holds her.

Nika considers his words. Ethan is listening to her, and she knows—truly knows—his intent is not to manipulate. Plus, if she goes ahead now, she won't feel guilty about saying no tomorrow. "No, no, it's okay, but if I feel ready to combust, I'll let you know. And then . . ."

The darkness of the room masks Ethan's expression, but his answer—gentle kisses in quick succession on her forehead, nose, throat, and belly—is enthusiastic, reminding her he is a virile man, which means he follows one credo when it comes to sex: the only bad sex is no sex at all. He presses up against Nika, his chest and legs aligning along the back of her. He's ready and probably has been for some time. Maybe even all night.

Within seconds, Nika settles on her back, and Ethan nestles himself between her legs. This won't be the first time she's gone ahead with sex even when she doesn't truly feel like it, and she's not the only person to have ever felt this way. Yesterday at the track, she overheard two women chatting about their lack of libido thanks to the approaching "change."

"Wow, you're ready," Ethan says as he moves against Nika like soft waves pushing against a shore.

Despite all the hormonal shifts, Nika still menstruates pretty regularly. "Well, I *am* midcycle."

Ethan stops his actions, and a frosty silence hangs in the air between them. "Can't you, I don't know, one time, say it's because of me? Because you want this?"

He's right, but it's too early for Nika to reflect on her words and where they come from. "It is, honey. It's because of you." She doesn't want to reflect on his words, either, or the disappointment most likely rising inside him right now.

He sighs and dips his face toward Nika's. The dim moonlight peeks between the curtains and highlights his furrowed brow. "You could at least act like you mean it."

Right once again, Nika thinks, but he's also not a perimenopausal woman with minimal desire for intimacy and increased sensitivity to heat. Even now, fire races along her belly, her thighs, her shins—any part of her in contact with her husband. Nika doesn't dwell there, instead swiveling her hips, bumping up against him and leaning in to press her warm lips to his sturdy chest. It's enough to get him to quit talking and move again. If he moves, he'll finish.

Afterward, Nika rolls out of bed, ready to begin her day. They're supposed to head to an annual brunch with the family up the street, and she offered to bring muffins and fresh fruit. The rest of the day will be filled with sports, grocery shopping, and laundry, along with anything else that always pops up unexpectedly in their married-with-kids life. Nika looks back once at Ethan. He's lying against the pillows, arms above his head, legs akimbo, a contented smile on his face.

"I love you, Nika," he whispers, extending a hand and grasping her fingers in his.

"I love you too," she replies, her heart sagging with heaviness. A good excuse for not wanting to have sex doesn't exist. So what about the next time the conversation arises? What will she say then?

chapter one

"All right, friends, it's time to pack up! What did we learn today?"

Twenty-five little hands from six- and seven-year-old first graders shoot into the air. The children wave their entire arms in big circles to get Nika's attention. Being an elementary school librarian is one of her toughest roles, but she loves it, daily grind or not. These kids—their potential, their energy, their giant hearts. They've certainly got hers right in the palms of their hands.

"Alanna? Go ahead."

"A book has a spine, like me."

"Yes, wonderful. And where is the book's spine?"

Alanna grabs an *A to Z Mysteries* book sitting in the table center and runs her finger down the length of the covered binding. "Right here!" she says and then lays the book down with a reverence of which Nika is proud.

"Indeed. And what else, friends?" Nika glances around the room. Gwendolyn, one of the youngest in the class, sits in her usual chair, hands on her lap, head cast down. She always has a lot to say, but most information requires a crowbar.

Nika kneels in front of her, barely catching the child's gaze. "Gwendolyn? What can you share with us today?"

She lifts her head, her large brown eyes wide. "Ms. Stewart, I . . ." She stops, looks around, and starts again. "A book has something called a *verso* in it. It's a page, but I can't remember what one."

"Nice job!" Nika holds her hand up for a high five. In usual Gwendolyn form, she returns the gesture by extending only her index finger, the tip of which barely kisses Nika's palm. "Did I talk about that word in this class?" She usually doesn't introduce the concept to her first graders. *Verso* and its definition are on the list of things to present to the fifth graders over the next few weeks.

A redness spreads across Gwendolyn's cheeks, and her voice drops. "No, but I saw the word over there." She points to Nika's lesson-plan pile on the media cart.

"Outstanding, Gwendolyn!" Nika defines the word and talks about its etymology, and while most of the kids don't care, Gwendolyn straightens her back and cocks her head, rapt with attention. Of all the children Nika sees on a weekly basis, Gwendolyn is by far the one most likely to become a librarian one day. Or maybe a research scientist.

"Ms. Stewart! Ms. Stewart!" Reggie draws attention with his high-pitched, dolphin-like squeal. He tips his chair to one side and then the other.

Without words, Nika slips a gentle hand on his shoulder, steadying him in place. She's seen too many accidents involving flipped chairs, children's heads, and the emergency room to let him continue his movement. "Yes, Reggie?"

"Jackson farted!"

The whole class erupts into giggles, which quickly turn to loud guffaws, and Nika can't help but stifle her own laugh. It's the end of the day—an unseasonably warm March first in Five Rivers, Ohio—so Nika lets them go on for a minute, and then, she claps her hands. "Class, class, class!" she says with each clap.

"Yes, yes, yes," the kids reply, a hush spreading over the room.

"Thank you for the information, Reggie, but next time, please keep it to yourself. A reminder to all of you—bodily functions should be taken care of in the restroom, please." Nika punctuates her sentence with a wink, and a collective, relieved sigh reverberates around the room. "Now, it's time to line up and head back to your classroom. I'll see you next week."

Being a librarian means Nika sees every student in the school once a week. From time to time, she allows the older students to come into the library to spend a half hour here or there researching and looking for books, but with a school their size—over 600 students in kindergarten through fifth grade alone—she doesn't have the space and time to allow browsing like the public library does.

As Nika pushes in random chairs, she regards the hallway. It's beginning to fill with the end-of-the-day rush, and little feet tap against the checkered linoleum, the swarm of older students eventually swallowing the sound.

She stands at the library door, arms folded, giving only a slight wave to those students who show interest. Reggie smirks at her, and Alannah blows her a kiss before she walks around the corner. As the bussers head to their buses at the front of the building and the walkers leave by the side door, an adult face pops up in the crowd. Rainey Delaney—the students are endlessly entertained by her name—Nika's dearest friend and confidante and Evergreen Elementary School's second-grade teacher extraordinaire.

"We're still on for tonight?" she calls out.

Nika looks at her watch, checking the date. Rainey has been trying to get her to give up the watch—"You have a phone with the date you know?" she always says—but old habits are hard to break. "What's tonight?"

"You know, the Sip and Savor at Wine Bar." With her arms above her and shimmying her hips like a hula dancer, Rainey scoots through the crowd toward Nika. The kids around her clutch their bellies in laughter.

"Shoot, I forgot," Nika admits.

"Come on. You haven't been out in ages, and I mean *ages*." Rainey places her hands on her hips and waggles her eyebrows, then takes one of Nika's hands in hers and flips it over. "This here," she says and traces the palm with her index finger. "Is your life line. And it's long. It means you need to live a little."

Rainey's words touch a nerve. Nika has been accused of not "living a little" one too many times, but in all honesty, Friday nights are her time to chill, to find herself again, to recharge for the new week, which always comes too soon. The students take a lot out of her, and so do her own kids. And Ethan? Well, as much as she loves him, he's another stratum of complexity in her very full life. Nika slaps Rainey's hand away. "Cute. I'm only letting you get away with this since you're my best friend."

"I know. Is my tactic working?"

Nika glares at Rainey out of the side of her eye. "Maybe."

Rainey fist-bumps the air, catching the attention again of a few second graders in the process. "I'm happy, friends!" She waves to the children and then whisks away, worming her way through the dwindling cloud of students. Before she can get too far, Rainey turns back and cups her hands around her mouth, shouting down the hall. "You need to come tonight. It will do you some good!" She raises her eyebrows again, and despite the distance, it's like she's looking inside Nika, as if she can see something Nika cannot or hasn't been willing to give up.

Come tonight. Is she talking about going to the Sip and Savor or something else?

Because of the distance between them and Nika's refusal to yell in the hallway—rule follower number one right there—she pulls out her phone, holds it up for Rainey to see, and then sends a text in answer to the verbalized question: *Okay, what time? I have some things to do here for the play. I'll check in with Ethan to be sure there's nothing outstanding on the calendar.*

Seven. Woot! Rainey's text reads. She blows a kiss and waltzes under the archway of the second- and third-grade hallway, her thick, black braid bouncing on her shoulders in time with her steps.

~

Thirty minutes later, when Nika digs her head out of boxes of scripts, set-design books, and permission slips for the play she's directing at the school, she texts Ethan: *You okay for dinner? We have leftovers in the fridge.*

Ethan quickly replies: *Yeah. What's up?*

Nika: *Rainey. She's pulling me to a Sip and Savor.*

Nika can only imagine what Ethan thinks. Wine and Nika have never fared well; even a small taste of the beverage causes debilitating headaches. Years ago, when Nika still attended church regularly, she explained to an overly nosy pastor why she didn't partake of the blood of Christ. Instead of understanding, he doled out judgment. Needless to say, she never went back to that church.

Ethan: *Wine?*

Her husband knows her well.

Nika: *Yeah. They have cider there. It will be fine.*

Ethan: *Good for you. Hope you have fun. Do the kids need anything from me?*

Lila and Alex are Nika's children from her first marriage, but genetics has never stood in the way of Ethan's concern for them.

Nika: *Both are headed to friends' houses. Staying through dinner. What about a sleepover? You okay if they ask about it?*

Ethan: *If their parents are okay with it, I am too.*

Nika's toe catches on a box she didn't see.

Ethan's text continues: *And then we'd have time to . . .*

The conversation is heading into let's-rankle-Nika territory, one she's not ready to explore. Not here in an elementary school library, not here at this moment in time. Maybe not ever. She's smart enough and old enough to know nothing good comes from burying your head in the sand, but sometimes, it's what she does to get herself through. So, she ignores what she *should do*—talk openly with her husband about her lack of desire, the hormonal shifts inside her body, the anxieties and issues plaguing her—and instead does what she does best, asks a question: *Didn't we do that a few days ago?*

Ethan: *Yes.*

Nika: *It might be late when I get back, so maybe.*

How many times can she crush this man's desires? Apparently, too many.

chapter two

Before Nika walks through the doors of the creatively named Wine Bar, she glances down at her shirt. She half expects to see detritus from her exchange with Ethan, when she buried her head in the sand once again, and she rubs at the fabric with her fingers. It's all in her mind, of course, but refusing to face some facts as often as she does can manipulate a persona in strange ways. Plus, dusting off something she's worn for the last twelve hours can't hurt, can it? At least a few lint or paper pieces or kid cooties hightail it to the floor, if nothing else.

Nika's tired eyes scan the room, and her glance falls on Rainey, sitting in the corner at a table meant for a small group. A genuine peace fills Nika's body and mind. If Rainey had planned a big bash with lots of unfamiliar-to-Nika people, she'd have found a larger table. Small gatherings are good; one-on-one meetings are even better.

Rainey lights up when she sees Nika, and she stands from the table, her foot tapping a beat to the bluesy tune filtering through hidden speakers. Even though they saw one another a few hours prior, Rainey pulls Nika into a giant hug lasting exactly as long as Nika needs it to. Rainey has applied mascara and lipstick—things she doesn't usually wear to school—and Nika wonders what her game is.

"Anyone else joining us tonight?" Nika can hope it will only be the two of them, but she knows Rainey. She's a people person through and through. Born with a phone in one hand, a good word in the other, she sparks conversation wherever she goes: grocery stores, airports, post offices. Years back, she almost got arrested for hitting a cop in a barroom brawl. Rainey hadn't intentionally connected her hand with the cop's face; the hit stemmed from animated talking on her part, and surveillance footage supported her claim. Before they left for the night, Rainey had the cop and most others at the bar, man or woman, asking for her phone number. To this day, she's still friends with some of those characters on Facebook.

Rainey sits and pats the seat next to her. Wine Bar has sets of low-top and high-top tables, but Nika and Rainey are both vertically challenged; Rainey left the high seats to the tall folks. Nika sits, then pulls out the menu, perusing the options for the evening, hoping they have a cherry cider on tap. She and Ethan tried one on their last trip to Traverse City, Michigan. It had been her favorite ever since.

"Not sure yet," Rainey finally says in answer to Nika's question.

Something about Rainey's tone worries Nika, and she glances at her. Rainey is still glowing, and Nika doesn't know why. Has Nika been so absorbed by her own situation that she's missed the details of her good friend's life? "Okay, fess up. Who did you invite? I know it's not Ethan. He's at home with the leftovers."

Rainey smiles. "Sitting on the couch in his boxer briefs, right?"

"Probably. Maybe crumbs in his scruff, tumbling onto his shirt. A beer too. He probably has a beer."

"Oh, girl!" Rainey slaps the top of Nika's hand. "I see it. I can so see it. But Ethan," she takes a sip of her wine, "he's yummy."

An image of Ethan sitting on the couch hovers in Nika's mind. Even in his shorts and ratty T-shirt, possible crumbs and all, he is yummy. She doesn't dwell on the thought. "And he's mine, so he's not the one you're expecting. Who is it?"

Nika's mind flits to the men Rainey has dated in the past few months: a tall, dark, man-bunned barista from the coffee shop around the corner from the school; a divorced, millennial truck driver—complete with gold front tooth— she met at a truck stop in Richmond, Indiana; a single, computer programmer dad from the pool she frequents in the summer. At close to fifty, it's doubtful Rainey will ever settle down—her words, not Nika's—but Rainey has a lot to offer a relationship. She backs up a friend ferociously until they tell her they actually made the egregious error someone accused them of. She'll also arrive at a friend's doorstep with a thermos full of homemade soup on any sick day. And cookies. She bakes them—everything from peppermint clouds to perfectly chewy chocolate chip—*and* drops them off, just because. The kids can't get enough of her, and Alex has already told her to save herself for him.

Rainey's lips pull into a sly smile, and she says, "You'll see."

Her words make Nika wary, but she has no choice but to sit and wait. A server floats by, asking if there's anything she can get her—a cherry hard cider it is—and after dropping the drink off, the manager arrives at the table. Apparently, word is out the establishment might be closing.

"All good here," Rainey says. "And I hope you aren't shutting your doors."

"We're not. I don't know who started the rumor, but that's what it is, a rumor."

"Rumors can hurt, relationships especially," a voice behind them quips. A tall, broad man with black hair and a salt-and-pepper goatee stands there, hands on hips, smile on his face. He's wearing a gray suit, casual yet refined, almost like he'd be on the cover of one of Rainey's preferred Billionaire novels. Something about him exudes warmth, and yet, Nika recognizes a certain smarminess emanating from him.

Smarmy Man moves toward Rainey, leaning in and giving her a hug before pulling a chair close and sitting down.

The manager seems to take that as his cue to leave, and he taps the table. "Let me know if you need anything, and spread the good word—we're here for the long haul, okay?"

"Will do," Rainey says and then turns to the newcomer. "Kenrick Ainsworth, meet my best friend, Nika Stewart. Nika, meet Kenrick."

Under the muted bar lights, it's difficult to see his face clearly—Nika's eyesight has been a thorn in her side since she was a child—but a quick quirk of Kenrick's lips leads to a full-on grin. Definitely a cover model for a Billionaire book. *Baby with the Billionaire? The Billionaire's Revenge?* Maybe *Falling for the Billionaire*—

" . . . to meet you, Nika." Kenrick extends a hand,

gripping Nika's cool hand with strong and sturdy fingers. The handshake lasts a smidge too long.

"And you as well. How do you know Rainey?"

"Oh, we go way back."

Nika turns toward Rainey and narrows her gaze. How has she never heard of this guy? What does Kenrick mean to Rainey?

Rainey nods. "I met Kenrick in college. Had a bit of fun, lost touch with him, then found him again. I'm sure I've mentioned him before . . ."

She doesn't get time to finish her sentence. A curly haired woman dressed in a black oversize sweater and leggings appears out of nowhere and slides in beside Nika before bursting forth with a lift of her hand and her own unsolicited introduction.

"Evangeline Baker. So good to see you again, R." She dips her head toward Rainey and then glances at Kenrick and Nika. "Should be a good night here. Wine Bar is a great place for gatherings." Her grin takes up her entire face, and she reaches for a menu before lifting her arm above her head, as if to call for the server. Nika's surprised she doesn't snap at the female server and say, "Garçon!" but her tactic works.

The server hustles over. "May I get you something?"

Evangeline twirls a dark curl around her finger. "A glass of Chablis, please." She rests her hands in her lap, then moves them to the table before grabbing a napkin and twisting it between her fingers.

Nika is starting to regret her choice of agreeing to this outing. First Smarmy Man and then Napkin Wringer. Normally, Rainey's friends are a delight, if not a handful, but it's been a long week, and Nika would much rather be sitting with Ethan on the couch—underwear, crumbs, and all. *Maybe*

I'll head to the restroom and let Ethan know he needs to save me.

"And you, sir?" the server asks Kenrick.

"May I please have a glass of your finest red? Whatever that may be."

"Do you—"

"No worries, really. I love to be surprised. So, surprise me." He winks at the server and hands her the menu. A blush spreads up the server's face—she can't be more than twenty-two or three—and with Kenrick's baritone voice, she's probably charmed.

Chatting with new people is often difficult for Nika, but because everyone knows Rainey, the conversation flows organically. Rainey shares the details of her Friday, a story Nika hasn't heard yet about one of her most creative—aka difficult—students, and Kenrick and Evangeline delve into their days as well.

With each sip of cider, Nika's mind roams, and her gaze moves from one corner to the next. An elderly couple huddles in a dimly lit booth, two half-full glasses of wine on the table before them. Two men—lovers or friends?—sit at the bar. One leans in and whispers into the other's ear; an intense blush spreads up the man's cheeks. Lovers it is. Or wannabe lovers. A server twirls from table to table, a genuine smile on her face as she takes orders and delivers them. Soulful blues music streams from the speakers and adds to the ambience, and Nika understands why people like it here. And the cider? It's as good as the Traverse City bottle. Next to her, her three tablemates continue to talk, snippets of the conversation reaching her ears.

" . . . therapist's notebook . . ."

"I'd love to be a fly on the wall during sessions . . ."

" . . . no one wants to talk about it."

"Even a one-night stand? You can't believe that! Sex is *never* just sex . . ."

The word *sex* yanks Nika's thoughts back to the table, and she waits for Evangeline to finish her sentence, but she lets it trail off, accompanied by a smirk and the widening of her eyes.

"What the heck are you talking about?" Nika says.

"Sex."

"I get *that*." Nika looks at Rainey. Nika's not a prude, but she doesn't know these people. Apparently, she chose the wrong time to zone out on a conversation. Or maybe it had been the right time, like a subconscious avoidance tactic.

"Where were you, Nika? These two were sharing a few tales from the crypt about their work week."

That description and the bits of overheard conversation tumble in Nika's brain, and puzzle pieces begin to align themselves.

"Wait a minute." Nika's gaze bounces between Kenrick and Evangeline. "Are you therapists? Sex therapists?"

Kenrick says, "*I* am," in a tone that conjures the word *supercilious* in Nika's mind.

"And did you first meet tonight," Nika turns toward Evangeline, "or do you work together? Are you a sex therapist too?"

Evangeline waves off the last question. "No, we just met! I can't wait to pick his brain. I've always wondered about the profession, and," her voice dips, "let's be honest—sex is *fun*!"

In Nika's imagination, Evangeline stands up, places one hand on her hip and the other in the air, then shouts, "Listen up! On the floor! With every pour you know we'll score!" *Rah-rah, sis boom bah!* At the table, the woman just smiles, her teeth glinting under the soft lighting.

"Of course, anything I say tonight has to be taken with a grain of salt," Kenrick says. "This isn't the office." There's the false charm again.

Was this a setup? Had Rainey ambushed her? Nika's heart thuds against her ribcage, and an itchiness spreads underneath her skin. If she's not careful, her breathing will change next, and then, a full-on panic attack. Her body knows she doesn't want to be here anymore, in a situation beyond her control, one she didn't facilitate; it's up to her mind to make the call to retreat.

As Kenrick and Evangeline, who turns out to be a Pilates instructor, continue their stories, Nika inhales deeply several times and places her napkin on the table. "Excuse me, this has been fascinating." She rises. "Sex is one of my favorite topics—I think it's important to understand the anatomy and physiology of it, as well as all the emotional components. In fact, I'm up front with my kids. There's no shame in sex." Nika steps away from her chair and scoots it in. "As much as I'd love to continue this conversation, it's time for me to go. The cider did something to my stomach, or maybe it's the virus going around Evergreen."

Evangeline perks up. "You work there too?"

"Yes. I'm the school librarian, and I direct the fifth-grade play. We're doing *Once Upon a Fairy Tale* this year."

"How lovely." Evangeline places her hands underneath her chin and doesn't look away from Nika.

Something about the gesture is unnerving. "Indeed. Perhaps we can meet again soon. Maybe I'll see you at the play." Nika musters a tense smile. Kenrick has the manners to stand, and she waves to them as she walks from the table, her unease apparent in her quaking hands.

Not more than five seconds pass before someone tugs

on Nika's sleeve—Rainey. Nika pulls her arm away. "Really? You aren't trying to tell me something, are you?"

Rainey has the decency to shrink back, enough to make Nika feel as though she's asking forgiveness. "Yes."

"Well don't beat around the bush!"

"I'm not!"

They move into the lobby of the bar. "That was sarcasm, Rainey. Clearly you aren't. Couldn't we have had a normal conversation about the topic I asked you to keep to yourself? Bringing in a sex therapist seems a bit extreme. And someone else who's so in love with sex? It's like you're trying to play matchmaker or something."

Rainey holds her palms up. "Listen. Yes, Kenrick is a sex therapist, and Evangeline, well, she is *enthusiastic* about the topic—"

"That's one way to put it."

"But I didn't plan this. I wanted to catch up with each of them *and* with you. Not once—cross my heart—did I seriously think we'd talk about sex tonight. We're best friends, Nik, and I wouldn't do that to you. I also wouldn't share what you told me with anyone else, unless you gave me permission. I would not betray your trust like that."

Nika and Rainey go back years, decades, to before Ethan, before Evergreen. Not once in those decades has Rainey lied to her. "Well, I appreciate your discretion and won't disown you, but they'll know something is up. My exit wasn't the most graceful."

Rainey rubs Nika's shoulder. "It's fine. I'll cover for you. You're my best friend. They won't give two shits about why you left. But I'm telling you—you *need* to address this, whatever it is. The convo back there," Rainey jerks her thumb toward the table, "triggered you. I've mentioned therapy before—no, not with Kenrick, with someone *you* choose. Not addressing your limited libido isn't fair to Ethan, but most importantly, it's not fair to *you*. Sex can be fun. It's not always, especially at our age. I want you to enjoy it, if that's what you want. You owe it to yourself to at least think about it." Her eyes plead with Nika.

As usual, when it comes to Rainey, Nika's resolve softens. "That's sort of what Ethan's saying, too, I think."

"And that, my friend, is why you need to keep him, why you need to see someone or come up with a plan. Your reaction tonight—thinking I might be trying to ambush you, the conversation making you so uncomfortable. Whether or not you realize it, something more than menopause could be involved. Maybe it's time to try and find out what and change it. If you don't try to make changes, what's to say Ethan won't make his own change and walk away?"

Interior: Michael and Evelyn Washington's Bedroom,
1984

NIKA, age six, wakes up from a bad dream and enters
her parents' bedroom. She moves to her mother's side
of the bed.

                      NIKA
                   (whispers)
             Mama? Are you awake?

                     Evelyn

                       ...

                      NIKA
                   (whispers)
                Mama? Ma-ma?

NIKA extends her hands to the mattress, and the
sheets feel cool. She moves her fingers back and
forth over the fabric, but the bed is empty. A door
creaks, and NIKA's eyes go wide in fear. She isn't
sure where her mother is, but she turns her head
toward the sound.

Light from the bathroom spills into the room, and
MICHAEL stands there in silhouette. He is naked, and
NIKA isn't sure what to do.

                     MICHAEL
             Evelyn, is that you?

                      NIKA
         It's me, Daddy. It's Nika. I had a bad—

MICHAEL
What the hell are you doing here?

NIKA
(in tears)
I ... I had a bad dream and I ...

MICHAEL grabs a towel and wraps it around his
waist, covering up what NIKA knows is his penis.
She's never seen it before, but it looks scary, like
a snake. Something she doesn't want to see again.

MICHAEL
Get the hell out of here, Nika!

chapter three

Ethan walking away had never occurred to Nika, probably because he'd waltzed into her life so effortlessly. They'd met at a set of dance classes Rainey had dragged Nika to as her sidekick; Rainey had been cast as the maid of honor for her younger sister's wedding and instantly proclaimed, "Dance lessons are a must!" Ethan and Nika were paired up the first week; they'd gone on their first date by the second week; he asked if it was okay to meet her kids by the third week. Over a decade had passed, and he'd been devoted to Nika, Lila, and Alex ever since.

But Rainey's words give Nika much to think about, and she's grateful for the fifteen-minute drive home. The night air, unexpectedly warm and redolent with the heady aroma of an early spring, helps soothe her frayed nerves, and she puts her car window down six inches instead of the normal three. The fresh, damp wind hits her face, spilling a sense of calm over her entire body.

Calm isn't something Nika comes by naturally; usually, anxieties hover like fireflies, blinking on and off, on and off. After her first husband left her with two young children and a pile of bills, the anxiety skyrocketed. Nika's dad moved in that year as well, several months after her stepmother left him. The dark night—all blues and grays and blacks—somehow emphasizes the pattern of repeated loss; is it possible Ethan might leave her too?

Nika parks the car in the driveway, and her phone lights up as she unplugs it from the charger, the glow chasing the unsavory thoughts away. For now. A text Ethan sent an hour prior reveals the kids have, indeed, been asked to sleep over at their respective friends' homes, which means Ethan and Nika can have alone time. What he'll want to do is obvious, but chatting would be better. It's been too long, maybe by seven years or so.

Nika walks toward the well-worn front door, and the house looks deserted, the front porch light flickering, the living room blinds yawning wide. The scene unsettles Nika, and out of habit, she checks her phone again. No new text alerting her to a change of plans. Perhaps Ethan simply fell asleep on the couch. *Crumbs. Underwear. Ethan.* She smiles.

After letting herself in the front door, Nika makes her way to the back of the house; a nightlight near the kitchen sink illuminates the counter, revealing dirty dishes Ethan forgot to put into the dishwasher. She sighs, but fatigue keeps her from doing anything about them. Her mind is spent, and she's worried: if her best friend thinks she needs help, maybe she does. Maybe this *is* about more than her perimenopausal state. Maybe she's seriously broken.

Nika places her purse on the counter and moves toward

the stairs. Everything is still shrouded in silence. Usually, giggles from Lila and her friends or bellows from Alex and his video games fight for dominance. Sometimes, the volume from Dad's television cuts through the cacophony. But Dad is out of state visiting a cousin in Los Angeles. Now, nothing but the plink from the kids' bathtub—it's been waiting for months to be fixed—reverberates in the darkness. Nika will need to put that item on the list for the plumber to attend to. Or maybe Ethan can take care of it tomorrow. Shoot, a YouTube video and Rainey would work as well.

The stairs creak as Nika nears the upper landing; their bedroom door is almost closed, but light flickers from the television, pulsing through the crack between the door and the doorjamb. One faint push, and the door opens. Nika takes two steps into the L-shaped room and glances around the corner at the bed. Her stomach drops, and she stands there, motionless. Speechless. Flabbergasted.

And Ethan? He's not standing. He's lying on the bed, pillows beneath his tilted head, penis in his right hand, sheet in his left. One grunt . . . two. That's all it takes for Nika to turn her back with the intention of fleeing. Of course, she figured Ethan took care of himself from time to time—most likely in the privacy of the shower as she prepped for the day downstairs—he's a typical man for God's sake. But until now, Nika had never witnessed the act and honestly, she doesn't *want* to witness it. Seeing her husband gratifying himself . . . Well, she can't unsee what she saw, can she?

A dumbbell thwarts Nika's plan to tiptoe out of the room, her toe snagging against its cast-iron edge. A snicker laced with embarrassment and pain erupts from her as she collapses onto the carpet. "Shit!" The whisper comes out louder than she intends, and a nervous chuckle rises in her throat.

A slight rustle of sheets. "Nika? Is that you?"

"Uh, yeah. Who else would it be?" She rubs her toe and clenches her eyelids shut so hard fireworks explode behind them. "Couldn't you have at least locked the door?"

"The kids aren't home."

"I know, but I don't need to see *that*." Using the dresser for leverage, Nika pulls herself to standing, shakes her foot, and then rubs her toe again with her fingers. This toe has been injured so many times, it's a wonder the nail hasn't fallen off already.

"Why not?" Ethan says, still on the bed, family jewels on display.

"Because I don't. And before you say anything, go grab some underwear. I can't do this right now."

Ethan's frown almost launches itself across the room. "When *can* you do this?"

Walking away is rarely the best option—her parents taught her that with their repeated actions—but Nika heads for the dark bathroom, places her forehead against the wall, and closes her eyes. Nika isn't a prude. People "tap into their potential" all the time, but Nika has always thought being intimate with yourself should occur in the solitude of your own room. Watching other people get off might appeal to someone else, but she's not one of those people. Ethan might say she doesn't *allow* herself to be one of them, but there would be a lot to unpack in that statement. Maybe too much, as unpacking has never been Nika's strong suit.

The nightlight's glow tumbling down the ivory wall reminds Nika of the streetlights against the falling snow in January. Peaceful. Soothing. She sighs. What should she say?

Soft footfalls sound behind her, and Ethan, still naked, slides up and threads his arms around her waist. He nuzzles his lips against the back of her neck, irritating the skin more than caressing it. Her nerves are jangled, and she's annoyed. Leaning forward, she moves away from the best thing that has ever happened to her.

"Did it bother you that much?" he says. "Me doing what I did?"

A moment passes as she thinks about what's appropriate to say. The penis itself is not the problem. But maybe his willingness to be vulnerable and open? Nika isn't like that. Never has been. Maybe never will be. "No, I guess not. It's . . . You surprised me. Really surprised me."

"You know these things happen." He pushes his groin against her back, his hardness still evident.

"I know."

Ethan grips Nika's shoulders lightly and turns her around so her back is against the wall and he's looking into her eyes. The muted darkness hampers her from discerning his exact expression, but enough light exists to punctuate the slight smirk—or is it disappointment?—on his lips and his softened eyes. His voice dips. "You could have watched . . ."

"Watched? I'm not a voyeur."

"If you were doing that . . ." Ethan raises his eyebrows.

Nika places a hand on his bare chest. It's warm, and she relishes his skin's softness. And yet . . . "Don't go there, please."

"I would have watched," he whispers.

An unsurprising answer, but Nika wriggles out of his grasp, darts under him, and gives herself two feet of space near the door. "You would have, wouldn't you?"

"Hell yeah, why not?" He crosses his arms over his chest, leans back against the wall, his still naked groin mocking her.

"But . . . but why?"

Ethan doesn't hesitate, as if he's thought about this topic many times before. Gracefully, he steps toward Nika and extends both hands to her shoulders, taking them in his gentle grip again. "Because I want to see you like that. Unguarded, honest, raw. I want to watch your lovely face as you break apart into a million pieces. I want to . . ."

Nika's ears itch, and she places both hands over her eyes. "Oh. My. God. Enough. Seriously. You sound like an overachieving romance novel."

Ethan furrows his brow, and his voice lowers. "I don't think so. What I said is true, and I'm not going to apologize for it."

Nika's tempted to move out of his grasp, but he's tenacious and doesn't let go. *That word again. Tenacious. Stronger than wild violets.* With a large exhale, she leans into the comfort, snuggling against his bare skin as he wraps his arms around her and pulls her close. Even this late at night, he smells clean: part laundry detergent, part deodorant, all Ethan. He deserves the truth, doesn't he? Or at least the truth in as much as she can give him?

"I don't know why those words bother me," Nika mumbles against his chest, then pushes him away and moves out of the bathroom, toward the bed. "I've had sex, clearly, and I don't mind the conversation about it," she sits on the mattress, "but seeing you . . . It's too much. All in my face."

In an ideal world, Nika would bare her soul, continue her thought and say, "I see what you want and what I'm not giving you, and that's why the words bother me. I can't do for you what you want to do for me, and that's why the words bother me. I have baggage I haven't faced and a whole lifetime of shame to get past, and that's why the words bother me. I'm tired, crabby, overworked, overwhelmed, and that's why the words bother me. I'm not feeling myself, and I'm not quite sure what else might be involved or what to do about it."

But this isn't an ideal world, and Nika isn't ready for the full conversation she should have about her insufficient libido and the harsh dryness of her vagina. The woeful fatigue. The low-grade, lurking rage. Her shortage of self-confidence. The backstory she drags around like outdated baggage due for the dumpster. Instead, she focuses on what she thinks Ethan will understand and looks up at him as he stands in front of her. "Sometimes, I feel like you want to have sex all the time, and I don't. I recognize the imbalance, I do, and . . . I'm trying to figure it all out—"

Ethan's eyebrows raise as a knock sounds at the door, and Nika scrambles to grab something—*anything*—to cover her naked husband.

"Nika, Ethan. You in there?"

"Dad?" Nika mouths the word at Ethan, who nods and then searches for his underwear. He darts back into the bathroom while she hobbles around the bed, straightening the sheet and grabbing some clean clothes. *Dad will assume we've been folding*, Nika thinks. And before she can turn off the television, her father pushes the door open and walks in.

"Oh, did I . . . ?" He tips his head toward the screen, which is still paused on The Teacher's Possession.

Nika grimaces. "Ugh, no, Dad. We have this free cable channel, and I surprised Ethan when I walked in, and so he paused the program, and I— Wait. Why am I explaining this to you? What are *you* doing here? I thought you were in LA."

"I was, but I came back."

"What? Why now?"

"Can I sit?"

"Sure." Nika gestures to the overstuffed plush chair in the alcove by the window. It's her favorite place to read, but it's also Ethan's preferred place to throw his clean clothes. Marriage sometimes equals compromise.

Dad sits and strokes the tips of his bushy beard. He's been gray for as long as Nika can remember, but the beard growth is relatively new. So is the sleeveless undergarment worn as a shirt and the—

A familiar, unwanted stench reaches across the room.

"Do I smell weed, Dad?"

"Well, that's what I wanted to talk to you about. The cops are in the kitchen. Can you come down for a moment?"

chapter four

Any day full of this much anxiety requires tea—the stronger the better, even at this hour. Dad and the two cops settle onto the chairs at the dining table, and Nika pulls out the tea kettle, filling it with enough water to go around. A sneak peek at the cops reveals nothing, and her imagination roams: They could be rent-a-cops. Or strippers. Maybe she's the victim of some enormous prank. Did Rainey have *this* up her sleeve?

One glance at Ethan standing between the dining room and kitchen, at his furrowed brow and his folded arms, the tension seeming to ooze from him, and she knows better.

"Cream and sugar?" Nika places the tea and tea accessories on the dining table and directs her question to Cop 1, the one with sandy brown hair reminiscent of a young Larry Wilcox from the CHiPs reruns. Rainey would love this guy. The thought that Nika needs a good night's sleep to work through the anxieties and slaphappiness crosses her mind.

"We're not here for tea, ma'am. We're here for him." Cop 2 nods at her father.

Maybe tea *wasn't* the best idea.

But then Cop 1 says, "Sort of. And yes, please. I appreciate your kindness." A slight drawl clings to his words, and questions about his origins surface. What brought him up from the South? Who helped seal the deal on his manners? Rainey would say Nika's building characters again for her great American novel or screenplay, and maybe that's the truth.

Nika covers a laugh with a cough. "And how about you, sir?" Nika's manners surface, too, and now, Cop 2 starts to waver—the slight uptick of his lips tells her so. Or, maybe he's trying to hold back his own laughter at the situation: sitting at a kitchen table at ten thirty at night, drinking tea, surrounded by the stench of marijuana rolling off an old man with a grizzly gray beard.

"I've never been much of a tea drinker myself, but with this nice selection, I think I'll go ahead. Cream, no sugar. Give me a moment, please." Cop 2 extends his hand over the tea basket and riffles through it, finally choosing a decaffeinated Chai—Nika's go-to after her morning coffee. "You wouldn't happen to have any doughnuts, would you?" he asks.

Ethan practically barks at the words. "You realize how close you are to making yourselves part of a cliché, right?"

His tone surprises Nika. Her husband is rarely rude, even when frustrated by inferior customer service or angered by unsafe drivers, but it's clear he's perturbed. By her earlier declaration? The interruption of their chat? Life with kids and responsibilities and parents always includes hiccups, sometimes too often.

Cop 1 nods. "Don't mind him. He does it all the time."

Cop 2 cocks his head, giving Cop 1 the side-eye.

Nika recognizes the camaraderie between the two. "How long have you been partners?" Glancing backward over her shoulder, she reaches for some napkins from the cupboard, all the while noting the subtle interaction, the body language passing between the cops at the table. They have something to say; now, they just need to say it.

Cop 2 clears his throat. "While I appreciate your hospitality, we're here for serious business." He looks at Ethan, then Nika, then her dad, who has the decency to cast his gaze toward the floor.

Clarity descends on Nika then as she moves back to the table: he's guilty of whatever they say he did.

Michael Washington has always been resolute and confident, the sort of person who knew what he wanted and how to get it. He stood firm on his beliefs, even when those beliefs were so clearly contradicted. But he's always been willing to accept defeat in the direst of times, almost like giving up to the inevitable when faced with a tsunami. What would happen here?

Nika tumbles into the last open chair and covers Dad's hand with her own. "Business like what?"

Ethan jumps in. "Can't you tell by the smell of him?"

Really? "Ethan, couldn't you be a little kinder?"

He huffs. "I could, but this is my house, too, and what kind of role model is this for the kids? Even worse, what if he had the kids in the car with him when he decided it would be fun to light up a joint? What if—"

"Hold on there, honey! You're starting to sound like me."

And he does. Nika is the worrier. Flu shots, skin sensitivity, BPA in plastic, lycopene in tomatoes. Anxieties could overrun her, if she's not careful.

Ethan narrows his eyes at Nika, then quirks his lips, a familiar gesture that dissipates some of the heightened energy thrumming throughout the room.

"With all due respect, Mr. and Mrs. Stewart."

"Nika and Ethan, please." Ethan and Nika speak at the same time, and Ethan winks at her. Nika's partner in crime is back.

"Nika and Ethan. We see this more often than you might think—"

"You see seventy-something-year-old men smoking weed?" Nika's mind flits to the homeless shelter downtown, the weathered, wiry men who stand with their backs against the west wall, one leg on the ground, one leg on the heated brick, squinting in the afternoon sun, lacy smoke curling above their heads. The thought flabbergasts Nika, but even she can admit to being naïve at times.

"We see worse than seventy-year-old men smoking weed, and that's off the record of course."

"I'd love to hear more of those stories, on and off the record," Ethan says, "but go ahead and tell us what's going on here. Or Michael, would you care to fill us in? I have to say—one of the last things I thought I'd be doing is sitting around a table talking about a weed issue with my father-in-law on a Friday night." He places his hands on the tabletop, tapping his fingers against the wood. "Actually," he continues. "I'll be honest—this issue never made it onto the list."

Nika's dad says nothing, simply dips his head lower before lifting it and looking right into Ethan's eyes. Does

Ethan see anything there? It's hard to tell—he simply blinks and remains silent.

"Hold on," Cop 1 says. "Before we sever any lifelong relationships, let's get the facts out, and we'll move on from there."

"Just the facts, ma'am," Dad says, and Ethan shoots him a glare.

Nika wants to laugh—it's better than crying or worrying over something they don't know anything about—but she also doesn't want to undermine Ethan and his feelings. Doing so wouldn't be fair to him. "Don't, Dad. This isn't funny."

"Oh, but it is."

"Well, yes, you're right, I guess, but we also need to take this seriously." Nika turns her gaze toward the cops. "Any way we can do this without him here? I feel like his parent, like he needs to go to his room."

The two cops smile and shake their heads. "No," Cop 1 says. "But I think you need to understand why we're here before we actually speak to, about, or with Michael."

"You're absolutely right," Nika says and takes one of Ethan's hands in hers. For the most part, they've always been a united front. They can be one here, now, when it matters. Everything else from before will have to wait—again.

Cop 2 dives in, says they spied Michael asleep in his car, which was parked legally on the curb. "We wanted to make sure everything was okay with him, and when we knocked on the window, he opened it. It was instantly apparent why he'd been asleep, so we escorted him inside to be sure he made it safely."

Nika frowns. "Wait, so, what did he do wrong?"

Cop 1 says, "Technically, nothing. Weed is legal in Ohio,

and he wasn't operating his vehicle while smoking or under the influence. He said he drove and parked and then indulged, and we have no reason to doubt him."

"Okay then, why are you here? Why did you come get us, Michael?" Ethan asks.

Cop 2 takes over. "We were on our way here, to speak with the two of you—"

Nika's world screeches to a halt, her breathing lurches, and she looks at her phone, hoping she hasn't missed a notification suggesting the kids need something. In this drama-filled night, the universe might pile the tension on, an unsteady stack of books ready to topple over. Thankfully, the screen is absent of anything new, but that doesn't mean—

"No ma'am, er, Nika. Don't go there. Your children, as far as we're aware, are fine. We're only here to get information. Alex, he's your son, right? He was at a party this evening, and we're wondering if we can speak with him."

As far as Nika knew, Alex was at a friend's house, not a party, but then again . . . Alex, usually open and honest in many ways, most likely has his secrets too. "Did you know Alex was at a party?" she asks Ethan.

He shakes his head, his brow wrinkled. "He said he'd be at Jake's house. If Jake is the one who had the party, then I guess I knew, but I assumed it was game night or something similar."

Cop 1 says, "And what's Jake's last name?"

"Robinson," Ethan and Nika say at the same time.

Cop 2 tips his head up. "The party isn't there, or wasn't, as it's been busted now. Is Alex here?"

Nika lets out a breath. "He's not." She opens the phone tracking app, something she rarely uses or even feels the need to use. "Looks like he's at Jake's right now." She glances up to meet Cop 2's gaze. "Is he in trouble? I have to tell you—I wish you'd have started with the kid issue. No offense, Dad," she looks at her father, "you're an adult, and he isn't. I—"

Her father lifts a hand and places it on her shoulder. "I get it, honey. No offense taken. And I think, if it's okay with everyone, I'll excuse myself and go to bed." He stands.

The air stirs, and another whiff of his pastime haunts seizes Nika, washing over her like a billowing breeze. The weed itself doesn't bother her; she's indulged before. But her father didn't think twice about how this might affect her and her family. What Lila and Alex might think or feel or do. Also, how much is he smoking and why? And how did she not notice? Nika mentally spackles another layer of guilt on top of the already thick stack . . .

Ethan reaches over and places his hand on Nika's thigh, a gesture meant to convey his concern, and she considers what he might be thinking. That he'll be here for her, no matter what happens. That they'll get through it. With him by her side, they will. This event? A mere radar blip, but it's a blip that seems to have come from nowhere, and one she'd rather not deal with right now. If she concentrates on Dad, she won't have the mental energy for her own needs. Or Ethan. Or their relationship. Nika sighs, an admittedly trite reaction, but the relief following almost overwhelms her.

"No, Dad. I think you should stay. You live here too."

Her father sits again, slouching in the chair like a petulant student.

Nika knows the feeling. All she wanted was a nice Friday night and look what she got. She focuses on the cops. "What can you tell us?"

Cop 1 grimaces. "At this point, not much. We want to get all the details before we divulge anything. What we can say is something went down at this party, and though no one was seriously hurt, drugs were involved. Weed and some other things." The cop turns to Nika's father. "Say, you didn't give Alex any of your stash, did you? Or did Alex know about your stash?"

A thick shroud of silence hovers in the air.

Oh no. It can't be. "What the fuck?" Nika glares at her father, heat moving through her body, ratcheting her blood pressure and tunneling under her skin. "Are you kidding me?" She jumps from the chair, walks to the foyer, throws open the door, and heads out into the night. The damp air and the gentle hum of a delivery vehicle a few houses up target the stress perching on her shoulders, and she breathes in and out, centering herself. The more she thinks about Dad and what he led Nika to believe (or not), the more her heart thumps and her fingers shake.

The screen door slams, and then Ethan's arms circle her waist. "It's going to be okay, Nika. It's not what you think," he says into her hair. He's tall enough to tuck her head under his chin, an action that makes Nika feel safe, protected. Especially on days when she can't protect herself.

"You don't know that. I know I need the details, but my dad's a weed junkie. Do we want someone like him living in our house? And Alex—a possible witness to a crime at a party?" Nika turns around, burrowing into Ethan's side. A hint of deodorant clings to his shirt, and she inhales a large breath of air, reveling in his essence, his presence, his steadfastness.

Right there, right now, the connection with Ethan is pungent, palpable, so robust and loud, it's almost audible. Capturing the connection and holding onto it should be a priority for Nika, for them, which means that despite everything else going on right now, the talk Dad interrupted needs to resume sooner rather than later.

chapter five

As much as Nika wants to stay in Ethan's protective, warm embrace and soak in the closeness, she's mature enough to know the time isn't right. With a quick squeeze of his middle and a peck to his lips, she steps out of his arms. "I need to be an adult here and get back inside," she says to him. "Let's go."

Ethan rubs Nika's back and reaches for her hand. She takes it willingly, choosing to tether herself to him once again. If she keeps allowing, better yet, initiating, these miniscule moments, will they add up to more? It's a hypothesis worth testing, and so easy to do.

Back in the house, the cops are talking seriously with Dad, who seems to be listening. From their vantage point in the living room, Nika can see him. Shoulders straight. Eyes fully open and alert. Head nodding. He's still a smart man and always has been. But he can be an exasperating man, too, and Nika wonders what else they might get themselves into by permitting him to live in the house.

"Nope," Ethan says, as if reading her mind. "He's staying."

"How did—?" She cocks her head and stops walking.

"I just know. I'm annoyed too. Actually, more than annoyed. Not about the weed. Honestly, he can do what he wants as long as he doesn't put anyone in danger and he smokes outside. But I would have preferred to know about the habit, and I think he needs to be candid—how much he's smoking and whether he has a problem. If he gave any to the kids. Years ago, we agreed to help him. If he can be honest with us, I think he deserves to remain here."

Two things spring to Nika's mind as she stares at Ethan's dark eyes and solemn expression. One, her husband might know her even better than she thought. And two, Ethan is a treasure. Truly. He'd hate to be called that, but what other husband would respond the way he did, resolute with his support because he knows his wife's father is important to her? A long overdue warmth spreads across her chest, and a smile tugs at her lips. "I'm a little surprised," she whispers.

"How so?"

"He's my dad, not yours. And you're being so generous to him. Not that I wouldn't expect it from you, but still. With Lila and Alex here, I thought . . ."

"Everyone deserves a second chance. Mostly."

"Are you sure you're not trying to get into my good graces . . . maybe to get into my pants?" A comment like that can go so wrong, so quickly, especially in light of their previously interrupted talk, so Nika leans in and kisses his cheek, hoping he understands she's kidding.

"Always. I'm always trying to get into your pants, but this

time, it's not even secondary."

A treasure, Nika repeats to herself and takes his hand, threading her fingers with his. "All right then."

"By the way," Ethan whispers in Nika's ear. "You wanna hear something funny?" He doesn't even wait for a response. "I always knew weed be best friends, and have I told you lately I juana grow old with you?"

Nika can't help but chortle.

~

The conversation looks to be over as Ethan and Nika enter the kitchen. Cops 1 and 2 stand, their faces stoic and restrained. "Ma'am," Cop 1 says, "I'm sorry. I should have thought before I asked your father. We don't suspect Alex had any weed or anything else on him—that's not why we're here. I *had* to ask Michael, and it looks like the answer is no."

The rumble in Nika's chest eases, and she sighs in relief.

"But," Cop 2 takes over, his hands on his hips, highlighting his overstuffed police duty belt, "as we said a moment ago, talk this over, and think about getting help if you need it, Michael. Resources are abundant." The cop turns to Nika. "As for Alex, we still need to speak with him." He hands Nika his business card. "It's late now, so when he comes home tomorrow, stop by the precinct or call and someone will come by."

"What happens then?" Nika asks. "Will Alex be charged with something?" The words alone barely leave her mouth, as if saying them might make them true. "Also, I apologize for running out of here. Sometimes my impatience gets the best of me."

Cop 1 speaks again. "We don't yet know what we're working with, so let's take this a day at a time. And again, Michael, consider counseling. Weed addiction is real, and it would be good to get to the root of why you're smoking. Furthermore," he glances at Nika and Ethan, "some think of it as the gateway drug. I'm sure you know this already, Mr. and Mrs. Stewart, I mean with teenagers and all."

Nika's heart leaps in her throat. Once the cops leave, she'll have to ask Dad about his interactions with Alex and Lila. If they know about his habits. If they've done weed with him. If he truly had no connection to the drugs at the party—

Again, Ethan must read her mind because he squeezes Nika's fingers, then loops his arm around her waist and pulls her toward him. "Thank you. We appreciate your time. Looks like we have quite the discussion ahead of us . . . Don't we, Michael?" A pointed look at Dad serves its purpose, and he frowns but nods.

Ethan escorts the police officers to the door, and Nika's mind churns. Maybe she needs to smoke some weed, allow the drug to loosen her up, erase her anxiety. Maybe Rainey is right, and she needs to go see a sex therapist. Maybe Nika at least owes Rainey a phone call and an apology for getting so angry at her. Maybe she needs to speak with Dad. When she risks a quick glance in his direction, he holds up a hand, silencing her.

"Can we talk about this in the morning?" His voice is raspy, gruff, like a scouring pad against a wood cutting board. The bags under his eyes and the drawn lines on his face tell a story, and she feels for him. He's been adrift for a while, ever since he retired from his plumbing business. He has no one besides Nika, Ethan, the kids, and his good-for-nothing stepdaughter, Mindy.

Having a weed-smoking father is something Nika never imagined, but she's not angry. He's an adult, and she agrees with Ethan—as long as he's aware of why he's smoking and he does it outside, it shouldn't be a problem. She understands her children will or already have tried the drug, but she doesn't want them to end up on the side of the road, sleeping off a bender. She continues to look at her dad, taking in his baggy clothes and unkempt hair. If Nika compares photos of her father from today with those taken last year, would she see a huge change? She thinks so. "Fine. Do me a favor and take a quick shower. Then, put those clothes in the garage. Or better yet. Burn them. I'll buy you something new."

"But these are my favorite jeans!"

"You're kidding me, right? You sound like the kids!"

"Hey, a great pair of jeans is hard to come by!"

Nika shakes her head. Her father is absolutely right, and she doesn't have the energy to argue. She waves him off. "Fine. throw them in the washing machine. I'll stay up and make sure they get clean—if they *can*. And we'll talk about this tomorrow."

"Good. I'm too tired anyway." An edge laces Dad's voice.

Tired my ass, she thinks, but she lets it go.

~

Nika's Dad moving in with them came out of nowhere. Her stepmom had taken off months prior—never to be seen or heard from again—and Dad had floundered. Which didn't make much sense because they had always led separate lives. She as a Mary Kay consultant who always chased the top prize (Mindy had missed the boat on the make-up gene), and he as a plumber who owned his own business. Dad did pretty well for himself, but the blue uniform and perpetually black fingernails were too much for her stepmom. When she left, she took half his money and all his dignity. Dad had been clawing his way back since then—with odd plumbing jobs and some counseling, but clearly, he'd been seeing the wrong sort of therapist.

As he shuffles toward the doorway, Nika stares ahead at the window, watching the stars wink at her, thinking about life. Amazed at the complications, the nuances, the little things that can and probably will mess with her head come morning. If she erects a wall now, perhaps she'll at least get some sleep. Sleep always makes everything better.

Ethan is slow to return, so she texts Rainey: *You up?* She waits for the three dots and is rewarded soon enough.

Rainey: *Yep. You okay?*

Nika: *Yes. Well no. But not because of you.*

Rainey loves the text, then adds, *I'm sorry, you know. I didn't mean to make you feel like I ambushed you. The thought never even entered my mind.*

Nika: *I know. And I had hoped to do some thinking when I got home but . . .*

Rainey: *But what?*

Nika: *But shit went down when I got here.*

Rainey: *Lila and Alex?*

Nika: *Thankfully, no. Ethan. My dad.*

How much should she reveal via text?

Rainey: *Like barroom brawl?*

Nika: *Again, no. Two things, which are NOT connected. Taking the self-guided tour *wink* and weed.*

Rainey: *OMG. I'm calling. Do you have time?*

Nika: *I do.*

When Ethan comes in, Nika is still on the phone with Rainey, who's laughing so hard, Nika imagines her literally ROFL. She holds up a finger to Ethan, who pauses, and she scribbles a quick note on a piece of paper: *Be up soon. Dad's in bed. Talking to Rainey.*

He nods and kisses the top of Nika's head. Any discussion with him will have to wait once again. She taps the paper and writes one more request: *Can you text Lila and Alex to check in? Let Alex know we need to chat and he should come home right away in the morning.* Ethan nods again, grabs his phone from the counter, and turns to exit the kitchen.

Before he leaves the room, Nika checks out his butt. His pants hug it quite nicely—they always have—and she smirks to herself as Rainey continues to laugh on the line. *Hold onto that thought, girl.* Nika thinks. *Hold onto that thought.*

chapter six

By the time Nika moves Dad's laundry from the washer to the dryer and reaches the bedroom, Ethan is asleep, but *The Teacher's Possession* still graces the television screen, bodies suspended in time. She pushes play and watches the performance. The picture quality surprises her. The last time she and porn met—in high school, at her friend's house, where said friend's brother and a classmate sat in the living room, mesmerized by the pumping action on a small screen—the picture had been grainy and smeared, though she could still identify the main star's swollen shaft. Nothing but shame, embarrassment, and a little creep factor suffused her then. This video is more tasteful, an artful premise, maybe, although she questions whether everything happening needs to occur without clothing. In school, no less. And no student that age would have *those* breasts. Plus, how often could the man perform within a certain amount of time? Why didn't porn stars have a refractory period?

When the camera cuts to the man's glistening tip, Nika hits the power button and stifles a snicker. Human reproductive parts aren't attractive. Functional, yes. Pretty, no, and no amount of tanned skin or oiled muscles will make her change her mind.

Nika brushes her teeth, throws her pajamas on, and checks her phone one more time for anything from the kids. A quick text to each—*I love you*—goes out, but Nika won't receive replies tonight. Or maybe she will, but she won't see them until her eyelids creak open in the morning. As she slides between the covers, Ethan's nakedness quickly becomes apparent. Still asleep, but naked. Nika laughs at his tenacity. (That word again.) She pulls the covers up to her chin and snuggles against his shoulder. He moves his arm over her but doesn't say anything. She has a reprieve tonight, and maybe she needs to thank the porn.

~

Ethan strolls into the kitchen the next morning, hair askew, eyes bleary, and points at her coffee. "I'm not sure why, but I need a boost more than ever this morning."

"Must have been your strenuous workout." Nika smirks before sipping the warm brew.

Ethan scowls. "What?"

"With the teacher character from the movie."

Realization dawns in Ethan's eyes. "Did you watch it?"

"Not really, but when I came up, it was still on. Paused, but on the screen. The woman sure is agile. So is the guy."

"Yeah, if we could—"

Nika stops him with her hand. "Don't go there. This topic is for later. Once I've finished my coffee, found my happy place, and had more time to digest the news—my dad is a stoner, and Alex might have witnessed a crime."

"Yep. That's your life." He splashes milk into his coffee and swirls the cup. Ethan never uses a spoon, though it would be more effective. "Fewer dishes to wash," he always says.

Nika sips her coffee again and swallows. "You know what the kids would say? 'Fuck my life.' And then they'd sigh. Long, loud, and low."

"You're right." Ethan takes the seat next to her and grabs the cereal box, the kind he's been eating for the last forty-odd years. "They would because they don't have the coping strategies we do. Even though they'd be right in some sense—I mean, who wants to deal with this shit?—they have a good life. *We* have a good life." At times like these, Ethan's social-worker side shines through.

"I know we do, but what do we do about Dad? I have to ask, again, if it's okay to have him living here if he uses weed regularly."

Ethan doesn't speak for a moment. He's looking out the kitchen window at, what? It's technically still winter, so the semi-barren, gray trees stand tall in the dingy brown grass, and a songless sparrow flits from branch to branch in the tree closest to the house. This is not Nika's favorite part of the year, but it holds anticipation and promise. And that promise is something she clings to each and every March like it's her life vest. Concentrating on the sights, smells, and sounds of spring as they unfurl, trusting that once again the earth will warm and open and bring forth vibrant, new life is what keeps Nika grounded at times. (What would a therapist say about that?)

"Sorry. I had to think," Ethan finally says. "I'm not sure what the right answer is. If we talk to them honestly about it, which is the way I'm leaning—they are old enough, after all—then we'll be doing the right thing, but we'll also be giving them information they might not be ready to hear. At least Lila."

Ethan has always been thoughtful about other people, a characteristic Nika found attractive from the start, one that's beneficial in his role as social worker. It's something they have in common, though Nika has been known to drown herself in her thoughts. Repeatedly. Especially when she turns those thoughts and insights toward her own life and actions.

Nika picks at the lint on her shirt. "I was thinking the same thing. But if we *don't* tell them what happened, we're doing the wrong thing. We're not informing them, when we could be using Dad to teach a lesson."

"Another teachable moment, huh?" Ethan smiles, which accentuates the crinkles near the corners of his beautiful brown eyes. "I had no idea all these moments existed until you, Lila, and Alex showed up in my life."

"You didn't even know what you were missing, did you?" Nika's words tease, but the look passing over Ethan's face is anything but casual or insincere.

"You have no idea." Ethan skims his hand along Nika's jaw then moves her chin forward. He places his lips on hers, coaxing them to open. And then, he plunges. It's been so long since they've kissed like this, slow and deliberate, with heat, passion. She wonders if he's been bottling it up inside, and if she's been the wrong one. But then, she thinks about how everything always comes back to sex for Ethan, and even though she needs to give him as good as he's giving, Nika can't. Not now. *Why can't I live in the moment? If I don't go see a sex therapist, I at least have to do something about this—*

Dad comes to the rescue. "Er, sorry to interrupt but . . ."

Nika pulls back from Ethan, who smiles again. She's not sure what the smile conveys, but when she glances at his pants, she knows he's going to be uncomfortable for a while.

He sees the direction of her gaze and whispers, "You can help me take care of it later." Then he adjusts himself, rises from the table, and walks to the coffee maker, pouring more coffee into his mug. "You want some coffee, Michael? It might not be strong enough for you—"

Oh my. "Seriously, Ethan?" Nika asks, trying to give him a meaningful glare.

Dad snickers. "It's fine. He has a good sense of humor. I've come to terms with where I am right now, and I'm grateful you're still letting me stay here." His expression quickly falls, and his eyes grow wide. "Wait a minute. What are you talking about here? Are you kicking me out?"

"Uh . . ." Nika starts. The night before, Ethan had stressed the idea of second chances, but Nika hadn't completely thought about the implications with the kids—

"Michael, as you so delightfully witnessed, our conversation, or lack thereof, was not concentrated on *you* this morning." Ethan winks at Nika, and a wicked smirk crosses his face.

Dad tumbles into the chair, and like the night before, Nika examines him. Stringy hair, sallow skin. *What is going on with him?*

"Dad, since the kids aren't here, I want you to speak frankly. What happened? Why the drugs? For fuck's sake, what's going on? If you need something, anything, why didn't you come to me?"

Michael places his arms on the table, his head low, and Ethan hands him the mug of coffee that started the conversation. He'll probably need it. Dad's never been one to open up to anyone, as far as Nika knows, but something of this magnitude has never happened either. Is he ready to be truthful? Forthright? With Alex and Lila involved, he might be.

"Honestly, I'm not sure what's going on. I've always dabbled with weed, even when you were a kid. It was something your mother absolutely hated, but she tolerated it, at least for a while. Then, I used it to relax after a long day. Owning your own business, bearing the weight of financial responsibility—it can take a toll on a person. And yes, I know your mother worked, and she made good money. I took my role as a father and husband seriously. Regardless of what your mother brought in, I wanted to support us.

"After she left, and then your stepmother . . . all my feelings of inadequacy took over. The weed—it calms me, slows me down, quells voices in my head. It allows me to enjoy life more." Dad looks up at Nika and takes a sip of coffee. Tears shimmer on his lower eyelids, something she's never seen from him before. This all might be too much, too early in the day for him.

This might all be too much, too early for her as well. Nika understands the idea of slowing down and quelling voices. After all, Ethan serves that purpose for her much of the time. Not until Nika met Ethan did her type A personality begin to veer slightly toward type B. And yes, she enjoys life much more now than in the past, regardless of life's stresses and the mayhem of menopause. The idea that Nika will need the names of sex therapists *and* family therapists settles in her mind once again. *Yeah, fuck my life.*

Nika takes a breath. "Here's the deal, Dad. I have a lot going on, and so do Ethan and the kids. But you're a part of our lives, so we'll all help you figure this out. Is now a great time? No. Is there ever a great time? We're always going to be busy with one thing or another, and as the kids get older and start looking at colleges, things might get better, and they might get worse. And yes, I'm getting ahead of myself . . .

"What I'm trying to say here, Dad, is we need to take this one step at a time. You know me. Let me think about this for a bit and come up with a plan. Yes, we'll discuss—because this is your life, too, not just mine. But you impact us, so we all need to be on the same page. In the meantime, we won't kick you out, but you better be on your best behavior—keep your nose clean, as they say."

Dad laughs, stands, and gives Nika a tight hug before shaking his head and leaving the kitchen. Ethan smiles and throws a chocolate candy her way. Milk chocolate hearts, one of her favorites, leftover from Valentine's Day.

She opens the foil, removes the chocolate, and stares at the writing on the inside: *Things have to fall apart for them to fall together.*

Interior: Liberty Boutique Hotel, Honeymoon Suite,
Rome, Italy, 2001

NIKA and BRYSON lie on their backs under the
king-size bed's rumpled covers, lazily looking at
the ceiling. NIKA stretches her hand toward
BRYSON and grabs his fingers. She smiles.

NIKA
What are you thinking about?

BRYSON
How lucky I am.

NIKA
We are lucky, aren't we?

BRYSON quickly flips over, positioning himself on
top of NIKA, who reaches out and strokes his face.
He places a soft kiss on NIKA'S lips, then pulls
back.

BRYSON
You know what else I'm thinking?

NIKA
That you'll love me forever?

BRYSON
(laughing)
Well, yeah, okay, but you know what? This whole
time we've been together—I never noticed the face
you make when you come.

                         NIKA
                      (frowning)
                       What?

                        BRYSON
         Yeah, it's like . . . I don't know. It's funny. I—

NIKA pushes him off, grabs the sheet, and heads to
the bathroom, where she closes the door. Sitting on
the toilet, she burrows her face into the sheet and
wipes the tears away. She stays in the bathroom
until she's sure BRYSON has fallen asleep.

chapter seven

Ethan and Michael head out to run errands, and Nika sits at her home office desk, rifling through her calendar for the upcoming week. Scheduling a talk with Ethan seems outlandish, but once the kids come home, she'll be overrun with familial responsibilities, and she still needs to speak with Alex and get him to the precinct. *In due time*, she thinks.

Monday's schedule looks standard, but Tuesday brings an after-school dentist appointment for Lila, and Wednesday is for music lessons. Maybe she and Ethan can chat on Thursday or Friday night, since Nika will *not* be attending another Sip and Savor; she has no intention of repeating embarrassment and anxiety again, if she can help it.

The memory of her Friday night gets her thinking about Kenrick Ainsworth and the sex therapy idea. Would one be able to help her with her lack of feeling? Two weeks ago, when she said yes to time with Ethan, she'd ruined the mood in spectacular fashion.

"Is it actually in there?" she asked.

He stopped his actions, sighed, and said, "Seriously? It's in there."

"Well, I can't really tell. For some reason, I'm not feeling it today. Actually, I don't feel much anyway."

"Have you spoken to your doctor?"

"Yes. Nothing's wrong with me. Blood work looked good, though yes, I'm in perimenopause. He told me to do some Kegels. They might help."

Ethan's answer? A quick thrust of his hips and then a quiet, "Do you want to stop? If you want to, it's okay."

Nika agreed to keep going, but she thought about that moment for the rest of the day, ruminating on the possibility of her body being physically incapable of feeling pleasure with another person. Shouldn't she have been able to feel something—*anything*—down there? Didn't she deserve a better answer than "do some Kegels"? What did this all mean for her—physically, mentally, emotionally?

Now, as Nika holds her planner in her hand, she wonders how to find an appropriate sex therapist. It's still early, and she's still alone, so she prepares to investigate. Up first: Kenrick Ainsworth. Nika pulls her laptop toward her, keys in the name, and waits as the page loads. Her need for a new computer is about as great as her need for a good lay, at least according to Rainey, but she keeps holding off on the purchase. Sometimes, Nika is stuck in her single-mom-life habits, scrimping and saving for as long as possible. With two incomes now, making purchases is easier, but she still doesn't want to blow through money unnecessarily.

She clicks on the link, and Kenrick's website spreads across the screen. Home tab, Services, About, Resources, and

Other. All usual website fare. What's not usual is the image: Kenrick in costume appropriate for . . . Mardi Gras? Shouldn't this be more about the patient? Why is he front and center? She scrolls to the About page and his credentials smack her in the face: licensed professional clinical counselor through the state of Ohio, Glenn State University graduate, certification for sex therapy through Glenn State University, and verified by the American Association of Sexuality Educators, Counselors, and Therapists. Because of the picture, Nika expects him to provide something about his personal life, whether he likes dogs or cats or horses or what he does for fun. He doesn't. As she's looking at his services, Nika remembers he's originally from England, and the thought pushes her in another direction. What made him stay in the United States? Why sex therapy? Would Rainey know the answers?

She's amazed at the list of people he's helped though. A trans woman from Kentucky gives him a glowing review, as does an Alabama couple. Did they travel to see him, or did they work together remotely? How will Nika know whether Kenrick or someone else is the way to go?

Nika clicks to a section of his website about his collaborations and finds another name there—Susan Harris—who also looks to be local. She clicks on the link to Susan's site, which loads easily. Susan's photo isn't front and center on the screen; instead, it's placed to the right, and she's sitting on a chair. Her site is all clean lines and classic style, and Nika guesses her home or office might look similar. She doesn't want to judge anyone by a website, so she doesn't, but first impressions matter, and she writes down Susan's credentials: another licensed professional clinical counselor, over twenty years' experience, good schools (University of

Dayton for her undergraduate degree and University of North Carolina–Chapel Hill for her graduate degree). As she's ready to move on, a question at the bottom of the screen catches her eye: "Do you need a sex surrogate?"

Nika gasps and glances right and left, as if someone might be observing her. Sex surrogacy? Is that what she *thinks* it is? She clicks the link, which takes her to an article about a woman who has sex with clients as part of a therapeutic approach. Uh, yeah. If Nika's desire to have sex with Ethan is practically nonexistent, why would she be willing to get naked with a third party? The idea intrigues her though—someone who can relinquish all their insecurities and fears about strangers and be intimate with someone they don't know. Share themselves at such a deep level. Ignore any vulnerabilities and be present in the moment. Nika would never be able to do anything even remotely similar, and maybe that's part of her problem.

~

Alex walks in the kitchen door without a care in the world, but Nika stops him before he gets too comfortable.

"Did you get your dad's text?" she asks, slipping the dish towel over the oven handle.

He presses the sensor on his AirPod, turning the sound off. "I did."

Oh ye, man of few words, now is not the time. "And?"

"And what? I didn't see anything. Yes, I went to the party. Yes, it got busted by the cops. Jake and I took off before that though." Alex grabs an apple from the fruit basket and takes a bite without washing it before picking up his backpack and heading for the stairs.

"Hold up," Nika says. "We need to call the police. They want to speak with you, ask a few questions."

He stops at the first step. "Yeah, but I have homework, and like I said, I didn't see anything." Alex presses the AirPod sensor again and ascends the stairs. Though rarely the sweet little kid he used to be, he's normally not so prickly.

Nika stares at his back, putting a plan into place. She picks up the phone and the cop's business card, then tells the person who answers the phone what she needs and why. "We'll send someone over within the hour, ma'am. We don't mind heading your way at all."

Alex might think he's too busy to do the right thing, but he's not.

~

Fifty minutes later, Nika answers a knock at the door. "Detective Brine," the man says and sticks out his hand to Nika, who shakes it. He has a strong grip and a kind face, and the fluttering under Nika's sternum abates. She invites him in and offers him a beverage, which he declines. Then she calls up the stairs to Alex, telling him she needs to speak with him.

Two minutes later, Alex is downstairs, disheveled hair hanging in his face, AirPods still snug in his ears. He looks like he's been napping, which is probably true. She points to her ear, a silent request to pop out the AirPods, and he quickly obliges. "This is Detective Brine," Nika says, "and he has a few questions for you."

Alex's gaze meets Nika's and holds it for a moment. A storm brews in his gray eyes, one that appears when he's confused or frustrated or angry. Nika tips her head and raises her eyebrows, but he says nothing. If there's an issue, she's not aware of it. She is aware that a detective sits on her living room couch staring at the two of them with interest, like he's ready to pounce with questions.

Nika places a hand on Alex's back and guides him to the

loveseat across from Brine. She sits close to him, right hand on his knee, and begins the conversation. "We don't have to worry about getting a lawyer, do we?"

"Mom!" Alex scoots away from her. "Really? This isn't *Law & Order*, you know."

A heat flushes Nika's cheeks. She loves her children fiercely but doesn't always love their reactions, actions, or behaviors. A temptation almost overtakes her—to turn to her son and tell him the only reason they're sitting on a couch with an officer of the law across from them is because of something *he* was involved in. She's been mothering long enough to know now isn't the right time. "Yes, Alex, I know, but I care about you and your rights."

Brine steps in. "It's a fair question, son, one I expect people to ask, so let's not be so hard on your mother, okay?" A grin follows, and it looks genuine yet somewhat practiced, like it's meant to put her at ease.

Alex doesn't move a muscle, but he also doesn't make a snide remark.

"Now," Detective Brine opens a small notebook, "I really am here only to get information from you. When we reached the, uh, gathering last night, multiple people said you were seen in the vicinity of the victim and possible perpetrator—"

Nika swallows hard. "Victim? Can we ask what happened? Alex got home a bit ago—he stayed with Jake Robinson last night. I'm guessing they were up late, since that's their usual routine."

Brine dodges Nika's question. "And does your usual routine involve going to parties with drugs and alcohol at them?"

Alex runs a hand through his hair and sniffs. "I've been

to parties with drugs and alcohol before. I'm not much of a drinker, and neither is Jake."

Not much of a drinker? Nika stifles a snicker at her son's very deliberate omission. He doesn't drink much because he learned his lesson the summer before, when Nika and Ethan had allowed him a "drink or two" at the family barbecue. Too much alcohol, too little food, too much sun. Alex ended up with more than a sunburn by the evening, and Nika had slept in his room, watched him breathe for much of the night, lest his vomiting get the best of him.

"And Jake. Who is he?"

"My best friend."

"What were you two doing at the party?"

Alex sighs. "This is going to sound so standard, but there's this girl." He looks at Nika, then Brine. "Jake has it bad for her, and she was going to be at the party."

Brine writes another note on the paper. "And was she?"

Alex frowns. "We looked for her, and someone said they thought they saw her in the kitchen, so we went there, but we didn't see her."

"And what *did* you see?" Brine's eyes are intense and sharp, and he's poised to capture anything and everything Alex reveals.

Silence reigns for a moment, and Nika's attention is drawn to Alex's ragged fingernails. He's been biting them again, a habit Nika herself has to deal with. Now, he taps them against his knee in an unsteady rhythm. Something is bothering him, but what is it?

"It's okay, honey. Tell Detective Brine what you saw."

Alex draws in a deep breath. "Honestly, a pretty large group was in the kitchen, and so much was going on. Music from the living room, people bumping and grinding. The refrigerator seemed to open and close almost on its own. Most of the people in the kitchen were guys, but a couple of girls I don't know were there too. Everyone seemed to be having a good time."

"Okay, and what else? Can you be specific about anything or any conversations you might have heard?"

Alex twists his lips then bites the bottom one before answering. "You know, the usual convos. Someone was talking about how hot a girl looked, another couple of people were swapping Fortnite stories. Some college guy was there—I think he liked being the mature one in the group. I don't know. He gave off a strange vibe. Jake and I"—Alex closes his eyes and says nothing, then opens them again—"we stood there for a while, watching a beer pong game. Yeah, but that's about it."

"And who played the game?"

"A few people. Some girls, some guys, the college guy."

"Did anyone look inebriated? Was anyone smoking anything?"

Alex laughs. "Drunk, smoking anything? Of course. It was a *party*."

Shaking his head, Brine snorts. "You got me there, so let's switch directions. Do you know where the weed or any of the other drugs came from?"

Any other drugs? What was this party?

Alex shrugs. "I honestly don't know. Stories float around about who deals what, but I don't know if the stories are true or where those people get the drugs."

Even in the elementary grades, Nika has heard tales about which kids might be involved at the high school. And sadly, the middle school is also affected. That's why she's pushed for better and more comprehensive programs on substance abuse, sex education, domestic violence, and the like. Programs using age-appropriate vocabulary spoken by nonjudgmental instructors. The school district pretends not to hear Nika's requests. *Now*, she thinks, *it might be time to take up the yoke again.*

Brine looks at his watch and stands, closing his notebook. "Thanks for the information. Like I said, you're not a suspect, Alex. We're trying to build a story. Yes, we have a victim. Someone spiked a young woman's drink. Thankfully, no one was seriously injured. We're trying to figure out who spiked it. So many drugs are out there these days, you know?" He places his pen in his shirt pocket and nods.

At the door, Brine hands his business card to Nika. "If he remembers anything else, please get in touch. No information is too small or trivial."

"The librarian in me approves," Nika says before saying goodbye to the detective and closing the door behind him. Regardless of the reason, it's always a little nerve-wracking to have the police in a home, and here she is, having seen Five Rivers' finest twice in less than twenty-four hours. She inhales deeply and shakes out her arms. Then she heads back to Alex, gathers him close, places a light kiss on his temple, and holds him. The embrace lasts for longer than she expects, and she is extremely grateful.

chapter eight

With everything the family needs to do that weekend—get groceries, transfer kids back and forth from acting classes and soccer and community service opportunities—Nika does not find the time to talk to Alex about the party or both kids about Grandpa. She wonders what they know. Lila and Alex can probably tell something is off, but right now, the situation is too raw. Having a stoner for a father? There *is* some humor in the situation. Had roles been reversed, Nika would have laughed as hard as her best friend. And yet . . .

Plus, Nika is still smarting from Friday night at the Sip and Savor. Knowing something about yourself and having someone hold up a mirror to you are two wholly different things. Which means she hasn't taken time to process the weekend in its entirety. It will certainly go down as one of her most memorable. Shitty and memorable? Yes. Oddly memorable. Sure. Something to write home about? No. But something to write about? Maybe. If she were a playwright of adult plays and not a director-cum-jill-of-all-trades for elementary school plays.

The thought guides Nika from the faculty parking lot, through Door 5 and into the quiet hallway. She always arrives at school earlier than she's supposed to, hoping to capture some quiet, Zen moments with the books. The library bustles from 7:50 a.m. until 2:55 p.m., almost nonstop. The time frame can take a toll on the most seasoned librarian, even those who love their jobs more than life. Which is Nika, if she's honest. On the other hand, if she didn't feel the job served more than a monetary value, she wouldn't be working here. In this library, she has a purpose, and these kids need her.

In reality, she needs them too.

Thankfully, the hallway remains empty as Nika makes her way to the library, unlocks the door, and flips on the lights. A shuffle of footsteps sounds behind her and—

"Nika!" Rainey's voice bursts the quietude and rings through the room. She enters, bag slung over shoulder, iridescent lunch box in hand, pearly whites a beacon of light in the dim library. The room is old, as are the light fixtures. The bulbs always require a warm up after their weekend sleep.

Today, Nika identifies with those lights a little too much.

"So," Rainey says. "What do you call a blended family that grows marijuana in their backyard?" Her eyes are bright and lively, and she's tapping her foot against the floor, eager to hear the answer.

"Shh." Nika places a finger over her lips. "I can't have the whole school know about this. Okay?"

"Okay, sorry," Rainey whispers. "But go ahead, answer

it." Her smile brightens even more, impish and mischievous and a little bit proud.

"I don't know."

Rainey frowns comically, her brows drawing low on her forehead. "You're not even trying."

Nika takes in a large breath. "You're right. I'm not. But try to see it from my point of view."

Rainey stops the foot tapping, her gaze still sunny. "Okay, I get it. But do you want to know the answer to it anyway? I think you'll like it . . ." She practically sings the words, and her lips curve upward.

"And you won't rest until I say yes, right?"

Rainey bats her eyelashes, and this time she curls her lip downward in a pout any casting director would be proud of.

"Fine." Nika closes her eyes and sighs. "Go ahead. What do you call a family like that?" Opening her eyes, Nika braces for it.

"A *joint* family! Get it?" Rainey doubles over, placing her hand against her stomach, and then glances up at Nika. "What do you think? It's a good one, isn't it?"

A slow smile cracks Nika's placid face, and she lets the levity wash over her. It's too hard not to when it's Rainey. And the joke *is* funny, especially in light of Ethan and her, the second marriage, the coming together, and Friday night's festivities. "It's funny. But I'm still a bit delicate right now."

"So, too soon?"

"Too soon."

"Fair enough," Rainey says and leans in and hugs Nika. "Let me know what I can do. Right now, I get the sense you want me to be quiet." She pulls away and holds Nika's gaze.

"That would be great."

Rainey smiles again and tosses her hair. Hair that always

looks fantastic, no matter the weather or season or if she's showered or not. She holds up her hand, almost like a scout, but she'd have never made it as one, or so she says. "Lips zipped and moving on." She glances at the clock. "Actually, I need to get going, but I think we should meet up soon. Figure out where to go with all this. If you want my help."

"All what?"

"Everything. I think you have more on your plate than you realize." Rainey gasps. "I'm sorry. You can handle anything. You know that, right? It's—you're my friend, and I care about you. And this weekend alone would do me in. At least what I know about this weekend."

"Speaking of which. How many other people know about Dad? Do I need to be embarrassed?"

"Eh, don't worry about it unless you have to, okay?" She backs out of the room. "See you when I bring the kids down. By the way, when does the play begin?"

The school's annual spring play normally takes place in late winter, but this year, thanks to construction on the gym—meaning the cafetorium has to serve three purposes instead of two—they are delayed. Auditions have been held, actors chosen, scripts passed out, and practices begun for *Once Upon a Fairy Tale*, a play written by a former student, now a novel writer. Set design is going well, props are right on track, and the students are enthusiastic.

"End of April, so under two months, if you can believe that! I need to stay after tonight to help with the castle. If you have time to spare . . ."

Rainey smiles. "I do. But I have a conference with a student and her family at three o'clock. I'll do my best to get down there right after."

As Rainey turns to go, a younger male teacher sees her

and smiles. He glances Nika's way, places two fingers against his lips, and sucks in, as if toking a joint. Her best friend would never have divulged such information to anyone, which means only one thing: news has spread.

Nika rolls her shoulders. It's going to be a long day.

~

At 2:57 p.m., Nika quickly places erasers back in bins, chairs in rightful places, and books on shelves. Her plans now consist only of pounding some nails in a few castle walls and listening to the Indigo Girls on her phone. Or maybe chatting with Rainey, depending on how much time she can give to the set. Moving a stack of books from beside her desk to the window shelf, Nika eyes her toolbox. She bought it after she learned that making adjustments to the bookshelves took less time if she did it herself—the school custodian is in constant demand for one repair or clean-up or another. She reaches for the box and sets it on the book cart she'll be bringing to the cafetorium. Next up? The earbuds.

Nika's head is deep in a filing cabinet drawer—she's found all accessories *except* her earbuds—when a voice sounds next to her ear.

"Do you have time to chat?"

Shit. It's the principal. Cole Hannon has been there four years, and he usually leaves her alone. They have an "I won't bother you, and you don't bother me" policy. As long as she does her job well—he really has no idea of the specific details—he leaves her alone. If he's here to "chat" as he says, it has to be about Dad or the party Alex attended. Can something a family member does affect her job? In a smaller town like Five Rivers, she wouldn't be surprised.

"Now?" She shouldn't have asked, but she does anyway.

"Now would be good. I know you have the play to deal

with, but—"

"Fine. Let me clear a few items. I'd rather we chat here." Nika's steadfast volunteer, Jane, just had a baby, so return books, though checked in, seem to be everywhere. Maybe instead of the castle, Nika should stay here and shelve.

"No worries," Cole says and drops into the student-sized chair. His large form fills it, and Nika makes a note to check all the joints and connections after he leaves. These chairs have been known to pull apart with too much weight on them.

"What's up?" She's known Cole for a decade, so she dispenses with the niceties.

"Well," he adjusts his tie, "Funny you need to get down to the play because I'm here about that very subject."

What? "Why?" She looks behind her and grabs a chair. "We're well into the process, and the whole school is looking forward to it."

"Don't get so defensive."

"I'm not." Nika shakes her head. "Actually, maybe I am, so say what you want to say and get on with it. I don't have energy for anything else."

As much as Nika loves this time of the school year, she's still reeling from the winter book fair, which induces more stress than anything in this dream job. So much stress that some librarian friends no longer hold the book sale. But a school year without a sale? Nika can barely fathom the idea—

"I know. Fine. I'll lay it out. A few parents have called about the play. They aren't sure it's, shall we say, appropriate, and I want to talk to you about it."

Appropriate? For whom? So many thoughts spiral in Nika's head, most of them expletive-laden treatises that would—no, probably could—get her fired. That, and Cole might only be the messenger. "Uh, what's wrong with the play? I got permission, from the board, to perform *Once Upon a Fairy Tale*. So, are you here of your own accord, or did someone send you? Like the board, who, might I remind you, *approved* the play. The one we'll be performing in two months." It's been years since anger like this coursed through Nika, and she wonders if her menopausal rage is mixing with this ire and threatening an overload. She takes a deep breath and discreetly holds it, hoping to dampen the fire to a spark.

Cole waves both hands in front of him. "No one sent me, but we can't have our librarian directing an inappropriate play."

The flicker ignites, spreads across Nika's back and shoulders, upsets her normal sinus rhythm, and she places a hand to her rapidly beating heart. "Whoa. Back up. How many parents? What's *inappropriate* about it? Have you looked at the script? Has anyone else actually looked at the script?" Her voice rises, and she leaps to her feet, crosses the short distance to her desk, and grabs an extra copy of the script. "This!" She shakes the papers in front of Cole's face. "This is the script. It's a *fairy tale*, Cole, nothing but a fairy tale for everyone. And my guess is a few parents are complaining, but what the hell are they complaining about? This school has a librarian, me, who is an upstanding citizen. One who helps our young students learn to think critically and judge information and news sources. I have done nothing but educate children, positively, in the time I've been here. And I'm the only one, besides Rainey, perhaps, who holds these kids accountable."

"Okay, who will hold *you* accountable?"

Oh hell. "Accountable for *what*?"

"The play. These parents, who shall remain nameless,

have a problem with the story, but I think you can easily fix it."

"A problem? Like what?"

Cole purses his lips and doesn't meet Nika's gaze when he mumbles, "They aren't supportive of the main characters. Princess, uh, Sayors and Rivena? Two girls."

Nika snorts at Cole's pronunciation of *Saiorse*. "S-A-I-O-R-S-E, but it sounds like Ser-sha. And what's the problem? Oh wait, I think I get it. They want to see a prince and princess instead of two princesses, don't they?"

Cole nods.

Blood rushes inside Nika's body, her ears burn, her teeth clench. She's ready to wind up her arm and clock this guy, but she loves this job, and Cole Hannon isn't worth taking out, especially because doing so won't fix the issue. "Let me tell you one thing, sir. I've gone to the board and the superintendent with my concerns about substantial issues in this district. I've received the nod and the 'thank you for coming in, ma'am' and the curt dismissal. The district doesn't want to know anything. They want to hide—everything. Drugs. Vaping. Sex. Racism. Sexism. Ableism. They don't want to provide proper information in the sex education classes. They're afraid to use the word *condom*, like it's vulgar. But if they used the damn word, they might not have fourteen-year-olds having babies and dropping out.

"And let's not forget the hell I raised about LGBTQ+ and identity issues. Oh no, they didn't want to hear my side at all on that one. Like this district doesn't have kids with two moms or dads or two moms and a dad. Did you know we have polyamorous couples in this district?" Nika lowers her voice and sits again. "If they choose to take up this battle now because they don't want to see two girls together—

because, dare I say, they're *homophobic*—they'll have a fight on their hands. A big one. Because they can't fire me—they *approved* the play, remember?"

"Stranger things have happened."

He's right. "Well, you know what? Let them fire me. Maybe I'll lawyer up."

Cole pinches the bridge of his nose. "Listen, I'm here out of courtesy. People are talking, so prepare yourself. While we might not be the best of friends, you're good at your job."

Good at her job? That highlight saves the conversation, one Nika no longer has time for. "With all due respect, this news has ruined my afternoon. I have a castle to help with and books to return to the shelves. I'll be sure to group all the books featuring queer families into their own little section. And how about this? I could have a spring-cleaning sale. I'll label the section as the 'five dollar and under' table. What do you think?" She narrows her eyes at Cole, hoping she hasn't gone too far with her sarcasm; he's still her superior.

Cole smirks. "You're funny, Nika. But in all seriousness, do we have those books? Can't you make it a prince and a princess and move on?"

"Of for the love of Pete. *Of course* books are out there," she waves her hands in the air in front of her, "books that help kids see themselves and their families. Books that confirm they're loved as they are, accepted as they are, but this is an *elementary* school, and I know what should and should not be on my shelves. I won't censor, but I *am* selective about what comes in. This library has *age-appropriate* books of *all* subjects. What about me being good at my job?"

"I had to ask."

"And you did. But I'm not moving on. Princess Saoirse

and her love interest—which really isn't a love interest so much—will remain, so I think we're done here."

No sooner does Cole move out the door and Alex and Lila walk in, faces flushed, talking animatedly about some subject or another. The two are pretty close, and even though they have their moments, they're still connecting as Nika hoped they would, like she wishes she did with Mindy. But it's been years, and that relationship? It's like having a piece of celery stuck between two molars at the back of her mouth.

The kids cross the threshold, and Nika throws her arms around their shoulders, pulling them in as close as she can. Alex towers above her by at least six inches, while Lila is maybe two inches taller. Alex, being his usual teenage boy self, pretty much leaves his arms at his sides, immobile, and Lila squirms to be let go, but in the end, the kids tolerate Nika's affection. Very few people are still in school, so there's no risk of being embarrassed by a hug from Mom.

"You okay?" Lila whispers. She's always been insightful, but maybe it's the way Nika clings to them both, inhaling their still innocent scents, much like she did when they were babies.

"I'm fine. It's been a long day, and since you weren't around for much of the weekend, I feel like I haven't seen you."

"Well, we're here now, and I have a lot of homework," Alex says, "so can we get going?" The weekend's prickly attitude is alive and well.

"How much? Because you know, I still want to talk to you. I *need* to talk to you." Nika lifts her eyebrows but doesn't explain.

"Latin, math, history, English. The usual. Some of the guys are meeting up to run." Alex plays soccer, but the winter session just ended. He's waiting for the spring session to begin, and he's taking it seriously. His behavior reminds Nika of Ethan—solid, resolute—and she's so grateful the kids have a role model like him in their lives.

"And what about you?" Nika turns to Lila.

"Math," she says, then cocks her head. "And a debate to prepare for."

"A debate? For what class?" Nika unlatches herself from her children and takes their book bags from their hands. A pile of *things* is growing in the corner, but they'll only be there for the duration of the afternoon. *Thank goodness.*

Silently, she begins handing the kids the items they want to bring down to the stage: a box of tissues, a pair of scissors, and a container of packing and duct tape. Last year, the tape came in handy when two fourth graders decided to spar, knocking over a line of cardboard trees the fifth graders had spent days creating. Sometimes Nika thinks she's less of a director and more of a fairy godmother for the play, which, this year, would be very appropriate.

"The debate is for advisory. We're supposed to argue cats are better than horses."

Alex lets out a huge guffaw. "Cats *are* better than horses, hands down. I could even tell you why." He opens his mouth to say more.

"I'm glad to see you have such a solid stance," Lila says, her eyes bright and tone confident as she places her hands on her hips.

Nika doesn't know where Lila's voice comes from or if she's helped cultivate it, but she's happy to see it. Maybe it's a product of being raised, at least for a few years, by a single mother. *Lila could probably go up against those parents a hundred times better than I could.*

"I'm just saying," Alex says. "Think therapy—"

"They have therapy horses. But not therapy cats, *Alex.*" Lila rolls her eyes, another habitual behavior for Nika's sassy teen.

"No, hear me out. It takes time and energy to find a therapy horse. You might not live in an area where you can even have horses. But cats? It's not hard to own one—thus therapy right inside your home. What about all the cat cafés? And some cats serve as support animals, bruh. Haven't you heard?"

"All right, kids! We can walk and talk, can't we?" Nika shoos Lila and Alex out the library door and locks it, then escorts them, boxes in hand, to the cafetorium. The cast and crew litter the stage, some kids on their phones, others talking to one another. Very little work is getting done, and for one moment, Nika envisions herself walking out the door, through the hallway, out of the school, and into her car, leaving it all behind her. At least for a few minutes.

She knows, though, how much this play means to the kids, to the school, to the former student who wrote the play, so she places her box on top of Alex's, tells him and Lila how to get things started, and says she needs five minutes. "I'll be right back. I forgot one thing."

Though no one remains to see her, Nika tiptoes down the hallway, unlocks the library door, slips inside, and takes a seat at her desk. *Five minutes. That's all I need,* Nika thinks, and she opens the tattered copy of *Bridge to Terabithia* tucked against the printer.

Nika's mood lifts.

chapter nine

Later that night, with the kids snug in their rooms, Dad asleep in front of his television, and Ethan playing a word game on his phone in the kitchen, Nika saunters to the bedroom. She pulls her laptop out, clicks over to Susan Harris's website, and roots around under Resources. There, she finds a questionnaire and prints it out, writing "Susan Harris Questionnaire" across the PDF before thinking, *Why do I call her Susan Harris?* Nika doesn't know any other Susans, and she hasn't even met this Susan, but in her mind, Susan Harris will always have a first and a last name. Like her friend Cindy Carpenter, another teacher in the district. When Nika refers to her, it's always by first and last names. The thought of her makes Nika smile, and she texts herself a note to plan something with Cindy Carpenter soon. A walk? A movie? No, a tea date. Cindy *loves* tea . . .

"Stop stalling," Nika mumbles as she slips her phone out

of reach. The questionnaire's first page includes a chart and at the top, a paragraph: *Directions: Sexual problems in marriage or long-term relationships can be multifaceted and complex. Honest answers to this survey will help us assess the nature of the problem and allow us to focus therapy on you and your specific needs. Please check the box that resonates with you currently, and remember, your responses are confidential. The survey will be shared with your spouse or partner only with your express, written permission. Wrong answers do not exist, so please be honest.*

"For the love of fuck. What have I gotten myself into?"

Nika's fingers actually shake as she holds the pencil, and she clenches her eyes shut. *The moment I begin the questionnaire, I'm committing to this project, aren't I?* A vision forms behind her eyelids—a monolith, dark, imposing, unscalable, daunting. But at the top sits Ethan, a relaxed grin on his face, hands waving ecstatically, and she thinks of the next thirty, forty, maybe even fifty years, and she can't, in good conscience, not address what's going on.

Or I can, but I certainly can't uphold a falsehood anymore.

Filling in her name, age, how many years they've been married, whether or not she was married before, and how often she and Ethan have sex is easy. Looking at those intimacy numbers, someone might not recognize an issue. Once Ethan got a vasectomy—he decided Alex and Lila were enough for him—the frequency of sex increased by 100 percent (which is sad, in and of itself). The only reason Nika does it most times now, though, is because Ethan wants it. An obligation of sorts, that good ole marital debt she remembers from elementary school.

"These ain't biblical times, my friend. Let's do this." Nika straightens the paper.

The actual document is almost thirty questions! Depending on the question, the answers hold different point values between 0 (strongly agree) and 4 (strongly disagree), with agree, neutral and disagree rounding out the line up. The higher the number of points collected, the worse off the person is. Nika charges ahead before nerves get the best of her.

1. Thinking about sex with my partner pleases me.

Thinking about doing it with *him* specifically isn't the problem, but Nika isn't pleased by thinking about it. Neutral, disagree? What does this question even mean? Next one . . .

2. Thinking about sex recalls unsavory memories.

There was that one time, but if Nika thinks about sex *lately*, she recalls unpleasant memories of Ethan's disappointment, her feeling of letting him down. Knowing she doesn't desire sex, doesn't feel it, doesn't like to have to do something she doesn't want to do. Do the past and the present balance each other out to equal neutral? Nothing here bodes well.

3. When my partner initiates sex, I eagerly agree.

Easy: Nika sometimes agrees, but reluctantly. So . . . disagree or strongly disagree? When was the last time Nika actually *wanted* sex?

4. Sex feels more like duty than desire.

Aha! Nika laughs out loud at having anticipated the next question. Yes! Sex does feel more like a duty. Strongly agree!

5. Sex repulses me.

No. It's useful, but it certainly isn't fun anymore. And skin-to-skin contact in her menopausal state—downright repulsive at times.

Repulsive? Well shit. Why am I doing this?

Nika closes her eyes, rocks her shoulders, and twists her

spine. A pop, a creak. *Ah. Much better.* She scans the questions, turns the paper over, and places it next to her on the chair. So many other duties beckon her right now, and she'd love to be anywhere but with this questionnaire at the moment. Maybe if—

Nika's phone pings. Against her better judgment, she checks it. Spam text. Dammit. She turns the ringer off and places the phone under the chair. She almost always follows through on something, and no matter how hard this questionnaire is, she's going to finish it.

She breezes through questions 6 and 7, which ask if sexual activity proceeds at its own pace and if the pressure to try new things during sex is bothersome. The answers? Fifteen minutes, baby, and not a minute over, and at this point, new things *aren't* anywhere near the table—just having sex is the priority.

8. Arousal occurs easily.

Nika briefly considers throwing the questionnaire to the ground, stomping on it, tearing it into pieces, and tossing it into the nonexistent fire. A fire. Which sounds great right now. Crackling logs, small bursts of heat, warming her toes and hands . . .

At least until the next goddamn hot flash. She tugs at her collar, allowing a sip of fresh air to caress her skin.

9. Arousal is sustained throughout sex.

Ha! The parts do what they're supposed to, but as for the brain . . . *How do I answer this?*

10. Other thoughts distract me during sex.

Nika should have read further before she answered the previous question. Here it is! She feels seen! Everything distracts her: soccer carpool duties, library responsibilities, what to make for dinner, where the kids will go to college, how much money they're putting into retirement, whether Mabel, their faithful Golden Retriever, is up to date on shots, Dad . . .

11. Scheduling sex isn't something I want to do.

Uh, hello? Planned sex is what it's all about! Finally, something to give her a shot of confidence.

12. In general, I satisfy my spouse and their sexual desires.

Nika pictures Ethan's face while they're in bed. The resignation, the masked disappointment. What they do might satisfy him physically—help him scratch the itch—but not emotionally. She *knows* this. Hence her attempt to understand what's happening with her. *I have to disagree with this one, strongly.*

13. In general, my spouse satisfies me and my sexual desires.

See answer to question 4.

14. I'd like for my spouse to be more emboldened in bed.

Ethan would be plenty emboldened if Nika wanted him to be. He'd dress up as whatever she wanted: billionaire, firefighter, the list goes on. And, he'd use whatever toys she proposed. *Wait, what was the question again?*

Questions 15 and 16 tackle what sexual activity includes and whether vaginal penetration is difficult or painful. Thankfully, penetration is not painful, though sometimes it feels like nothing. It could be a cucumber in there for all she knows. And the dryness is more than she can take some days.

17. We both experience orgasm during sex.

When was the last time Nika orgasmed during sex? It's not for Ethan's wanting to try. In Nika's world, they only have time for one of them to finish, and since it means more to Ethan, she chooses him.

That's an awful answer, isn't it?

18. My spouse takes too much/too little time to orgasm.

What a loaded question and terrible pun. Too little?

Never. Too much? It depends on the day. He's a fifty-something-year-old man. Nothing he does is quick.

19. I take too much time to orgasm.

See answer to question 17.

20. I cannot orgasm with my spouse, but I can alone.

Nika has the capability of having an orgasm with Ethan, but she often doesn't want to bother. And as long as he's not reading this, yes, of course, she's done the job herself.

21. I orgasm too quickly.

Again, see answer to question 17.

22. If I or my spouse does not orgasm, it's an issue.

This is one to talk to Ethan about. For Nika, she doesn't care, but his day is probably better if he finishes.

23. My spouse and I agree on what "good sexual activity" means.

How to answer this one?

24. My spouse and I cannot discuss sex without arguing.

Nah, fighting isn't something Ethan and Nika do. And since Nika now understands sex is a means of connection for him, at least in some capacity, maybe he'll be as open to talking about it as Nika hopes to be.

25. Overall, I am satisfied with our sex life.

No? Yes? If Nika were single, she'd be absolutely 100% thrilled to not have sex again. But she's not single, and she loves her husband. So therein lies the problem. Outside of bringing in a concubine . . .

26. Overall, our marriage relationship is very strong.

Before reading these questions, Nika would have answered yes, and she'd have defended that answer. She'd have said they communicated well, respected one another, understood each other's hopes and fears and vulnerabilities. Now, after reading these questions . . . Disagree.

~

The next day dawns with fog so thick, the district calls a two-hour delay. Nika creeps into everyone's rooms and shuts off alarms, thankful for the quiet morning hours before the kids awaken, before Ethan trudges across the room and down the stairs to look and see what's on his schedule for the day, before Dad wakes, asks for coffee, and then forgets to put the milk away. She opens her laptop again, looks at the printed questionnaire, and thinks, clearing her mind of thoughts. She's trying, she really is. But this questionnaire brought up more than it resolved and—

A creak sounds to Nika's left, and she glances up as she closes her laptop and turns the questionnaire over. It's Ethan, with his mussed hair and puffy eyes. Mornings have never suited him, and she's surprised to see him awake.

He moves around the back of her chair, enfolds her in his arms, and leans his face into her hair. "You smell good," he says. "You always smell good."

"Glad you think so. Check in with me the next time I exercise. You won't like the smell then."

"Of course I will, and if I get to see your tight little—"

Nika unwinds his arms. "Okay, stop."

"Why? I like how you look, especially in those leggings. All curves, which I like." He tugs a nearby chair close to hers, takes a seat, and runs his hand through his hair.

Nika sighs. "I'm glad you like how I look. I'm not sure why I told you to stop. Habit maybe?" She should at least indulge him, let him know something in the words themselves bother her, but she doesn't. "Maybe so the kids won't hear?"

He looks around at the empty room, still veiled in darkness. "Uh, I know you know this, but they aren't here. Why wouldn't you want them to hear how much I appreciate you?"

Appreciate me or my body? "You're right and . . . never mind." Nika doesn't want to ruin the day, so she changes the subject. "What are you doing up this early?"

He settles back against the chair and then stretches his arms forward, which delivers a small *pop*. He's always been a little tight in the morning, and his stretches can veer toward the elaborate. On several occasions, Nika has accused him of behaving like a peacock, and his usual reply? If he's stretching with his clothes *on*, he's not being a peacock. Then, he usually emphasizes the last syllable of *peacock*, and the accusation changes.

"You know, you're being such a man," she'll say.

"I am, and *you're* generalizing." Ethan always delivers the line with an endearing wink and flash of his dimple.

Nika sniffs at the thought of that conversation, the familiarity of it all; they're too young to be predictable, and yet, they already are.

"Actually, I couldn't sleep." Ethan rubs his hand across his stubbled jaw. "I've been thinking about your dad."

"Dad?" Usually, Ethan shuts things like that off so well. "Why are you thinking about him?"

Ethan leans his elbows on his knees and drops his head. "I'm not sure. As you know, I'm not a saint, but what is he doing and why is he doing it? He has a decent life living here, so why jeopardize it? He should have known we'd find out eventually and we'd be a little concerned. Anyway," Ethan lifts his head and catches Nika's gaze, "I'm thinking about him and where we go from here. Your dad's been quiet about everything, you know?"

"What about Grandpa?" Lila's voice sounds over Nika's shoulder.

"How does this keep happening? Not only did you both sneak up on me, but you're taking a part of my *alone* time. There's a *delay*!"

Lila moves Nika's laptop and papers to the side table and sits on her lap, threading her thin arms around Nika's waist and placing her head against Nika's chest. She's warm and still soft, the way children often are when they haven't fully woken up. Lila doesn't say anything and snuggles in closer to Nika, who tightens her arms, relishing the moment and knowing it cannot last forever.

"Do you think you could go back to sleep?" Nika whispers as she rubs Lila's back with her hand. "This rarely happens in March. The school district has given you a gift."

"I always get up at this time," she says. "Or at least I'm awake. Normally I lie in my bed and stare at the ceiling while I think."

"About what?" Nika asks.

"Anything. Everything."

"Better watch out, Lilabug. You're starting to sound like your mother. Her brain never shuts off." Ethan winks at Nika, a wide grin on his face. He's always accused her of thinking too much, and while the comment might hurt some folks, it doesn't hurt her. Because it's true.

Right then, Kenrick's business card near Nika's computer draws her attention. It's face down, thank goodness, and it's covering a note she jotted to herself about Susan. She can't see what words are visible, and she doesn't think it's a big deal, but with an observant kid on her lap, she can't be too careful.

Nika slides her left arm from behind Lila and sneaks the card under her computer. If her daughter notices, she doesn't say a thing, but the movements don't get by Ethan.

"What?" he mouths.

"Nothing." Nika frowns and shakes her head.

"It's not nothing. If you didn't want me to see—"

"Mom? I'm hungry. Can you make chocolate chip pancakes this morning since we have more time?"

Nika nuzzles against Lila's head and looks at Ethan, imploring him with her eyes to let the topic drop. Whether or not Lila realizes it, she's saving Nika from an uncomfortable conversation. Nika will share the card and the idea of therapy with Ethan—*when she's ready.*

He quirks his lips and winks, then extends a hand to Lila's head and ruffles her hair. "Your mom is probably tired, and I'm happy to make the pancakes today. What do you say?"

Ethan's words are meant for Lila, but Nika knows what she'd say if he'd addressed her: She *is* tired. She's had a long week, and the week isn't nearly over. She's grateful for his kindness and for seeing what she doesn't feel like having to say aloud. Instead, she says, "Thank you, honey. Be sure to save me one!"

Lila sits up, still on Nika's lap, and leans in, giving her a peck on her cheek. "Sounds good. Can I help?"

Ethan musses Lila's hair again, then tugs her hand. "I wouldn't have it any other way, kiddo."

Lila and Ethan saunter off to gather the pancake ingredients, and within minutes, they're lost in the process. The sounds of measuring and mixing float from the kitchen to where Nika still sits. Ethan loves chemistry, and he explains why he adds baking powder to the flour and what the baking powder will do. He specifies to Lila how much batter he uses to make his "perfect" pancake. By the time Nika comes down to the kitchen, flour dusts the counter, milk puddles cover the cutting board, and a small test pancake lies on the floor, waiting for someone to get it or for Mabel to lap it up. Oddly, Mabel is nowhere to be found, so chances are Nika will take it on.

Ages ago, she would look at the mess and sigh, annoyance simmering in her blood at yet another task to add to her list. Now, time between daughter and father is precious—that she knows—and a splendid warmth spreads in her chest like melted caramel: *I wouldn't have it any other way either.*

chapter ten

Nika often feels like she rides the sine-cosine curve. Not because math plays a large role in her life: she likes the subject, but she's certainly not blessed with a math brain, as they say. But Nika appreciates its crest-and-trough nature, the ascent and descent, the oscillation, and its endless nature.

For many months, mostly after Nika's first husband exited without a word as to why, leaving her with two kids and no child support, she hunkered in the curve's dark pit. Day-to-day functioning was difficult, but with a little help from her dad, a lot of help from Rainey, and probably a dash of sheer luck, the kids and Nika managed to climb the curve and stand at its apex. For the most part, since meeting Ethan, they've remained there.

Once Ethan entered the picture, it was easier to see the good in people, the peace that could surround a marriage, the generosity of friendship, and the stability that came with truly loving another person. Over a decade has passed, though, and Nika doesn't always consider the bookshelf half-full. And, it takes a lot of coaxing and convincing to get her to believe the bookshelf isn't going to fall. As she bustles between her librarian and director roles, cataloging new titles for the collection, culling the seldom-borrowed books from the shelves, marking the stage with masking tape, and answering a round of questions from two more parents concerned about the "appropriateness" of the script, Nika realizes the shelf is, at the very least, sagging. Which means she's going to need everyone in her family on her side. Which also means she needs to be sure Lila and Alex are on the same page as their parents.

The opportunity comes after school and violin the next day. A rare period of time when all three are home and sitting at the dining table. The kids with their homework in front of them, Nika with a recipe book and pad of paper. They've been stuck in the recipe rut for a while, and with spring hovering, she wants to make a fresh start.

"What about slow cooker chicken tortilla soup?" Nika asks as she looks at the ingredient list. She can always substitute tofu for the chicken if the kids would prefer it.

"Does it have chunks?" Lila asks. Aside from vegetarian chili and white bean soup, she enjoys her food chunk free.

"You shred the chicken, so yes, there are chunks, sort of."

"Then thumbs down from me."

"I'd try it," says Alex. "As long as it has some flavor."

Nika makes a note to consider the recipe. If she asks Dad about it and he's interested, she'll go ahead. He loves leftovers for lunch, and between his appetite and Alex's, leftovers rarely last long. Maybe now, Nika knows why.

Weed. Munchies.

"What about a chickpea crust pizza?" Nika leans in with raised eyebrows, curious about their responses.

"Uh, what's wrong with regular pizza crust?" Alex asks, his brow furrowed.

"Nothing."

"Then why change it?" Lila adds.

Nika doesn't argue about how some change is good, how it can be useful for growth and enrichment. She doesn't want to dwell there. "Agreed and enough said. Moving on—"

"What are you up to?" Dad says as he walks into the kitchen, his steps heavy, tired.

Nika discreetly breathes through her nose, trying to tell if a stench accompanies him or not. Today, it's not there, and she's not sure how he's spent his day. Being in this little comfort zone of contentment with the kids, she doesn't ask him now. "Looking at recipes, and the kids are doing homework. Will you be here for dinner tonight?"

"Maybe. I have a thing I want to go to."

Nika stops flipping the pages of the recipe book. "A *thing?* What sort of thing?"

Dad pauses, like he doesn't want to tell her, like he has a secret, like the time he was too ashamed to admit her stepmother had left, just like her mother. But then he shakes his head and looks directly at her. "At the church. It's just a meeting."

His answer surprises Nika. Is it an anonymous addiction group? She doesn't want to ruin the mood, even though Lila is looking at her with questions in her eyes. "Sounds fine. Text if you're going to be late. We're having pulled pork tonight anyway, and it's in the crock pot. You can eat later if you want."

Dad leaves the room without answering, which prompts further silent questions inside Nika's mind. What was the point of him being there? Did he purposely drop the hint he's headed to a church meeting? Is Nika supposed to think everything is fine?

"What was that all about?" Alex says.

"What do you mean?" Nika scribbles a few page numbers on the paper as a reminder to go back to those recipes.

"A church meeting? Grandpa doesn't go to church, so what's it for?"

Now's the moment, dropped into her lap like a divine gift. Was *that* her dad's intention? When the front door clicks into place, Nika prepares her thoughts about her father, about what happened, about where he needs to go from here.

"I'm not sure exactly how to say this, but . . ."

The kids stop typing, glance at Nika, and tip their chins up. Both of them. The gesture is so their biological father, and in moments like these, Nika sees him. His dark eyes, his cockiness. A twinge settles in her chest—her ex is not the sort she wants to remember right now—but he gave her these two, and she has no regrets.

Nika blows out a breath and moves a strand of hair away from her mouth. Heat rises inside her, from their undivided attention or a hot flash? Nika isn't sure. "The other night, the night of the party, when you were at your friends' houses, your grandpa came in the house and surprised me."

"Surprised you?" Alex says, his eyes wide.

"What do you mean?" Lila leans in and drums her fingernails against the tabletop.

"He . . ." How much to tell? The kids are fifteen and seventeen. Will the news corrupt them? Then images of everything that goes down at her own school, even in the younger grades, fills Nika's mind. The things these kids have seen and heard and experienced. Foul language, food scarcity, neglect, shooter safety drills. The truth wins out. "Two cops showed up at our door to talk to Alex, but they found Grandpa asleep in his car. And he might . . ." Nika pauses again. It's hard to admit her dad might have a drug problem, much less say it to her children.

"Might what?" Lila says. "Come on, Mom!"

"Might have a—"

"I'll say it," Alex chimes in, slapping the table, "a problem with weed?"

Nika's hand moves to her chest, and she cringes at the words, at the truth. Those words came out of *her son's* mouth. It's always different when it comes to your own children. "Yes. How did you know? Did you hear something about it at school?" Would they be talking about a district employee's father?

Alex and Lila look at each other, speak silently like they sometimes do, and nod. They're two years apart, so why does this behavior seem so natural to them? Despite the heavy conversation and the feeling she's treading in deeper waters than she's used to, Nika's heart melts. These two. The best—

"Mom. I hate to tell you this, but we've known about Grandpa for a while," Alex says.

Nika's gut clenches. "You have?" Have I been so busy, so selfish, I wasn't paying attention?

"Yeah," Lila says. "I didn't know for sure, but I asked Alex and he agreed."

"Why didn't either of you come to me?"

Twin pink spots tinge Alex's cheeks. "I don't know. Maybe I thought you knew about it? Maybe because weed isn't a big deal—"

"Whoa. Back up, buddy. Weed *is* a big deal. I know you think it's not, and I'm not trying to make this into a 'don't do drugs' spiel, but weed can be and is as impairing as alcohol. If your grandpa drove a car after smoking it, he'd be under the influence. I have nothing against him smoking, but to bring weed into a house where two impressionable teenagers live? That's my biggest issue here."

"I don't think he brought it into the house," Alex says.

"How do you know this?"

Alex looks at Lila. "We'd have smelled it. Really, Mom, the only way I know is because I saw him cross the driveway and head behind the house, smoking. But he stayed outside for a long time afterward, and once he came in—you were gone that day—he made sure to take a shower, open the windows, and spray air freshener."

"He was sneaking around behind my back."

"Yep."

And her kids covered for him. Nika isn't sure whether to be proud or angry. Clearly, they're loyal to their grandfather, but they didn't openly communicate with *her*. She had to do better. "Well, okay then. How do you two feel about your grandpa smoking weed?" And in an effort for pure honesty: "Are either of *you* smoking it?"

She tried the drug herself, years ago, in a batch of brownies so sweet her teeth ached as much as her stomach screamed for snacks. But experimenting in college and experimenting in high school are two very different things. *Aren't they? Yes, they are.*

A moment of silence hangs in the air, sharp and pungent. A bright pink flush now moves up Lila's cheeks, and she glances at Alex, who shrugs.

"No, we're not. I tried it once at a party, but it made me

feel sick, and I had to skip my workout the next day. You know—smoking weed is what Grandpa does," Alex says. "Some old folks do puzzles, collect stamps, play golf, polish rocks. Grandpa? He smokes weed."

"Yeah." Lila rolls her eyes and looks at the table. "I see it as stress relief, actually."

To an observer, this conversation might sound laughable. Stress relief? How did these kids get to be so nonchalant? And yet . . . "I had a feeling you'd say that. Is anyone bothering you about it at school? The news has already spread about it, unfortunately."

The kids glance at one another again before Alex says, "No one has said anything to me."

Lila shakes her head. "Me neither."

Nika lets the moment linger, probing her children's gazes for any fabrication, any lies about what they've discussed, but she doesn't see it, doesn't feel it. "Keep me posted, okay?"

They both nod, and her thoughts whirl again. To her dad. To Alex. To the play. To the possibility of seeing a therapist. To what's to come—

"Hey, Mom?" Alex says, bringing Nika back to the present. "What does all that have to do with a church meeting Grandpa is going to?"

"I don't know. I thought maybe it was a narcotics anonymous group, and he was too embarrassed to mention it. Or he didn't want to say anything in front of you. Do you think he knows you know?"

"I doubt it," says Alex. "But I guess a meeting like that would make sense."

"I don't know what makes sense anymore." Nika cocks her head and flashes a quick smile at her kids, batting her eyelashes at them the way she did when they were young.

Lila and Alex both groan and roll their eyes, and then Alex says, "Mom?"

"Yeah?" Nika takes in the huge grin crossing his face and making his eyes crinkle. Again, so like his father.

"Do you think maybe for dinner this week . . . we can have *baked* potatoes?" Alex whispers.

Nika begins to write the request on her list but then pauses. "You didn't, did you?"

"He sure did." Lila lifts up a finger, and Alex quickly stands and places his hand against it.

Nika is touched once again by their camaraderie, their connection. A true one. Solid, strong, singular. It has its ups and downs and takes work to maintain it, but it's there.

Nika's emotions bloom. It's always a good day when you learn from your children.

chapter eleven

After the chaotic delay on Tuesday and the heart-to-heart chat with the kids the night before, Nika arrives early on Thursday to get her bearings, to remember how much needs to be accomplished before, during, and after school and how long everything will take. The play is coming together—it always does—but a few of the students are still "unsure" of their roles, and going off book down the line might be a struggle. Thankfully, one of Alex's friends hopes to be a theatrical director one day, and he's signed on to help out, which will allow Nika more time to put out fires. With the play, with her family, with the library, which has seen its fair share of issues lately, especially with respect to her library holdings. If Cole would take on the role of principal the way he should . . .

Nika laughs to herself at the idea of Cole stepping into a role she isn't even sure he wanted. Since he's been here, he's allowed more autonomy than his predecessors. Nika actually appreciates that trait for her job, but being hands off when it comes to kids and performing the role of principal? Not the ideal approach. The teachers are beginning to think about a revolt, and while Nika supports them, it's in her best interest to stay in "her lane," as Cole likes to say. What he has against her, Nika will never know.

Nika unlocks the door to the library, her spirit high and light, grateful for every book that will surround her in their embrace, but her heart sinks when something crinkles under her foot: a business-size envelope, next to which lay two books. *And Tango Makes Three*, a picture book about two daddy penguins raising a chick, and *Pride: The Story of Harvey Milk and the Rainbow Flag*, are in tatters. Pages ripped out, covers torn off, paragraphs blacked out. They aren't her library copies, but her heart aches as she rips open the envelope and finds a Love Is Not Love pamphlet, with a bloodred X over a rainbow.

This had to be the work of an adult then, one who knows about *Once Upon a Fairy Tale* and the love shared between two girls. Cole wouldn't do this, would he? Abuse of power couldn't possibly be something he'd follow through with, and he'd already come in and raised Nika's ire. What would actions like these serve?

Nika pinches her chin and thinks about leaving. For the day. The week. The rest of the year. She thinks about screaming and running to the office and hauling anyone who will listen into the library. after which time, she'll give them a piece of her mind. She thinks about the world, the unfairness of life, the 1984 Depeche Mode hit "People Are People," and how the world still hasn't made much progress. Then her thoughts land on Gwendolyn, Alanna, and the other students, and she closes the door and texts Ethan: *You aren't going to believe what happened.*

He's probably still making sure the kids get out the door—they don't need much help these days—but a moment later, the three dots appear, and then: *Do you want me to guess?*

Nika: *I'll save time.*

She snaps a picture and sends it to him.

Ethan: *Who did that?*

Nika: *Wish I knew.*

Ethan: *Take pictures. Document everything. I'm not sure those pricks will believe you if you don't.*

Nika: *You're right. If I have to, I can open late.*

Ethan: *Better yet, screw the library. Take a day off.*

A day off sounds good, but how fair would that be? She says so to Ethan.

Ethan: *To whom?*

Nika: *The students.*

Ethan: *It always comes back to them, and that's only part of why I love you. I can swing by soon—do you need me?*

Having Ethan as support, to buttress both her mood and her confidence, would be fantastic, and yet, Nika needs to speak to Cole, pronto.

Nika: *I appreciate the thought, but I need to do this myself. Once I've documented and talked to Cole, I'll decide what to do about opening.*

Ethan: *Good idea. I'll see you this evening. I love you.*

Nika responds with a kiss emoji and an *I love you.* Saying the words is no issue for her, but showing love in the way Ethan wants . . . God, they need to chat, don't they? Really talk about things? Yes, but it will, once again, have to wait.

She places her phone onto the table and assesses what she has in front of her. The book demolition cleaves her heart, threatens to split it wide open. The question is—did the perpetrator leave any clues? Rainey would be the one to tell Nika. She's always been a fan of police procedurals, and no case is ever too small.

A quick text confirms Rainey's presence in the building. *I'll be down in two*, Rainey writes.

Two minutes later, almost to the second, Rainey peeks her head through the doorway. Nika didn't tell her anything, only that she needed to see her for a few minutes.

Rainey's gaze lands on the books. "What the—"

"Right?"

"I'm not sure what to say. What is this? Who did this? And *why* would anyone do this? What's wrong with people?"

"Apparently, it's to get back at me." Nika points to the center table. "Along with the books, they slid a pamphlet under the door."

Rainey moves to the table and picks up the pamphlet, then frowns and reads aloud from the first page: "The phrase love is love seems to be everywhere, and those who use it condone love between people of the same sex. But love is not love, and Scripture tells us so, unequivocally condemning homosexuality."

Rainey's scowl deepens as she flips through the pages, pauses at pictures, and reads to herself. "This is stupid. I mean, this is one person's point of view. Not even all Christians abide by this, not to mention a whole host of other religions don't. But leaving this here. Why? All because of the play? It doesn't make any sense."

"I guess they wanted to leave a message, as if those," Nika waves a hand at the butchered books, "didn't make enough of an impact." She picks up the remains of both books, cradles them against her chest, as if her love for books can repair the damage.

Rainey looks at the pamphlet again, then up at Nika. "This means you have a dumb criminal on your hands—Darwin and all—and my guess is, they left a calling card."

The flippancy of Rainey's comment makes Nika laugh so hard, tears come to her eyes, and she blinks them back, fearful the mirthful tears might morph into angry, sad tears—all part of menopause's magic.

"Listen," Rainey continues. "My student teacher can take the first hour for me. Let me go check in with her," she glances at her phone for the time, despite the large, primary color clock on the wall, "and I'll be back. We can scour the books and papers for clues!" Rainey shakes her hips and pumps her fists in the air.

"Thanks, Velma," Nika says. "Hey, if you see Cole, don't tell him. I'll do it in a minute."

Rainey leans in for a hug. "No worries, Nika. We'll get through this." She skips out the door, almost taking Nika's heart with her.

~

Cole is in his office, coffee cup nestled between his large fingers, ESPN on his computer screen. Does he even know how to access all the files he's supposed to oversee? Sometimes, Nika wonders. Today, she doesn't have time to worry about him and whether he's doing his job or not. She taps on his desk, tries to make her face stoic, serene, hopes he'll see she means business. Her emotions swell inside her, and a heat erupts across her skin as she thinks about how she found those books. She wills back whatever is happening to her—panic attack, hot flash, pure anger, whatever. "Cole, I need you in the library. Now, please."

Cole looks up and cocks his head to the side but says

nothing. He does the right thing by placing his coffee mug on his desk and following Nika to the library without complaint, his strides next to her long and fluid. A large rush of air releases from him when he sees the books, and he places his hand up to his bearded chin. "What happened?"

"Someone slipped them under my door. They aren't ours, but I don't tolerate book destruction." Nika leans over and grabs the pamphlet. "They left this too."

Cole takes the paper and scans it. "I'm not even sure what to say."

"How about, 'We'll find the person who did this, Nika, and we'll make them pay!'?"

He chuckles—*that's fair*—and looks at her. Though she has issues with Cole Hannon and his role here in the school, his gaze is nothing but sincere. "Glad you can keep your sense of humor. I'm not sure what the protocol is here. They didn't trash anything of yours? They're trying to send a message, it seems. Right?"

"Right, and I suppose even if I report this to the superintendent, she and the board won't want anyone to know this happened. This will be yet another little story they tuck into the very deep closet in the board offices."

"Nika—"

Nika slices the air with her fingers. "No, please let me finish. Someone came in here after school, after I closed up for the night. Another teacher? I don't think so. A parent? Probably. What if a student had been with me and saw this? How to explain to them why someone decided it's okay to deface books and leave religious propaganda in a public school?" A large gulp of air helps dampen Nika's anger. "Plus, I want to get a good look at these books and papers— *now*—so opening is going to be delayed by an hour, which affects the kids. *That's* why I'm angry. I can take the scorn, the venom, the ridiculousness of the situation, the very narrow-minded and sanctimonious people who are likely behind this. But you mess with me, *not* my students."

Cole places a large hand on her shoulder. Nika knows he means well, but his touch releases an agitated ripple through her backbone. "Look, that's why you're the best person for this job. We might not see eye to eye, but I'm certainly not going to take out one of my best people. Document everything, which I'm guessing you've done or are going to do, and we'll go from there."

Nika thinks about her bank account and how this job helps keep the kids in braces and athletics and instead of calling the board or the police to report noncriminal activity, she makes her way back to the library, prepares a cup of tea, tapes a note reading, "We'll open at 9 a.m." to the door, and settles in for the long haul.

~

By 8:43 a.m., Nika and Rainey have scoured the detritus, looking for anything to reveal the culprit. No hidden receipts or random price tags—the books could have come from any bookstore, could have been bought by anyone, which only cements the theory that the whole idea is to make an impression on Nika herself. Her jaw clenches again at the thought, and Rainey places her hand on Nika's forearm.

"You need to stop, hon. What's done is done, and I think we need to let this go for now." Rainey points to the computer screen. She had the great idea to try and find information on the pamphlet, but they quickly realized they were barking up the wrong tree, as Velma might say.

"*You* need to stop," Nika says. "Look at the time. You have a class to get to."

"Yes, but this is more fun somehow." She looks at Nika and holds up a magnifying glass in front of her right eye. "So much more fun!"

"Where did you even get that?"

"From *Diagnosis Detective.*"

Kids of all ages love the book, including, apparently, big kids like Rainey. "You are such a nerd."

"Sure am! But you love me."

"That, I do. Now, why don't you get going? I need to open soon. For the most part—" Nika's gaze travels the room, landing on the tall shelves, short tables, and the carpeted floor. "We're good here. Tomorrow, hopefully, will bring a good, destruction-free day."

"Okay." Rainey slips the magnifying glass into the book's sleeve. "I'll at least put this back on the shelf so you don't have another thing to do."

"Thanks."

Nika moves to the computer, pulls up the schedule, double checks which class is next, and the hustle and bustle of the late morning gets under way. Thankfully, nothing eventful happens after that. Nika runs out of bookmarks, which is a good *and* bad thing. Good because she has many interested students, bad because the students like to trade their bookmarks on the playground, which keeps them busy and out of trouble. Today, though, Nika doesn't worry. She doesn't even care that the last of the volunteers never makes it in to help. While she could not get along without volunteers, the push to finish this day is gargantuan. So powerful, she's beginning to think she deserves a personal day tomorrow. Fridays are traditionally lighter days, and a substitute wouldn't have to do too much. She stops in her tracks, thinks about a day in bed—*alone*—and warms to the idea of taking a day of leave. No one would need to know the *why* behind it.

As Nika hands two books to the last child in the library, she sighs, and the worry sitting like a weight on her shoulders lightens. The decimated books sit at the forefront of her mind, but now, she wants to clear her head of Cole, the library, her dad, the weed, possible sex therapy. She plugs the earbuds into her phone, turns on The Killers, and lets herself be swept away.

chapter twelve

The night Nika formally met Ethan, she'd been listening to The Killers in her car on the way to the dance studio. After class, she hopped back into her car, turned up "Mr. Brightside," and sang at the top of her lungs until a tap on the window startled her. Nika rolled the window down as an embarrassed flush spread throughout her body.

"Your siren's call, I see." Ethan, who had introduced himself when they'd paired up, leaned down and made eye contact.

Nika covered her heated face with her hands, too mortified to answer.

"It's okay, you know. I like The Killers," he said.

"You do?" Nika spoke through her fingers.

"I do, although I'll admit—I wasn't aware of them when they first burst on the scene. I don't know what I was doing in my life then, but it wasn't listening to alternative rock."

"Ha!" Nika uncovered her face and smiled. "I remember when I first heard 'Mr. Brightside.' I thought, this is great. Who wrote this? Wonderful new song. Then, I looked it up. It was three years old! I guess I'm in the same boat."

In a fit of unknown bravery, Nika hopped out of her car to stand near this almost-a-stranger man. As they leaned against her car, his sensitive intensity coiled around her in the same manner it had inside the studio, when they danced, their warm bodies pressed close to one another.

"Well, you have a few years on me then."

"Guess so. Favorite song of theirs?" she said.

"Oh, tough one." He placed his finger to his chin, tapped it once, and then spoke. "Have you heard 'Between Me and You'?"

The title didn't sound familiar. "No. How'd I miss it?"

"I don't know if it's a Brandon Flowers song or the whole band, but anyway, check it out."

"I will. Did you know they wrote a song for the *Twilight* movie?"

"They did? I'm sure you're not surprised to hear I didn't see the movie. Didn't hear the song."

"As a librarian, I have a love-hate relationship with the book. It's difficult to write one book, and the author finished a series that people loved, which is testament to her. She wrote a story people wanted to read."

"But? I sense one loud and clear. Mostly because you said you have a love-hate relationship with it." He tapped his head. "I'm smart like that." Ethan had the decency to blush before smiling.

"*But*, the books . . . Oh, I hate to disparage any author, so I won't. An agent knew no one would care about any issues because they'd love the story. At the end of the day, a world where everyone reads is better than one where they don't."

"Spoken like a true librarian. I'd love to hear more about your job. By the way—" He reached out and moved a stray hair away from Nika's face, a gesture so trite, and yet, it instilled a shimmer in Nika's already fluttering heartbeat. "Would you be interested in going out? Maybe grab a bite to eat before class next week?"

Without knowing it, Ethan had chosen well in terms of opportunities. Nika already had a sitter scheduled so she could take the dance classes, and even though he knew nothing about Alex and Lila, she appreciated the easy setup. But dating wasn't on Nika's radar, and she had no intention of getting married again. Having been burned to ash once was enough for her. Lila and Alex deserved more, and so did she. So, her first inclination to Ethan's request was to say no, but then she thought of what Rainey would say: a quick dinner before a class wouldn't hurt, especially since it came with a time limit.

"You're a smooth talker, Ethan. Quite the segue."

"So I've been told." The tips of his ears turned red, making him look younger than she supposed he was.

"Sure, I think I can swing dinner. Do you have a place in mind?"

"I have a few, but . . . any foods you don't like?"

"Nah. I'm not a big meat eater, but otherwise, I can be happy almost anywhere."

"Great. Then what about the Kennedy Grill?"

"Perfect. I'll meet you there. Is five thirty too early?" She'd still have time to sit with Alex and Lila for their early dinner, one of her most treasured times of the day.

"Nope. Makes sense. We would *not* want to miss class,

would we?"

Nika twisted her fingers together. "Actually, I'd be fine missing class. You saw me in there, didn't you?"

"You did okay. I could tell you didn't really want to be there but—"

Well how embarrassing. "You could? It wasn't you. Dancing isn't my thing."

"Then we'll make it your thing, or at least make it *look* like it's your thing. How about it?" A smile. Words laced with hope and promise.

Nika's heart flopped in her chest, once, twice, three times. Sappy sentiment but what a delightful change to feel something so innocuous, almost potent and positive. "Sounds great." Nika tapped her car. "I should get going, but I'll see you next week."

It wasn't until after Nika had arrived home and spent a few minutes in the driveway, thinking of Ethan—the natural sheen of Ethan's hair, the light scruff covering his jawline, the strong chest she'd been pressed up against—that she realized they hadn't exchanged numbers. If she had to cancel, she'd call the dance place and ask them to relay a message to him. But he hadn't pushed her into exchanging numbers, as if he'd read—*clearly*—she was on new ground by even accepting a date. Maybe everything would be okay.

~

Nika ends up taking the next day off. Ethan heads to the office early after kissing her softly on the lips and smiling, telling her to enjoy her peace and quiet. The kids hear their conversation as they get shoes and backpacks on, and they both look at her with furrowed brows. Lila puts a hand to Nika's forehead and then follows it with a kiss, the way Nika would assess whether Lila has a fever.

"She seems fine," she says to Alex.

"Then I don't know what's wrong," he replies.

"You can stop pretending I'm not here," Nika says and takes another sip of coffee. She's still on her first cup, but she might indulge in two full cups today. Along with a slice of homemade banana bread. Warmed. The thought of the sweet snack sends a tingle through Nika. She is far too dependent on sugar-infused items in the morning.

"Oh, did you hear something?" Lila asks.

"Do you want to eat dinner tonight?" Nika directs the question at Alex and Lila, but she's smiling.

Lila leans over and hugs her while Alex extends a fist for a usual daily bump.

"I'll see you after school. I might have a list of things we need to do today, but we'll get them done before whatever else you want to do. Sound good?"

"Well, no, but I know you don't really want to hear that," Alex says wryly before hoisting his backpack on his shoulders. "See ya, Mom."

The two leave, and the silence strengthens Nika. She wants to know where Dad is, but the house's setup doesn't always make it so simple to ascertain. It's why they bought this house in the first place. With an in-law suite on one side toward the back, it's easy for him to come and go without anyone knowing about it. Clearly, he's been using that to his advantage, but Nika ignores that for today. Instead, she lifts the coffee to her lips again, takes a slow sip, and marvels at the sun streaming through the kitchen windows, making beautiful patterns on the quartz countertop.

Her phone dings with a text from Rainey, asking if she's coming in.

Nika: *Nope.*

Rainey: *Good for you. I'm walking to the office now. Going to check to see who's subbing. OMG. You're not going to believe this.*

Nika: *What?*

Rainey: *The library is closed.*

Nika: *Why? It doesn't make sense. I put the job up last night. Someone should have taken it.*

Rainey: *Yeah, well, the doors are closed, and the lights are off.*

Nika hadn't told anyone what happened, except for Rainey, Ethan, and Cole. So . . .

Rainey: *Hold on. I'm going to*

The screen is dark for a minute, and impatience gets the best of Nika. She keys in, *Going to what?* More silence from Rainey makes Nika's heart thunder, the sound reverberating in her ears. She stands from the table and paces. If she's not careful, her thoughts will spiral. Mabel looks up from her bed, blinks, and closes her eyes again as if saying, "Nothing to see here, lady."

Nika: *Hello?*

Finally, her phone buzzes.

Rainey: *I went around to the side door. It wasn't locked. And I went inside . . .*

Nika: *And?*

Rainey: *I crept into the dark room . . .*

Nika: *Not funny, Rain!*

Rainey: *And I . . .*

Nika's had enough. She clicks on Rainey's phone number, and Rainey picks up instantly.

"I really am funny, aren't I?" Rainey says.

"No." Nika manages to keep her tone deadpan. "Now what's going on?"

"You're not going to like this, but I found another book, and yes, it's been destroyed."

"Is it one of mine?"

"Doesn't look like it. Hold on."

A text comes in from Rainey with an image attached. Nika clicks on it and gasps. It looks like *Maiden & Princess*—a beautiful picture book about finding true love in an unexpected person—had a showdown with Edward Scissorhands. There's no plastic sleeve, which means it's not one of hers. But still . . . "What the fuck?"

"I know, right? This is beginning to piss me off." Rainey sighs over the line. "You know what? The admin gets here early. Maybe Cole told her to keep the library closed for the day, and she canceled the sub job. Makes sense, yeah?"

"I guess so, but why was the door unlocked, and who put the book there? Furthermore, why can't they have some balls and confront me?"

Rainey laughs. "You're asking a lot, my friend, and you know it. Conflict avoidance seems to be the norm these days, and don't get me started on communication and respect."

"I won't," Nika says, then looks out her window. "Guess what? I'm not there, so I don't have to worry about this right now, do I? If this happens again, though, I guess—"

"If it happens again, we're calling authorities of some sort. In the meantime, take a rest, enjoy your day. I might still do a little snooping."

"I wouldn't expect anything less."

Interior: Pius X Elementary School, Sr. Margaret's
Fourth Grade Classroom, 1987

NIKA fidgets in her seat among a group of fourth
grade girls. SR. MARGARET draws on the chalkboard.

SAMANTHA
(laughing)
What are you drawing? An elephant? A bull?

SR. MARGARET
Enough! It's a picture of what's inside you, what
makes you a woman. This is the uterus, and these
are the fallopian tubes. After a woman and man
join as one *after* marriage, a baby will grow in
the uterus.

NIKA
(whispers)
Join as one? Oh my god.

SAMANTHA
My sister is having a baby, and she's not—

SR. MARGARET
Samantha! Remember, ladies, premarital sex is a
sin, a mortal sin. You must turn away from
temptation, but after marriage, well then, ladies,
you must commit and comply.

SAMANTHA
What? What do you mean?

SR. MARGARET

We'll discuss conjugal or marital debt another
time.

NIKA goes home after school and rummages through
her mother's books. She pulls out a large volume and
runs her finger over the index, hoping the words
will jog her memory. She stops when she gets to
conjugal/marital debt.

NIKA
(whispers)
A *right* to sexual intercourse? What does that even
mean?

chapter thirteen

Dad is nowhere to be seen, so Nika pulls up information on Susan Harris. Maybe going to visit a woman would be easier than talking to a man about her . . . issues.

Nika even hates to call them *issues*. Aside from Rainey—who isn't married and seems to find joy in every date and every sexual position—Nika knows she's not alone. People don't talk about the subject too much, but if you get in the right group at the right time and maybe involve some alcohol, it's easy to find out a good number of women are crabby, worn out, and affected by all the menopausal wonders. They're also tired. Extremely tired. Of the patriarchal nature of life and society. Tired of having to put out for the spouse. Ugh. The *spouse*. Yes, that's what Ethan is, what she is to him, but the word reminds her of the book chapter she read on conjugal debt, of the phrases "right to sexual intercourse" and "the obligation to give it to them." Nika shivers: better call for an appointment.

As if the stars align, Susan has a cancellation the next day, and "would she like to take it?" Alex and Lila will be occupied on Saturday—workout and homework, respectively—which means Nika can get to her appointment easily. Her fingers shake as she writes the appointment on her trusty paper calendar. Yes, she's one of those. The date will go on the computerized calendar, too, but there's nothing like pages. As a librarian, her preference shouldn't surprise anyone who knows her.

The receptionist on the line is kind and warm as she takes personal information and leaves Nika with one thought: be ready to work. Nika clicks to end the call, and she thinks, *What have I gotten myself into?*

Her phone rings, and without thinking, Nika reaches for it. Maybe it's the receptionist calling her back. Maybe another client beat her to the time slot, and she'll have to reschedule. Maybe Susan is no longer taking on clients. She'd jump for joy and never think about it again. Okay, not really, and the number is . . . not Susan's but Mindy's. Nika's whole body deflates at the idea of speaking with her stepsister, but the phone stops ringing before she can answer it.

Mindy came into their lives a long time ago. Nika's parents' divorce became final when she was twelve, and within two years, Dad had moved on to another relationship with Kathleen, which included Mindy, then ten years old. The four years between Nika and Mindy were enough to sustain a gap, though maybe *chasm* was the better word. While Nika was beginning high school, nervous about a larger academic campus and unsure of herself, Mindy was still back in her last year of elementary school. The big fish in a small pond without a care in the world. Her mother gave Mindy everything she wanted, and Dad didn't have the heart to stop either of them.

Living with Dad, Kathleen, and Mindy for four years had marked Nika. She'd often said to herself, I'll never divorce! I'll never bring two families together! I'll never allow any stepchildren to treat anyone as badly as Mindy treated me or Dad.

The naivete of being young. While Nika didn't have stepchildren, she *did* have a lot to learn, like understanding love doesn't always work as planned, and it can hit you when you least expect it.

But Mindy? Nika never understood why a grown woman in her forties hung on to her past so adamantly. Without responsibilities—she wasn't married nor did she have any children (thank goodness)—Mindy's life revolved around herself. She held a steady job—Amazon delivery person—but the rest of her time, at least from Nika's perspective, held very little meaning. Mindy's social media pages were littered with this party and that, this drink and that, this vacation and that. This year alone she'd flown to California. Twice. And then Barbados, an Alaskan Cruise, and New Zealand.

Each time Mindy posted about a new trip, Nika thought to herself: *How much does a delivery person make?*

"She's single," Ethan would always chirp. "She probably hoards the money and goes traveling. It doesn't take much to live on if you do it right."

Ethan would know, having been single without children for years before meeting Nika. "Do we drain you?" Nika had asked the last time the subject of Mindy came up.

"*Draining* isn't what I'd call it. I chose you, and I chose the kids. I chose this life. Do I have less money because of it? I probably will, but it's not something I think about. You contribute, financially and in countless other ways, so stop the nonsense." Then he kissed her on the nose and took off out the door.

What could Mindy want now? Has she heard about Dad? Should Nika call her back?

The phone rings again, and this time, the ringing does not stop. *Voicemail or answer?* Nika asks herself that question twice before answering the call.

Mindy launches right in: "I have a job for the kids, if they want one."

A job with Mindy. Nika sucks in a breath. "What do you mean?"

"I have a couple of kittens, and I'm headed out of town. I wanted to know if they could come over and check them while I'm gone. You know, food, water, scoop the litter."

The kids love cats more than anything. Except for Lila, who would say macaroni and cheese wins out over cats by a hair. But Alex has always been the animal whisperer in the house, and it's been a hot minute since they had a cat. "I'm sure they'd love to help. Do they need to come over every day?"

"I'll be gone for about ten days, but every other day would be fine for Olaf and Cheetah. Cute as buttons, feisty too. Little claws and *so* fuzzy. Maybe you could bring the kids over to meet them first."

"How about today after school? The kids get out at three." Having taken a day off, Nika might as well get something else accomplished. That philosophy would be lost on Mindy, whose mantra seemed to be: If I have the day off, why not party?

"Sure. See you about a quarter after three."

Nika holds the phone and looks at it, narrowing her eyes.

She didn't even ask Mindy where she was going or when she'd be leaving. They didn't have any solid plans to go anywhere, but exact dates would be great. Nika will have to ask when they go over.

The phone rings again. Nika sighs and picks it up, even though the number doesn't look familiar.

"Mrs. Stewart?"

"Yes."

"This is Detective Brine of the Five Rivers Police Department."

Nika's breath hitches and her fingers shake, and cold shivers move up and down her spine. She hasn't seen Dad yet today, has no idea where he is or what he's up to. Maybe she should have asked him about his schedule, but he's a grown man with his own house entrance. Playing parent to her parent isn't something Nika thought about before.

"Ah, good morning. What can I do for you?"

"Would you be able to come down to the precinct? We'd like a word with you."

"Can I ask what this is about?" Nika tries to keep her voice from quivering too much.

He ignores her. "Would you be available at eleven thirty?"

Nika looks at the clock, which reads eleven on the nose. The precinct isn't far, and she doesn't need to wash her hair. A quick shower and change of clothes will suffice. "I can be there at eleven forty-five." Give herself more time to let the squall inside her chest abate. The worst he can say is no.

"Good. We'll see you then."

Brine ends the call, leaving Nika with questions and a roiling in her gut. Something might be seriously wrong; she might not be the only one with issues.

Maybe she should have gone into work today after all.

~

The only other time Nika has been to the police station was the summer before, when she dropped off Alex's leftover wisdom teeth removal medication. Alex's teeth were impacted, and their presence would deter his other teeth from aligning properly, even with the planned-for braces.

Today, an overwhelming doomed feeling strikes Nika as she pulls open the first set of double doors. Gray coats everything: the walls, the floor, the chairs. Sterile, clinical. But sad too. Depressed, dreary. She wonders about all the events these inanimate objects have witnessed, what despair they've seen—the horrified faces of family members and tears of friends—and she reminds herself not to go there. Life's events can mire her down quickly if she lets them.

Nika pushes a button next to a window with metal shutters and waits.

A receptionist answers. "What can I help you with today, ma'am?"

They must have a camera, Nika thinks and looks up to the corner, smirking at the technology. "I'm here to see Detective Brine. I have an eleven forty-five appointment."

"Please have a seat. He'll be right with you."

Nika settles into a chair and reads the limited paraphernalia on the walls. A nonemergency phone number. What to do if you feel threatened. How to rid your home of medications. She's not sure what she expected, but it's not this. Someone inside these walls would need this information *before* they got here. Then again, these posters plant information in the head, like seeds in the ground, something to come back to when needed. Nika doesn't have time to dwell on the thought, though, because a tall man with familiar piercing dark eyes buzzes through the door.

"Thank you for coming in on short notice, Mrs. Stewart."

"You're welcome, but Nika is fine."

"Nika it is, then. Please come this way."

She follows Brine down a series of cool-air hallways to an office area toward the back. Or, she thinks it's the back because she can't tell where they're headed. It's like a true dungeon and labyrinth all in one, and suddenly, a heaviness settles in her chest, alternating with a light tapping, like her heart is on a timer, ready to blow when the clock reaches zero. *I didn't tell anyone where I was going, so no one knows I'm here. What if I don't come back? What if I'm not home when the kids get home? They know I'm supposed to be there—*

They stop before the water cooler, and Detective Brine gestures to it. "Would you like some? We also have coffee."

"No, I'm good. Thank you. Would you mind telling me what this is about?"

"All in due time, Mrs. Stewart. All in due time." He tips his chin up and dismisses Nika.

If he weren't an officer of the law, she'd kick him in the heels, or at least say something snarky and unrefined, but she refrains. And then she thinks: *What would Rainey do?* She'd probably be staring at his butt, deciding if he was her next conquest or not. In fact, this guy *is* Rainey's type. Nika will have to dig out his business card and give it to her.

When they reach his glorified cubicle, Detective Brine gestures for Nika to enter. Here, the walls still scream sterile, but the click and clack of computer keys and the voice level of those on the phone lend vitality to the scene. Her gaze lands on a window with a small jade plant on the sill. The leaves, tinged brown, are parched, like the plant has been neglected a little too long. Nika itches to take a Styrofoam cup and water the poor thing, but she holds back. Instead, she switches her attention to a woman a few cubicles over, who looks up from her work and sends Nika a quick smile. Nika returns the gesture, then glances around the rest of the place. Everyone else is doing their thing, not noticing her or her jittery hands, the trembling overtaking her knees. For them, it's simply another day in the precinct.

Nika settles into the chair and tugs on the end of her shirt. She considers herself strong and powerful at times, confident at others, but right now isn't one of those times. Trying to keep the pleading tone out of her voice, she says, "Please. I need to know what's happening. It's been a little stressful at my house, and this . . . well. I don't need this."

"Stressful?" Detective Brine lifts his eyebrows. "You don't say."

That's a bit too . . . What, comfortable? "Wait. With all due respect, did I detect some attitude there? What don't I know?"

"We took the drug-sniffing dogs into the high school today, and we found something."

"Okay. And how does this involve *me?*" How had she convinced herself she would have an absolutely stress-free day with everything—?

"Well, we found drugs in your son's backpack."

"What?" Nika brings her right hand to her heart and grips the chair's arm with her left hand as blood thunders in her ears. Images of Alex as a little boy come to mind. Floppy hair, toothless grin, chubby cheeks. An even mix of dare devil and comedian, the kid who keeps her on her toes. "No, you did not, sir. There's been a huge mistake. Alex would not— I don't even know what to say."

"Actually, he said they aren't his, but we see things like

this all the time, ma'am, and in most instances the teenagers are trying to get out of getting in trouble. It's likely they *are* his drugs."

"Well, I'd beg to differ. I'd know my own son! He didn't do this. He just didn't."

"Are you sure?"

Brine's words make Nika question herself. Does she know Alex? She knows how he likes his scrambled eggs—made with milk but only a little butter in the pan—and how he loves eucalyptus candles, though he won't admit it to his friends. Alex wanted to grow his hair long for years but didn't have the courage to do it. He was relieved when Ethan welcomed being called Dad, and he'd do anything for Lila, Ethan, Nika, Mabel. Even Grandpa.

But Nika also knows kids in general, knows they surreptitiously slip things past their parents. Even the attentive ones. And even when people think they know most things about someone, they don't know everything. *Can't* know everything. Plus, she had no idea Dad—*her own father!*—partook of weed on the regular, so maybe she doesn't have a clue about anything going on in her house right now. Maybe she's not only a shitty daughter and a shitty wife, she's a shitty mother.

Nika's head falls into her clammy hands, and she closes her eyes, blowing out a breath, trying to tamp any other anxious thought from exposing its claws. But in that moment, a hot flash threatens, so she sighs and adjusts her collar, letting the air move against her damp skin. "Detective Brine," Nika finally says, "there are so many things I see daily, none of which surprise me, but I would be *very* surprised if those drugs are my son's. Shocked even. Did you give him a drug test?"

"We need your permission. He's a minor."

"Okay, so where is he? You're not allowed to transport him separately, are you? Shouldn't I have been called? When can I see him?"

"Soon."

"And that means?" Nika's rage simmers, swells to a boil, then she dials it back by taking in steady breaths and holding Brine's gaze. "Listen. I'm an upstanding Five Rivers citizen and a valued school district employee. I'm a taxpayer and a volunteer, a mother, and a wife. I'm a neighbor and a friend, and I deserve better treatment than you, Detective Brine, are providing. You give me an answer I can use, or I'll find someone else to help. Do you understand?"

A hand falls on Nika's shoulder and squeezes. It's Ethan. The universe will right itself with Ethan here. Since meeting him, he always applies salve to Nika's wounds, always makes sure to assess the damage and help repair it. With Ethan—

"Honey?" Ethan's dark eyes brim with worry, and his voice shakes. "They called me, and I met him at the school. He . . . Alex confessed."

chapter fourteen

Nika's stomach clenches, and acid rises in her throat as Ethan's words register in her brain. Confessed? Alex? A-L-E-X?

When Alex was four years old, Nika would joke around with him, using the letters of his name to tease him. Always Learning and EXamining. A Little Energetic Xylophone. He'd been the kid most likely to flush the toilet pass because he wanted to see how it would affect the swirling of the water, and a few weeks ago, he admitted to taking litmus paper into the bathroom and testing his urine during the pH lab.

So, despite what she thought moments before—*parents don't know everything about their children*—Alex with drugs doesn't match Nika's mental picture of her child, unless he was "experimenting." But his behavior lately hasn't supported drug use, at all. Plus, Nika is certain Lila, who loves him fiercely, would have ratted him out if she knew anything.

And yet he confessed.

Ethan takes a seat next to Nika and grabs her hand, squeezing her fingers and pulling their clasped hands to his lap. He doesn't let go, and right then, Nika feels his worry. Ethan might be doing a magnificent job of looking untroubled, but his gesture—something in it—reveals so much.

Brine rises. "Mr. Stewart, can I get you something to drink?"

"Water would be nice, thank you."

"I'll be right back."

Nika allows her gaze to follow Brine as he moves deeper into the precinct, then turns to Ethan and shrugs.

"I'm sure he wanted to get out of here for a moment. Give us time to chat," Ethan says, his voice muted against the office chatter.

"You're probably right. He wouldn't tell me why I was called down here, and with Dad and the party, honestly, I was confused."

"I would have been too."

"So how did you get lucky enough to get the phone call to meet Alex? Don't take this the wrong way—you *are* Alex's father in every way, but I'm the one who birthed him. Shouldn't *I* have had the right to the information first?"

"No offense taken." He leans over and strokes her cheek then places a kiss on her forehead. "Sounds like Alex told them to call me, probably so you weren't worried. And when I spoke to the school on the phone, they said you'd been informed."

An exhale leaves her body, and she's only slightly relieved by his statement. "Informed? Ha! I'd like to know what the truth is here."

Ethan raises his eyebrows. "The truth? Do you think he did it?"

"I don't, but what else could it be? Why would he confess?"

Ethan doesn't hesitate. "Alex is a lot of things, but he doesn't use drugs."

It's not Ethan's words, it's the way he says them. The conviction in his voice, the set of his shoulders, the depth of his eyes. Nika's reminded why she fell for him in the first place, which involved his wholehearted loyalty to Lila and Alex. How much they captured his heart right from the start. She leans over and places a kiss on his lips. Gentle, sweet. Painful, really, because she knows he wants so much more outside of this place. But it's enough, for now.

"Thank you," Nika whispers.

"It's the truth," he says.

Detective Brine comes back with water—two of them—and hands one to Nika. "I thought it best to bring one for you too. The bottled water is better than anything from the water cooler. Hope you don't mind."

"Not at all," says Ethan. "Thank you. What comes next?"

"We're getting all the information from Alex, but possession for anyone under eighteen is considered a misdemeanor. Depending on what happens here, he might have to go to court. He might end up with probation, drug counseling, and there's something called *diversion*, which we won't get into now. Since he confessed, well, the prosecutor might not go lightly on him, but at the same time, this is his first offense."

First offense. Nika wants to say it's not even an offense. It's a mistake. An error. An injustice. Brine doesn't want to know Nika's way of thinking though. If he did, he would have asked. "When can we take him home?"

"Soon."

Soon turns out to be two hours later, and the rest of Nika's day off is for naught. Alex approaches Nika and Ethan, his face pale and drawn, his shoulders slumped, and his hands tucked deep into his pockets. The look screams despondence, not guilt, and Nika is tempted to shout obscenities at the top of her lungs and hurl her hefty bag at anyone within a five-foot radius. Instead, she wraps an arm around Alex's waist and pulls him in, keeping a constant pressure against him, as if she's afraid he'll float away.

Detective Brine holds a plastic bag out to Ethan and Nika. "We're keeping the backpack, but Alex requested his phone, computer, and a few other things we're allowing him to take. We'll be in touch—make sure to sign papers on the way out."

Nika snorts. "And the way out is? It's a maze in here."

Brine chuckles, the first sign of lightheartedness Nika's seen from him. "It really is. Sorry for any confusion." He points to one of the doors with the large, red EXIT sign over it. "That door will lead you to the receptionist who will have the papers for you."

He tips his head in Alex's direction. "We'll see you soon."

Tears perch on Alex's lower eyelids, but he furiously blinks them away. He mumbles a quiet "thanks," and Nika imagines it's not quite the word he was looking for, but Alex has always taken his manners seriously, much to Nika's delight. What does one say in a situation like this anyway?

"I appreciate your help," Nika says and extends her hand to Detective Brine, who shakes it easily but offers no warmth.

The car ride home weeps with quiet, drips with

desolation. The last thing Nika wants to do is cause Alex any more angst by talking. If she knows her son, he's probably trying to process everything right now. Shit, Nika herself is trying to process everything because she truly believes those drugs *aren't* Alex's. She glances at him in the passenger seat. Eyes closed, pale cheeks. Finger tapping incessantly against his thigh as they listen to NPR. Terry Gross is speaking to an up-and-coming author on her latest novel and changes in the publishing industry, and in usual Gross fashion, the interview draws Nika in, away from the heartbreaking reality next to her. When they're in the driveway and the garage door opens, Alex hops out of the car and hustles inside.

Ethan exits his own car—he's pulled up alongside her on the driveway—then shares a glance with Nika. Ethan speaks first. "I'll say it again—there's no way those drugs are his."

"Then we need to keep that at the forefront of our minds and tread lightly, right?"

"Yeah." He nods, then shakes his head. "You ever think we'd get caught up in two different drug stories in such a short amount of time?" Ethan jingles the keys in his hand then turns them over and over, their clink contrasting with the swallow's song filtering through the air.

"Nope, not at all. I wonder what lesson life is hoping to teach me this time." Life works that way for Nika; when she tries to address one issue, something else comes along. *When will I have time to take care of myself?* Nika thinks. *What if—*

"Say no to drugs?" Ethan laughs.

"Really?"

"Yes. I had to, and I'm sorry."

Nika can't help smiling, and the moment's gaiety eases the acrimonious lump growing inside her chest.

~

Lila is sitting at the kitchen table doing her homework when Ethan and Nika walk in. Alex is nowhere to be found, which means he's hiding in his room. Nika knows he needs his space, but she wants him out here, with them, so she texts him to come out and do his homework. He's quick to respond, almost as if he's had enough for the day, as if he knows there's no room to challenge Nika.

He pours himself into a kitchen chair and places his things on the table. Gone is Nika's confident, true Alex. A somber cloud surrounds him, casts dark shadows, and this being? He's not Nika's son. She places her hand on his back, rubs circles, and then leans into a hug. Alex has never been one to shy away from her when she's adamant, and thankfully, he doesn't do it this time either. He tilts Nika's way and presses his body up to hers, a silent gesture of trust. Or surrender.

"You need anything, kids?"

"No, but what happened to *him*?" Lila says. "He looks like death."

Nika tries not to keep anything from either child. When their dad left, she explained the situation in terms their young selves could understand. When Ethan came on the scene, she did the same. "We had a meeting at the police station. Dogs found drugs in his backpack."

Lila doesn't miss a beat. "Bullshit."

Nika's watching her children the whole time, her gaze flitting back and forth, and while Alex's head is pointed downward, she sees him flick his eyes up at Lila's words. He widens them for a millisecond as he stares at her, like he's communicating silently.

"Exactly what *we* said." Ethan sits in the chair between Lila and Alex. "And you confirmed it," he says to Lila. "What

I want to know is, what are you doing with drugs in your backpack? And why would you confess they're yours?"

Lila blanches, and her eyebrows draw together, then she points at Alex. "You *confessed?* Are you an idiot? Come on, bro. I expected better of you."

In another universe, Nika would be laughing at Lila's attitude, at her carefree demeanor, at her confidence and swagger at calling out her older brother. But her words hit Alex hard, and tears form in the corner of his eyes.

Alex *never* cries.

"Okay, okay, Lila," Nika says. "I agree with you on all levels, but Alex is hurting, and while I know you're trying to support your brother, you might need to be more sensitive. What do you think?"

Lila peeks at Alex and sighs. "I'm sorry," she says without Ethan or Nika prodding her. "It's—those drugs *aren't* yours."

"They are. Those are my drugs. Just live with it, okay?" Alex whispers as he closes his eyes and rests his head against the seat back.

"Live with what?" Dad says as he walks in the kitchen. For being older, he's quite the stealthy ninja; Nika rarely hears when he's approaching.

Alex's head whips around to look at his grandfather, then he jumps up from the chair, gathers his things, and bolts from the room.

"What did I do?" Dad asks.

A look of comprehension washes over Ethan at the same moment realization dawns on Nika. "Those drugs *aren't* his." Nika whispers as she places her hand on Dad's forearm. "Either Alex thinks they're yours, or they really are."

chapter fifteen

"Lila, would you mind going to your room for a moment?" Nika says.

Lila must understand the situation's gravity, for she doesn't argue. "Can I take a snack? Some peppers and a cheese stick?" Ethan hates crumbs in the bedrooms, and Nika appreciates Lila's awareness.

"Yes, and a cookie is fine too," Ethan says with a tight smile.

"Thanks." Lila leans in as she passes the table and gives Ethan a kiss on his cheek.

Nika's heart melts until Dad leans back in his chair, something Nika has asked him not to do several times. She doesn't want him or the chair getting hurt, but she's not willing to deal with the battle right now. *Break the chair, break your hip, whatever, but please find me some peace.*

"What did I do? I mean, I've tried to stay out of trouble

for the past few days. Can you give me a clue?"

Nika assesses her father's face, his posture, everything from the top of his head to the tip of his toes. Nothing about him screams he knows what she's talking about, so she fills him in on what happened at the precinct.

Dad's eyes widen in shock when Nika reaches the part about the drugs in Alex's bag. "And how might I be involved? I have my own weed stash, but I certainly wouldn't give any to Alex. Like he'd even ask."

"Well," says Ethan as he scratches his chin. "Alex confessed. He said the weed and pills were his."

"What the fuck? I might not be the smartest, but your kid has a helluva lot of intelligence, and he's not doing drugs. I don't know what he's doing, but it ain't drugs."

"We agree with you." Ethan gets up, pours some leftover coffee into his favorite mug, and pops it into the microwave. Thirty seconds later, he's back at the table, holding out a cup for Nika to sip from, steam spiraling from the lip of the mug like a twirling dancer.

"So, what do you think he's up to?" Dad asks.

Nika glances once at Ethan, then locks eyes with her dad again. "To be honest, if those drugs aren't yours, I think he thinks they are and is trying to protect *you*," she says.

"What?"

Ethan takes a seat again. "The only other person would be another kid—"

"But he doesn't hang with that crowd." Dad finishes Ethan's sentence, and Nika is astounded her father might be more aware of what's going on in her child's life than she thought. Maybe Dad deserves some slack, deserves to tell his story, the whole of it. It's something to consider.

"I agree, but it must be a kid or you. Those are the only

explanations, right?" Nika says. She taps her chin in time to the second hand of the old analog clock sitting on the kitchen shelf. Her dad had given it to her when she was younger, and for some reason, she's never been able to part with it.

"They might not be the *only* explanations, but protecting your dad makes more sense than some kid," Ethan says. "Because if he confessed to the cops—which we know he did—then he must be concerned about the person he thinks he's covering for."

Dad scratches his cheek and pulls on his beard, which is veering into Grizzly Adams territory. Add to it his threadbare undershirts and the state of his other clothing and . . . Nika makes a mental note to ask her father how he's doing.

"You know what?" Nika says, "I think we need to talk to him."

"Be right back." Ethan stands and leaves the room.

Dad leans in and takes Nika's hand. "I'm so sorry. I didn't mean for any of this to happen. I know—"

"Dad, I get it. You brought weed around the house, but the blame isn't all yours. I mean, I'll place part of the blame on you if Alex thought he was protecting you, but I won't place *all* of it. Okay?"

"Deal," Dad says and then snickers. "I'm sure this isn't how you thought your day off would go, is it?"

"Not at all. In fact, my plan was to sit around and maybe prepare a little for an appointment I have tomorrow." Dad can't help Nika find a sustainable and fulfilling connection with Ethan. He can't help her channel her menopausal irritation or uncover a more robust libido, and even if he could, how bizarre would that be? So, she doesn't elaborate.

Then, Alex walks into the room and sits in his chair, his head hanging, dark hair flopping over his eyes.

"Honey. Look at me." Nika reaches out to touch his fingers, and he pulls away. A little more sharply, she asks him to look at her again. His eyes are tinged with red, and she reads remorse written all over them. "We think the drugs aren't yours."

"They *are*." He's emphatic, but again, he won't meet anyone's eyes.

"They aren't. And while it's noble you want to protect someone—because that's what we think you're doing—we want you to know the drugs aren't your grandfather's either."

Alex's head snaps up. "They aren't?"

"No," Grandpa says. "I would never leave anything like that in a place you two could get it. And if I couldn't find a bag of something—let me be clear, I've only used weed—I'd admit my problems to your mother before I let you take the fall."

The words cause more tears to course down Alex's cheeks, and he begins to heave.

Ethan snatches a prescription bag from the table, removes the medicine, and hands the bag to Alex, telling him to breathe into it and rubbing circles on his back. Moments like these, as difficult as they are to witness, confirm once again that Nika chose correctly when she said yes to the date, to the engagement, to the marriage, to this life she's so incredibly lucky to have.

Two minutes pass, and Alex steadies his breathing, wipes his eyes. "Then whose drugs *are* they?"

"I don't know," her dad says, "but I think you need to be honest with the police this time."

Nika's entire being brims with fatigue, and the thought of another trip to the police station does nothing but set her on edge. Outwardly, she's sure she's fine, but inwardly, she's fuming, churning, and plain exhausted.

Ethan takes action. "Why don't Grandpa and I take Alex back and you stay here. Someone should be here for Lila anyway, in case she has any homework issues, and we can call you if we need anything."

"Are you sure?" Nika wipes her hand across her forehead. Maybe she's coming down with something, or maybe stress is getting to her. Or maybe it's her blood vessels expanding, which will lead to another hot flash. Either way, she's grateful for Ethan's flexible schedule and his gesture. She turns to Alex. If he wants her there, she'll go.

Alex doesn't hesitate. "It's fine. I think Dad's right about this."

"Then keep me posted. I'll be here."

~

After the boys leave, Nika pokes her head into Lila's room. She's on the bed, papers strewn across the covers, earbuds in. Lila doesn't see Nika, who stands there watching—marveling, really—at her child. While she looks a lot like Alex, all knees and elbows and wide eyes, Lila has always been a sunnier person, and happiness follows her everywhere. Nika often wonders if the divorce and remarriage had any unpleasant effects on the kids, but looking at her daughter here, in her comfortable habitat, surrounded by books and stuffed animals and art supplies, she hopes any negative outcomes have been outweighed by the positive. At least for now. *Something* will send Lila to therapy someday—Nika is sure of it, and it might even be something she or Ethan does—but for the most part, they have a happy kid. A feral, fierce, deeply rooted love unfolds inside Nika's chest, and she walks into the room.

Lila looks up and plucks an earbud out. "What's up?"

"Not much. It's just you and me here now. Do you need anything?"

"Hot cocoa, please?" A smile spreads across her face. "With whipped cream?"

Years ago, Nika began keeping cans of whipped cream in the fridge. The frothy concoction did wonders for mood lifting. Feel like a treat without really having one? Add whipped cream to the strawberries. Only overripe bananas left in the bowl? Add whipped cream. Want to pretend you're at a fancy restaurant? Make hot cocoa, add whipped cream, and throw on a few chocolate shavings. A taste of ambrosia in an often-unpalatable world. Maybe Lila doesn't see it that way, but Nika does. "Sure. And chocolate shavings?"

"Oooh, yes please, if we have them."

"I'm sure we do. Give me a couple minutes."

Lila thanks her and puts her earbud back in, then settles in again with her homework. In no time, she'll be finished with her work, and she'll ask Nika to check it. It's the same approach every day, and Nika rarely has to ask her daughter to do the homework. It's a part of Lila's process, her routine.

Nika shakes the thoughts out of her head and makes the cocoa, filling a mug for herself too. When Lila tells Nika she's good and won't need her help for a while, Nika lets her know she'll be in her bedroom, calling Rainey. It might help disperse some of the uneasiness roosting on Nika's shoulders.

Rainey must hear something in Nika's voice, for she tells her she'll see her in fifteen minutes and to put more hot cocoa on. "Do you have any Bailey's?" Rainey adds before she hangs up.

chapter sixteen

Rainey rushes in like the Tasmanian devil, a scarf trailing behind her as she comes to rest near the kitchen table. As she sits, she begins to unwind the fabric, which seems to have no end, and Nika wonders how long it is, where she got it, and how it lays so nicely around her neck in normal circumstances.

"It's amazing, isn't it?" Rainey says as Nika stares at her.

"It is. How—?"

"It's a very fine material, so it almost adheres to the body when wound properly. I don't want to risk spilling any cocoa on it right now—it's my favorite."

"Noted. I love it too. Here—" Nika extends her hands. "Let's hang it on the hooks so it doesn't have a chance to get spoiled. You never know what might happen in this household these days."

"Speaking of which . . ." Rainey waggles her eyebrows

and sips the piping hot cocoa in front of her. "What in the heck is going on? This is almost like a Housewives of Five Rivers sort of thing!"

Rainey and Nika have been friends forever, so there's nothing she wouldn't tell her. But where to begin? So much seems to be happening lately, and Nika feels like a discombobulated mess, an untethered buoy in the sea. But Rainey already knows about the opposition to the play and Grandpa, so Nika regales the afternoon's misadventures. As Nika tells the story, Rainey's facial expressions change. At any other time, watching her would be pure entertainment. Today, not so much.

"Holy crap. What a lot to take in. And to think I once thought intimacy was the only thing you had to worry about!"

"Indeed. Funny thing is, I called Susan today to see about setting up an appointment, and I have one for tomorrow, but I wanted to prepare before I go. As you can imagine, my day got away from me."

"Uh, yeah, I can see that. The only prep you need is to reserve judgment, and you might want to be honest with Ethan. Let him know you're going, if you haven't already.

Nika shakes her head. "I know. But I'm not sure what to do. I mean, we have to get Alex cleared of these charges, and we need to figure out whose drugs they are. And Dad? I need to make sure he's going somewhere to get help, and the play? Well, I still don't know who destroyed—"

Rainey lifts her hand and snaps her fingers. "Whoa. Hold on here. I know you're Ms. Responsible, but let's review something. One," she holds up her left index finger, "your dad is an adult. I think he'll follow the rules, if you set them. Two, we have police for a reason, so let them do their job. Your dad said they aren't his. He isn't going to lie when Alex is involved. He might not always do the right thing, but your father loves your children—I have no doubt—and he would never hurt them. If Alex is cleared of any wrongdoing, you shouldn't have to worry about this situation for too much longer."

"I guess you're—"

"I'm not done."

"All right, bossy."

"And three, the library and the play—as long as the situation doesn't escalate, let it go for now. If it does happen again, we'll figure out next steps."

"What about you, Nancy Drew?"

"Oh, I didn't say *I* wouldn't still worry about it. I'll carry the burden on this one, but I don't have all the responsibilities you do. What I'm saying is, try to be at peace and let everyone worry about their own things. Which means you worry about you, do your prep, and go to your appointment tomorrow. By the way, how did you decide on the one you're going to?"

Nika tells Rainey how she found Susan Harris via Kenrick's website. "I wasn't sure about going to see a man regarding any issues I might have."

"Would it have helped to know Kenrick is gay?"

"Nah. He's so good looking, it's off-putting. Like you expect him to have this active, amazing sex life, which might put undue pressure on me."

"You know, you could have an active, amazing sex life too—"

"I know! That's the problem. I realize Ethan would do anything I want, within reason. He's up for experimentation. He'd try any position, anywhere, with anything. Probably with anyone if I wanted to, which I do not. It's a hard limit for me, as they say. Honestly, a magnificent, wonderful, mind-blowing sex life is right there for the taking!"

"*But . . .*"

"But I'm not sure I want it. I'm tired. I'm crabby. I'm angry. I'm *dry*, for fuck's sake—in places I didn't even realize I had! This body can do without sex for the rest of its life, and it hasn't even technically reached menopause yet. At least I'm pretty sure it can." Nika imagines a happy space, a bedroom all to herself. Waking up refreshed each morning, padding down the hall to Ethan's room, where she gives him a peck on the lips and then goes to make coffee—

"Oh," Rainey says, eyebrows raised, "I'm not sure I've ever felt this way. I'm not invalidating your feelings—"

"Don't worry about it. I think part of the feeling comes from birthing kids, which wears everything out. My breasts have been suckled beyond recognition, and having vaginal births shattered my pelvic musculature to smithereens, causing . . . What, dysfunction? Or maybe my brain is dysfunctional. I don't know. And if we add perimenopause to the mix . . ." Nika tips her head back, looking at the ceiling. For what? Guidance? A sign? The neck extension feels fantastic, like stretching after a deep sleep. Then, she glances at Rainey, who's leaning back in her seat, laughing.

"Are you laughing at me? Are you trying to make me feel bad?"

Rainey composes herself. "Not at all. In fact, I'm amazed. You're stronger than you think, and I sincerely mean it. If I had two kids, a second marriage, a dad living with me, a full-time job, and all the rest of this shit going down, I might not be interested in sex either. So maybe it's *not* just you."

"Nice try. I've been feeling like this for a while, and you know it."

One of Rainey's standby gestures is to take Nika's hand in hers. She does so now. "Yeah, but even if the peripheral shit is recent, I'm sure there were a few other things keeping your mind occupied. I get it—I really do. Me telling you to let go of the mess in your brain and enjoy yourself with Ethan would be invalidating, so good on you for making the appointment!"

"Will you go with me?" Going alone to a new place is something Nika has always avoided, if she can help it.

"Don't you think Ethan should go?"

"Maybe, but not the first time. I need my best friend there." Nika flips her palm and squeezes Rainey's fingers.

"And he's not?"

"No, he is. But you're my best *girl* friend. I need you. Not him. Eventually, I'll bring him with me."

Rainey leans in and hugs Nika. "Okay then, I'll be there. Power in numbers, right?"

Nika certainly hopes so.

Interior: Pius X Elementary School, Sr. Lydia's
Fifth Grade Classroom, 1988

NIKA twirls her hair as she sits with the rest of
the fifth-grade girls. SR. LYDIA, a new hire, stands,
frowning and with chalk in hand, at the front of
the classroom.

SAMANTHA
(raises hand)
We're going to talk about sex today, right? My
sister has sex.

SR. LYDIA
And how do you know that, Samantha?

SAMANTHA
(laughing)
Well duh, she had a baby last year. She's pregnant
again too!

SR. LYDIA
Congratulations to her and her husband.

SAMANTHA
Oh, she's not married. She graduated high school
last year. And the father left. I don't know who he
is.

SR. LYDIA
(covering her mouth)
That's enough, Samantha. We won't discuss
fornication in this classroom. Good Catholic girls
don't go around having sex before marriage! Didn't

anyone teach you sex is for procreation while married? Fun has nothing to do with it.

NIKA
(raises her hand)
If sex isn't any fun, why is everybody doing it? And why would we want to do it anyway? Just to have babies—

SR. LYDIA
I will not condone such insolence, Nika Washington, so march yourself to the office right now and tell them I sent you.

Forward to NIKA, sitting outside the principal's office, knees trembling. EVELYN walks out of the office, glares at NIKA, then points to the door.

chapter seventeen

It takes everything in Nika to hold herself together until her appointment with Susan Harris, but the hours slide by with few bumps, as if the entire universe is looking out for her. The police must have believed Alex's story, for they put a pin in any possible charges against him until they finish their investigation. Ethan assures them they'll help if they can because "as parents, we'd like to get to the bottom of it as well." Nika's mind begins to wander: Is this episode connected to the books and pamphlet in the library? Is someone trying to get back at her through her children?

Saturday dawns bright and foggy, opening like a new book: creaky and tired until the spine breaks and then, all at once, the pages freely fan out. Nika cuts short her usual Saturday morning run/walk so she can shower and eat before heading over to Susan Harris's office. It's in a tidy building on the north side of town, in an area housing small shops, boutiques, and salons. Nika's not even there yet, and she already feels out of place, lightheaded. But Rainey's voice rings loud and clear in her head—she "needs to do this." For herself and for Ethan, but mostly for herself. And Rainey will be meeting Nika there anyway, so it's not like she can bolt.

Parking is easy, thank goodness, and Nika walks over to the Four Corners Paper Company. If paper is needed, this is the place to look. Standard white copy paper, children's birthday party invitations, graduation announcements, parchment, cardstock. You name it, they have it. She's always wanted a real reason to go in and get some paper. So far, the only time she's been inside was for wedding announcements. Ethan and Nika had decided to elope, taking the kids of course. But they didn't want to confuse anyone, so they'd sent out a short announcement, letting friends and family know of the changes and new address.

As Nika stands looking in the window, a bright card catches her eye, and she thinks a new bookmark for the library is in the cards. She chuckles at the inadvertent pun then turns to see Rainey rushing up the street.

Coffee in one hand and keys in the other, Rainey hustles, her cheeks flushed, eyes glowing. She reminds Nika of Lila: always a force to be reckoned with, a burst of positivity, like a rain shower of Skittles.

"Hey, girl," Rainey says. "I almost brought you coffee, but I knew you'd be up at the ass crack of dawn. You've probably gone for a jog, thrown in the laundry, done some weeding, eaten breakfast, showered, and paid some bills. Maybe even more."

Nika twists her lips and says nothing, hoping her expression says it all.

"Oops. Sorry. I know, I know. I was *teasing* you." Rainey

cocks her head to the right. "Have you considered maybe I'm jealous? I can barely keep myself on track, and here you are, taking care of three, wait, four, other people and yourself rather well."

"Not so well—hence our foray here." Nika points up the road to the miniscule sign with Susan Harris, LPCC and a bunch of other letters behind her name. While she doesn't broadcast sex therapy on the sign, Nika imagines a gigantic, cherry red, blinking arrow hovering above her head as she and Rainey walk the few steps toward the building, and her cheeks warm. "I'm getting too hot. Can you tell?" Nika turns toward Rainey.

"Holy fuck. Your face is the color of your beloved beets! What happened?"

"I was going to say hot flash, but this feels different. Tightness. Pressure. My chest, my, my—"

Rainey sets her coffee down and grips Nika's shoulders with her fingertips, driving them hard into her skin. While the action doesn't hurt, it's enough to draw Nika's attention there and away from her rickety breathing. "Breathe in and out, slowly. This is something you can do. You're not the only one to come here . . . You realize this, don't you? This is Susan's *job*."

"I do. In my head, I do." Nika breathes deeply through her nose and tries to focus on the chirping birds in the gutter above her. "Please, can you tell me one odd thing about you?"

Rainey snorts. "You've seen me. What do you mean?"

"I mean with respect to sex. Don't take this the wrong way because I *do not* imagine you getting it on, but I always think you're a sex goddess. No issues. Completely open to all things. Always having fun, never feels like a chore. Does it ever? Feel like a chore?"

Rainey lets go of Nika's shoulders, reaches for her coffee, and looks toward the sky. "I'm thinking, not putting you off."

Nika takes in two large gulps of air and moves her neck two more times, cranking it right then left. She blows out a slow breath and glances at her watch. Ten minutes and they should get inside. "Don't tell me what I want to hear. I'll be okay if it's always good for you."

Maybe I'll be okay.

"No, that's not it. I don't think about it much anymore—whatever happens, happens. Plus, I don't think I take sex as seriously as you because I wasn't raised in a prudish Catholic household, *and* I'm not using it for connection. For me, it's the opposite—a way to let off steam or have fun. If I'm not feeling like having fun, or I don't think it's the right person, well, we end the date, and I guess what I can say is . . . Sometimes, sex feels like a science experiment. Press this button, insert X here, then turn Y. I'm not sure why—because it can feel that way even with people I've had plenty of fun with. At those times, I go with the flow and don't kick myself. I know I'll be back to fine form in no time."

Nika holds the outside door open for Rainey. "Maybe you've found the key. Maybe I'm perseverating on the negative aspects—it doesn't feel the same, I'm tired, sometimes I don't want to do it—which of course might cause a downward spiral, or an outward spiral, or something infinitely larger than it is." She doesn't bring up her lack of confidence . . .

"Hopefully, Susan can help." Rainey punctuates the sentence with a nod, extends her hand to the inside door handle, and pulls open the wooden door.

It makes a slight swish, a susurration drawing Nika forward into a bright reception area, abundant with natural light from the skylights overhead. A small fountain stands in the corner, the water flowing over the rocks in a gentle and soothing melody. The chairs welcome them. So large and puffy, like Nika might sink into them and never be able to get out.

"Thank you for coming," Nika says.

Rainey points to the long wall at the back. "You're welcome. I think this used to be an apothecary of some sort. Carried all kinds of beauty tools and makeup, even had a salon in one section. I'm not sure how they split up the building's interior because this seems nice, but this light would help in terms of beauty routines."

Nika is grateful for the details and conversation and knows Rainey is trying to set her at ease. They each choose a chair, and then Nika thinks better of sitting and checks the receptionist window, which is devoid of any person. A small computer rests there, with the express instructions to go ahead and sign in. Nika does, heaves a sigh of relief, and returns to the chair.

"Step one. I signed in. No going back now."

"This is going to be fine. Totally fine."

"I know, but I'm nervous. It's one thing to admit you have—I don't know—issues in general. But these? So many ways I can be embarrassed, and you know I *hate* embarrassment."

"But you also have a long life ahead of you, presumably with Ethan, right?"

"That's the plan."

"Then don't focus on the negative here. You're always talking about learning opportunities. Take this as one of those. And hey—I'm proud of you."

Nika glances around the room, at the soft blue walls, the abstract paintings with splashes of red, green, and orange, the potted succulents, and the stacks of magazines, most with *Psychology* on their covers. The office smells like clean laundry and comfort. It's an office, yes, but she feels at peace here, at home. "I can do this, can't I?" she says to Rainey, who smiles and touches Nika's hands with gentle fingers.

"Yes, you can, and you will. I'll help in whatever capacity, but there's a limit to what I'm willing to do." She winks.

Nika groans. "Don't go there, sister."

Rainey laughs and takes a sip of her coffee. It shouldn't be long now, and Nika will go in and see Susan Harris, LPCC and whatever else she's qualified for. As Nika stares at the waterfall, mesmerized by the water's arc, she thinks about Susan and their session. Maybe she'll tell Nika she's not actually sexually repressed but she doesn't know how to have fun. Maybe she'll talk about how to relax, how to let the mind wander, how to refocus on the bigger picture and let go of the minutiae. Or maybe she'll tell Nika something else is wrong: like she has anxiety or depression or ADHD or an overactive imagination. Maybe—

"Nika?" Rainey says, the tremor in her voice drawing Nika's attention her way.

"Yeah?"

Rainey points to the window, which opens to the side parking lot. The morning has cleared enough now, and it's easy to see her concern: a blue sedan, much like Ethan's, with a man who looks exactly like Ethan getting out of the car.

Nika's palms feel clammy, and her stomach turns; she hiccups. "He could be here for something else. But what else is out there to bring him in here?"

"Not sure," Rainey whispers.

"Do you think—?" The door to the office opens, and Ethan walks in.

chapter eighteen

One of the first characteristics Nika found attractive in Ethan, besides his deep, soulful eyes, was his intuition. His ability to know about her with only a few details. Her favorite song, distaste of dancing, which toilet paper brand she preferred to buy. To this day, she still doesn't understand how he picks up on some things. No other guy she knows can do it. But Ethan—he knows. What she's thinking. What she's doing. What she's feeling. Except with respect to sex, intimacy, and proper communication, apparently. Which is sort of funny, and not, at the same time. Ethan standing in front of her now, in the therapist's office, is funny, and not, at the same time too.

"What are you doing here, honey?" Nika says as she stands from the chair.

Ethan frowns, a look of startled confusion written all over his face. "What do you mean? This appointment was on the calendar."

Shit, shit, shit. Nika closes her eyes, envisions the sticky note, her paper calendar, her phone as she keys in the appointment onto the *digital shared* calendar. It's not the first time she's added an appointment without consulting him.

Nika flicks her gaze to Rainey, who has averted her own elsewhere, to her phone. It's her way of giving them privacy without really giving it to them. And they don't need it. This is *Rainey.* Even Ethan considers her a good friend. Now, she's a good friend who knows too much, but Nika doubts Ethan will care.

"Hey, Rainey," he adds, without an ounce of hesitation.

She smiles and waves and goes back to her phone.

"Anyway . . . Susan Harris? LPCC? What's going on?" He takes a seat next to where Nika stands, and she sits back down, sinking into the chair, letting it enfold her, encase her, embrace her. If she scoots back far enough, will it swallow her?

"I know what you're doing," Ethan says quietly. "You're trying to get away again."

"What do you mean?"

"If you're in a therapist's office, there must be a reason why. The chair can't get you away from *here.* The present time. You, me, Rainey. This office."

Well. How's that for knowing her? "I was fine until you got here. Okay, not fine, but you know." Her cheeks warm again. Married ten years, and she's feeling like a nervous freshman on her first date. Something bubbles in her stomach, and she swallows thickly.

"Maybe this isn't what I thought then. Do you want me to go?"

Rainey loops in. "Told you he was a keeper!"

Nika glares at her, and Rainey snaps her gaze back to her phone. "Okay, I guess—"

"Ms. Stewart?" A voice from behind her rings out.

Nika looks up. It's Susan Harris, in the flesh.

"It's so nice to see you," she says and walks over. "And who else do we have here?"

Aside from the four of them, the office is empty. Nika introduces Rainey and Ethan, and Susan gazes at all three of them in turn. Then she says, "Did I not get the message? Is this a threesome?"

Nika cannot help but burst out laughing. Even Ethan's eyes crinkle with laughter. The word *threesome* isn't the problem for him. He's always said he loves Nika and is happy with *only* her, but if a threesome is something she's interested in, he'd be willing to try it. Spoiler alert: she's never had an interest.

After Nika recovers from her surprise, she wonders about Susan Harris and her approach. Despite the lack of other clients, should she have voiced her confusion in the reception area, or was it an ice breaker?

Rainey stands and pats Nika on the back. "I'm only here for reinforcement, Susan. Nice to meet you, but I plan on staying out here. With my phone." She holds up the device for all to see.

Ethan stands and extends his hand, taking Susan's fingers into his grip.

Nika imagines his firm handshake; it has always symbolized strength and vitality to her, a confidence she doesn't often have. Susan's grip is probably as steadfast as his.

"Nice to meet you," Ethan says and then turns to Nika. "And I'm a one-woman man. This one, right here." He smiles at her, and something in his demeanor leads Nika to believe he's uncomfortable. But as much as she wants to take his discomfort away, this isn't about him, and she cannot worry about him at this moment. A voice at the back of her head reminds her that not holding him as priority, by always moving him to the side, is a part of the problem, but she hushes the voice. *One thing at a time, lady.*

"Nice to meet you too, Ethan," Susan says. She looks at all of them, a kind smile showcasing a flickering dimple. "By the way, I would never have said what I said in a full waiting room or even one with a few folks in it, but you're my only Saturday appointment. Shall we?" She gestures to Nika.

Sweat breaks out under Nika's armpits, across her brow, at the nape of her neck. A steady thrum picks up inside her body, and she tamps it down with a few short breaths. *No big deal. It doesn't matter what you say to her. She has to have seen worse.*

And with that thought in mind, Nika follows Susan Harris through the reception door, to a short hallway, and into another warm and cozy room. A deep slate blue covers walls trimmed with white, and the couch looks ready to prod a person into divulging secrets. Again, abstract paintings—only three—line the walls, and mismatched lamps on twin side tables bathe the room in a buttery glow. They've left Ethan and Rainey behind—Susan said speaking with Ethan is a part of her plan, but she'd like to begin with Nika first. The question is, is Nika ready to speak with Susan?

"Would you like some water? Maybe tea or coffee?" Susan says near the office threshold.

"No, I'm good, thank you."

"Well then, please take a seat."

Susan shuts the door and moves toward her chair, which is stationed behind a tiny desk-like table with a computer on it. She pulls up what looks like some information—probably whatever Nika told the receptionist yesterday—and then stares directly at Nika. Susan's piercing gaze intrigues her. In this lighting, her eyes are dark, cavernous, almost parallel holes Nika cannot see the bottom of. Not menacing, but odd. Even odder, Nika doesn't feel strange sitting here. At least not yet.

"So," Susan says and leans in. "I know you know about me already, so I won't waste time there. However, is there anything you'd like to ask?"

"Other than how will this session go? No. And please know I'm not really about attending more than one session."

"You're not? Didn't you make the appointment for yourself?" She looks at her calendar and down at a printout. "It says right here you're the one who booked it, and among other things, you want to discuss your sexual relationship with your husband. It also states this therapy will be for you, not couples therapy."

The woman's office is thorough, and Nika isn't sure if she's offended her. "Sorry for my bluntness—one of my greatest flaws. What I mean is—while I *should* be here, every cell in me is holding a protest sign right now, so I might go running from this room and never come back. You wanted me to be honest, right?"

Susan flashes a thumbs-up. "I appreciate full honesty, especially between these walls. Otherwise, my job will be so much more difficult. And one thing: *do not apologize*. Tell me this—are you a serial apologizer?"

Nika doesn't hesitate. "Why yes, I am."

"Then we need to rid you of the habit along our journey too. Sometimes, there's a reason to apologize, and it's important for us to do so. If the situation doesn't call for an apology—if you're not the problem, or you didn't hurt anyone—then try to find something different to say."

The words *our journey* strike Nika as humorous. Maybe she assumes she's going on this with Nika—

"And another thing. We need to be partners in this journey. Not partners in the traditional sense, but I cannot help you unless you're ready to take my metaphorical hand and let me guide you. Are you ready?"

Is Nika ready for someone who seems to read her mind? Will she *ever* be ready? Isn't that the problem? She's ready for so many things but facing who she is inside, at the very core of her being? Utterly and downright terrifying. She doesn't know if she can do this, but she thinks of Ethan, the future. His happiness, her happiness. *Their* happiness. *Yeah, I'm ready to at least listen.* "I guess I'm as ready as I'll ever be."

"Okay then. What I like to do right from the beginning is let you know what to expect."

"Great. I'm a planner and organizer and someone who hates surprises. I'm sure you're not shocked, are you?"

Susan laughs. "No, I'm not. I appreciate all those qualities, but we need to get you to let go of some of them."

"Then you have your work cut out for you."

If Susan doesn't appreciate the snark, she doesn't show it. "Anyway, let's discuss what will happen as we go forth. Normally, I make sure nothing physical is at play, and it says here you have a clean bill of health. Nothing wrong but perimenopausal?" Susan waits for Nika to nod. "I also like to send forms ahead of the first appointment—intake forms going over services, cost expectations, insurance, HIPPA, and sexual history, including both positive and negative experiences. Since you booked this appointment yesterday, you don't have those forms yet. I'll send them home with you today, and you can email them back or drop them off when you're finished."

Nika nods again.

"Those forms will take time. They will ask you questions about your schedule—no matter how planned out it might be—what you're interested in, your current job, any past jobs, what your day-to-day routine looks like. It will also have a region asking about your likes or dislikes and of course, a section delving into the current situation with your sex life."

A heat rushes across Nika's face at the mention of *sex life*.

Susan doesn't miss a beat. "I see you might be a tad uncomfortable here. Does talking about sex pose a problem? Because we might have to get over *that* hump first to help you."

Nika's inner child snorts at the use of the word *hump* and Susan's tone. "No, no. I always say I'm not a prude, and I'm not. Sex can be a glorious thing, and the naked body doesn't bother me. I see the body in more scientific terms. Its capability amazes me." Nika pauses, tries to assess how to say the next part, wondering what it will sound like to Susan, then chastising herself for being worried about it. "I'm not turned on by the body. I'm not sure why I should marvel at my husband's penis each time I see it—which is something he seems to do—and I guess talking about my sex life with you will be slightly uncomfortable until I get used to it. I'll do my best though."

A genuine smile lights up Susan's face. "I *really* try to avoid blanket statements, but I've worked with a lot of men, a lot of couples, and many men *do* marvel at their own penises. Every day. It's like, 'Wow, look at this toy.' I'm not sure why, but I believe our brain chemistry is different. They're like kids in the candy store every time."

This woman didn't bat an eye at my naked body comment, and she infuses humor into the discussion. Perhaps I'll be okay.

"Anyway," Susan begins again, "once I look at your forms, I'll have a better sense of who you are and what you're looking for out of therapy. A better sense of how I can help you. And, at some point, I'll be asking Ethan some things, too, provided you approve. Looking at your forms helps customize the sessions, if you will, so they're tailored to you. What I do with one person might not be right for another."

The approach makes sense, and Nika is curious about the intake forms, how they might differ from what she found online. If she'll feel as low about herself and her sexual health as she did when she answered the online questionnaire.

"Any questions so far?" Susan asks.

"Well, what happens after the forms? After you customize a plan for me?"

"Then, we begin taking the first steps. And while I will want to see you again, we can schedule appointments in-person or via Telehealth. Whatever works for you. I can't remember exactly what you do again . . ."

"I'm an elementary school librarian, so my days are pretty full."

"Yes, they are. Full and mentally draining at times," Susan says. "I'm sure the job, as lovely as it might be, can take a toll on your sexual health. All jobs do."

She's right. "Indeed. So, what happens now?"

"Well, today, since he's here, I'd like to hear from Ethan—with your permission of course and only after I've heard a bit about your story—condensed is fine."

Nika nods.

"And then, I'll make a recommendation for this week or

two until you return the forms. After looking at your responses, I'll provide a comprehensive analysis of how to move forward, some exercises to get you moving in the right direction, and how I will be involved. Along with what you'll need to do—alone and with Ethan. He will need to be involved in this, of course."

Of course. "Don't worry, I figured as much."

"Okay then. So—what's going on? What brought you here?"

What specifically brought her here? The fear of losing Ethan? Deep inside, underneath all the cottony layers cocooning her soul, she knows he'd stick whatever this is out. What *really* made her pick up the phone and make the appointment? The fear of losing herself?

"Well, I guess my problem, in a nutshell, is I don't like sex."

"You don't like it? Or you don't like to talk about it?"

"Oh, I don't mind talking about it. I'm pretty up front with my kids. I just don't enjoy it and haven't for a while, and I'm not sure when it started to happen, though perimenopause certainly isn't helping."

Susan nods. "Duly noted. How long have you been with Ethan?"

"We've been married for ten years. We knew each other for over a year before that. And no, we didn't live together before we got married. I had two little kids at home. I didn't think it was proper. We did have sex though."

"Okay. I appreciate the background. Another question: Do you not like having sex, or do you not like having sex with Ethan?"

Nika waves her hand. "There's no one else I want to have sex with, Susan, if that's what you're asking. The act itself is part of the issue right now. I guess I'm here to find out why."

The smooth swish of Susan's pen against paper as she jots down notes is the only sound in the room. "I'm going to go ahead and give you these forms, and I'll send you out to the waiting room. While you start on them, I'll bring Ethan in and ask him a few questions. Nothing major. And then, you get those back to me," she points to the papers in Nika's hand, "preferably via drop-off, because of the sensitive info, and we'll go from there. Can you have them back to me in about a week and a half? If so, we could meet two weeks from now. Same time. Would that work for you?"

Nika pulls up the phone calendar, knowing full well any useful details are all on the paper one attached to the refrigerator. But Susan makes her a little nervous, and she needs to look away, focus on something other than this room, this therapist, what she's getting into by embarking on this "journey." Susan might think Nika is looking for space in her schedule, contemplating her words. In reality, Nika is hauling herself from the edge, which looks sharp and menacing right now. She breathes in through her nose, and a tickle rises inside of Nika. Something in the air—mold, essential oils, Febreze, who knows what?—swarms her respiratory tract, and she scratches at her throat.

"Are you okay?" Susan asks.

Nika nods, blinking back tears.

"Are you sure?" Susan stands and moves toward Nika. "This might be a panic attack. Have you had one before?"

Nika can't speak. She can barely take in air, her breaths short and shallow. She stands and looks at Susan, eyes feeling dry and crusty, heartbeat thundering in her chest, skin on fire. So much fire. "Ethan," Nika spits out. The last thing she remembers is the feel of the couch beneath her as her legs buckle.

chapter nineteen

A warm washcloth against the forehead. Velvety fingertips whispering against her cheeks. Rhythmic movement, a gentle tug at her hand. Coaxed back to the land of the living, Nika opens her eyes and blinks. Ethan kneels over her. Eyes cloudy, jaw set, eyebrows drawn into a crinkled line. He's mumbling something, but she can't catch what it is.

"What happened?" Nika says, the edges of her vision still blurry.

"I think you had a panic attack. Has this happened before?"

"Not for a while. I mean, I felt a little high energy before I walked in here, and Rainey had to talk me down from the rafters, but otherwise, no. Maybe."

"That clears it up," Ethan says, deadpan, then smiles. "Are you okay?"

"I'm not sure. Do I look okay?"

Susan Harris comes into Nika's line of vision. "You look okay but definitely pale." She extends a bottle of water. "That was a first for me. I'm sorry if I did anything to cause—"

"No," Nika interrupts. "Sorry, but no. You didn't. It's been a real, what shall I say, challenging time at home lately? I think I might be overwhelmed. This, whatever happened here, will have no bearing on my going forward."

"Do you think you can stand? Are you ready to head home?" Ethan says.

With her arms, Nika pushes herself to a sitting position. This couch and its marshmallow pillows could be her home forever, nestling her in warmth, comfort, safety. "I'm good now. Yes, we can go home . . . but didn't you have to speak to Susan?" Nika glances back and forth between Ethan and Susan.

"Don't worry about it, honey. We can talk later, right?" Ethan looks to Susan, who is jotting something down on paper.

"Of course, by phone will be fine. Also," she hands Ethan a piece of paper, "this might be useful. It's called the three-three-three rule. If you feel anxiety or panic coming on, identify three objects near you followed by three sounds. Then, move three body parts. It can help ground you. Of course, if this continues to happen, you should tell me, and we'll talk about other coping strategies. Now, are you sure you don't want anything—crackers or juice? Again, I'm so sorry this happened."

"It's fine. I'm fine." Nika shakes her feet and hands, takes a deep breath, and moves her neck this way and that. "Overwhelmed, I think." *And repeating myself.* The intake forms are on the floor, and Nika picks them up, folds them over, and shoves them into her bag, which still leans against the clay-colored couch.

Susan angles in close to Nika saying, "If parts of the paperwork are too much, tell me. You have my phone number, and my email address is at the bottom of the page. I can gather information in a different way, if needed."

"Thanks."

Nika and Ethan turn to leave, Ethan with his warm hand at her back, Susan trailing behind them. Even with this episode, a hopeful feeling lingers in Nika's chest, gurgling gently. The first step is admitting a problem exists, and today, she's there. Admitting it and taking another step to do something to fix it. She's being *proactive*, not *reactive*. An empowering thought, one that makes Nika believe everything will be okay.

Even me. Even me.

Rainey looks uncharacteristically discombobulated when they meet up with her in the reception area, hair askew, teeth worrying her lip. She rushes over, wraps her arms around Nika, and whispers in her ear. "I was so concerned. Don't do that again. I can't lose you."

Nika can't lose Rainey either. Or Ethan. Those two ground her in indescribable ways, more solid than cables to a bridge, and Nika blinks emotion away. "I'm pretty sure I wasn't in any danger of being lost, but I will *try* not to do it again. Scout's honor," she says to Rainey, pressing her arms around her and then pulling back.

"Lot of good that would do! You were never a scout, asshat!"

"Okay, mom's honor. You know how seriously I take that role."

"I believe you." Rainey snatches Nika's fingers in hers.

"Do you want me to drive you home, or are you going with Ethan?"

Nika appreciates Rainey asking her, and she's torn. If this episode scared Rainey, it might have scared Ethan too. She should think of how he might feel and ride with him, but everything is still so tender, and Nika needs to consider what's best for her. Being with Rainey seems the safer choice.

Once again, Ethan proves he knows her well. "Hon, if you want to go with Rainey, I'm good with it. Then I can stop off at the store for a few items, and we'll come back later and get your car. What do you think?" He moves in for a comforting hug and kisses the top of her head before lightly brushing her lips with his. A light flutter of wings almost, nothing that asks or demands anything. A brief but tangible connection.

But he's in her space and taking up too much of it. Nika stifles the urge to place her hands on his chest and push him away. "Sounds fine." Nika turns to Susan. "Sorry to make a mess of your Saturday, but I'll get on this and get back to you. Did I tell you that two weeks from today should be fine?"

"You were sort of occupied," Susan says with a wink.

Once again, Susan's easy humor draws Nika in. She's always been able to make a joke of herself, and in this case, she would have said something similar if the roles had been reversed. Maybe this partnership will lead to something good. "Then count me in. I'll be in touch."

~

Rainey peppers the ride home with incessant talking about inane topics. Rumors of the Duke and Duchess adopting another dog. An update on the social media habits of Carly Camden and her socialite family. Chatter about what's happening at school, who had a spat in the teacher's lounge, and which teachers are talking about retirement in the new school year. "And Cole," she says. "Are you ready for what I heard yesterday about Cole?"

"Great question. Am I?"

"You are. While I should feel bad about spreading this rumor, I'm going to say up front I think it's true, so I'm stating a fact and not spreading gossip."

"Well, you might be spreading gossip, but it's true gossip. Are you sure it's true?"

"I won't reveal my sources, but yes."

"And it's not the Magic 8 ball?"

"Not this time."

Nika bursts out laughing, so grateful for the conversation's frivolity. "Go on."

Rainey looks at Nika for a brief moment before glancing back at the road. "Well. Sources say Cole is dating . . . Danielle Perkins—"

"Danielle Perkins? I knew she had trouble with her husband and all. Did they get a divorce?" Danielle had come to Evergreen two years prior as a fifth-grade teacher. Her students ran roughshod over her, and by April of the same academic year, she'd asked for a transfer and gotten it. Now, Nika understands why.

"Not only did they get a divorce, but he gave up custody of the kids! So she found a new place—right around the corner from Cole and his kids. Word on the street is she'll be moving in within a few months."

"That all seems pretty quick, doesn't it?"

"*Indeed*, my friend. And here's the kicker: apparently their relationship began to bloom while she was still at Evergreen."

Nika gasps. "While she was still at the school? Isn't that against the school district's code of ethics? I certainly don't care who's cavorting together, but I'm a little put off by flaunting the rules, er, the code. Cole trying to keep me in line . . . Well, the fact gives me some leverage going forward, if I need it. Plus, he was her superior!"

"I hadn't thought about that," says Rainey. "I find it so interesting—Danielle comes in and can't hold her job together but leaves with a man and some new kids. Then again, maybe she found the important parts of life. If she's happy with him and the kids, then more power to her. Maybe she's found the secret to her own happiness."

Unexpected tears prick Nika's eyelids. Something in Rainey's words, her confidence, the idea of personal happiness, raises an alarming question. What if Nika's not happy? Is that what her lack of desire is trying to tell her? Even worse, what if she doesn't love Ethan anymore? What if she doesn't love him *enough*? The idea of a second failed marriage causes acid to churn in her stomach, and she swallows hard, staying silent, hoping it stays put. *If I keep it inside, it can't possibly be true, can it?*

"Yes, maybe she has," Nika says, and she leaves it at that. The morning wiped her out, and she's tired. Knackered. All the anticipation, the panic attack—maybe two—the shock of seeing Ethan there. It's all too much. She needs a long soak in the tub and hot peppermint tea, possibly even a nap.

Rainey must sense her mood, for she switches gears, somewhat. "Do you know what Susan wants to ask Ethan?"

Nika taps the window's edge with what's left of her chewed fingernail. "I have no idea. My plan is to find out when I get home."

"And you're going to go back? To Susan, I mean."

Nika flutters her eyes closed. "Yes. I have forms to fill out—and yes, I'll let you know if anything funny comes up on them. I'm kind of looking forward to filling them out. Walking on the wild side, doing something I thought I'd never do. Hell, it might be fun!" She opens her eyes and catches Rainey's gaze.

"That's the spirit, friend." Rainey pumps her right fist in the air. Her nails are short but manicured. Today, a pearly aqua covers them. Not a hangnail or torn cuticle to be seen.

They're silent for the remainder of the ride. As they pull into the driveway, something settles over Nika, almost like a mist on a rainy April day. Benign, anodyne, dare she say, peaceful? She feels lighter, like the proverbial weight has been lifted from her shoulders. Cliché, yes, but some clichés ring true because they're so appropriate.

"Do you want me to come in?" Rainey says as Nika opens the car door.

"No, I'm good. I appreciate you going with me. Panic attacks aside—which of course, I'm hoping won't happen again—this is the right thing to do."

Rainey taps the steering wheel with her hand to the beat of whatever is playing on the radio. "Well then, my work is done here! I have some very big plans for today." She waggles her eyebrows then places a finger to her lips. "And you do too, don't you?"

Nika's not entirely sure what she means, but Rainey has never looked so mischievous, and she has to wonder . . .

"Not that. I mean the forms, silly. Although, I'm sure Ethan would love for you to—"

"Stop. Don't go there. Not today, not right now."

Rainey tips her head back, lets out a deep and true chuckle. "That's fine. Enjoy the afternoon. And remember this: It's a marathon, not a sprint. You'll get to the finish line eventually, whatever that finish line may be."

chapter twenty

Nika wants to ask Ethan what Susan Harris will talk to him about. Whether or not she's allowed, she doesn't care. Whether or not Ethan will know if she's allowed—well, that's another question. But Mindy is sitting on the side stoop, phone in hand, sour look on her face, like she expected Nika to be there. It's not a particularly warm morning, and Mindy isn't wearing a coat, so Nika hopes she hasn't been sitting there too long.

Nika climbs out of the car, and Rainey wishes her luck with Mindy before she closes the car door. "Mindy!" Nika calls as she saunters up the walk. If her life were a movie, portentous music full of minor chords, chromatic notes, and eerie intervals might be playing right now. But her life, despite all the recent drama, is no movie. Too ordinary, pedestrian.

Mindy looks up and gives a succinct and half-hearted

wave. "I'm here to drop off the keys. I was about to text you."

"Shit. I forgot!"

Nika and the kids had gone over to Mindy's apartment to meet Cheetah and Olaf. The trio had fallen in love and after hugs and kisses and several rounds of zoomies, brought on by the laser pointer, decided they'd be thrilled to check on the cats while Mindy was away. Mindy needed to make an extra copy of the keys and would deliver them this morning. With Mindy in front of her, Nika remembers all of it. But she suspects she neglected to write Mindy's name down on the paper calendar as a reminder, and clearly, she didn't put it on the shared calendar. Otherwise, Ethan would have reminded her.

"I'm so sorry. It's already been a busy morning. I hope—"

Mindy stands up. "Nika, it's no big deal. I haven't been here long, and I probably could have knocked on the door. Your car is usually in the driveway, so I figured I'd wait."

Nika and Ethan's old house has a two-car garage that only adequately houses one car. Ethan's car, being the newer of the two, won the coveted garage parking spot.

"Well, come in. Would you like to? The kids are here— at least they should be. They might be sleeping. But if you have any last-minute—"

"No, don't worry about it. I have the keys." Mindy holds up a key ring with two keys on it. "One is for the front door, and the other is for the shed. They have no reason to go into the shed, but I'd rather be prepared than not." Mindy hands the keys over. "I have all the instructions written down. They're pretty easy as far as pets go—of course, they like to have some attention. Kids can head over any time, sit and do homework or whatever. This paper," she extends a page to Nika, "is also on my kitchen counter."

The paper reveals vet information, Mindy's cell phone number, and how much food and water the kittens should get. It also has instructions on grabbing the mail, taking out the garbage, and checking the herbs in the kitchen window. The fact sheet is comprehensive, which impresses Nika. Mindy's never been the sort to worry about much or be proactive. Maybe Olaf and Cheetah's presence will positively impact her stepsister.

With a slight upturn of her mouth, Mindy turns to leave, gets halfway down the walkway, and looks back at Nika. "And thanks, by the way. I appreciate the help."

The sullen look on Mindy's face is hard to read. Does she *really* appreciate the help? Or does she just know the proper thing to say? Mindy has always been an enigma: her motivation, her intention, her stance—unclear most of the time. As much as Nika once wanted a sisterly relationship with Mindy, she cannot fathom what that would look like now. Had they met without Dad's connection, they'd have bounced away from each other the way magnetic poles do. But the kids like cats, as does Nika, and helping Mindy, regardless of the state of their relationship, is the right thing to do.

"Have fun," Nika says. "If you need anything else, call or text."

Mindy turns back once more. "Let the kids know the mail can sit on the counter or the kitchen table. Either is fine." Her shoes scuff against the brick walkway leading from the house.

Nika stares after her. *What's the rush, and where are you going?* These days, with cell phones and social media, almost no one needs to tell anyone where they're headed. Knowing she can check Mindy's posts later in the week, Nika lets her go, but an intense curiosity hums inside her, and she almost stops Mindy before she leaves the yard.

~

Nika enters the house and finds Lila and Alex in the kitchen eating breakfast. Alex's phone sits in front of him, his cereal bowl to the side. He's careful not to drip his milk onto the phone, but the table is fair game. Always has been. Lila munches on toast with a side of strawberries. Both look tired.

"Why are you awake? I thought you'd still be asleep. Also, did Mindy ring the bell?" Nika drops her purse onto the counter and shrugs off her coat, placing it on her designated hook. These hooks make life more manageable, in Nika's opinion, but she's often the only one who uses them.

Without looking up, Alex says, "She didn't. I'm helping the scene shop with a few things today. They're putting together the stairway for your play, remember?"

"That's right." Much of what they need is ready and waiting in the stage wings, but the castle stairway proved to be a thorn in their fairy-tale sides. Nika called in a favor from the high school. "What time do you need to be there?"

He taps his phone. "In about forty-five minutes."

"Okay. And what about you?" Nika pours herself a cup of coffee and looks at Lila.

"Cora and I want to work on our debate. I was thinking of seeing if she'd like to come here, but her mom's gone, and her dad wants me to go over to her house. Is that okay?"

"Sure. Please let me know when I need to drop you off. Actually, would it work to drop you off *after* Alex?"

"I think so," Lila says.

"And what do you say about getting a license soon, Alex? You'll have more freedom, and so will I!"

Alex slants a stony gaze her way before shoveling another spoonful of cereal into his mouth. Another drop of milk hits the table with a soft plink, and an easy grin crosses Alex's face.

He did that on purpose, Nika thinks, taking a sip of coffee and shuttling her mind to other matters. It's a good thing she needs to get them someplace, or she might spiral inward. Nika is a thinker—or an overthinker, as Rainey would say. Spending so much time in her head probably isn't the best thing, but it's the way she's built. Can she change that?

"By the way," Nika says as the kids put their plates and utensils in the dishwasher. "Mindy dropped off the keys to her place. Watching the kittens starts today."

Alex, a true animal lover, doesn't show much enthusiasm, but Lila jumps up and down and claps, her mouth in a smile that will likely stay all day. Speaking of smiles, Nika's thoughts move to Ethan. Where is—

A clunk, the slap of metal, and Ethan strides in the door, small bag in hand. He leans over and kisses her cheek, then moves through the kitchen and out toward the living room. All sounds indicate that he hangs his coat in the front closet—his place of choice—takes off his shoes and rummages around in the bag. Nika isn't sure what he's up to, but she doesn't bother asking. All will be revealed soon enough.

"Ethan?" Nika calls. "Alex is going to help at the scene shop, and Lila is going to Cora's. I'm going to leave soon to drop them off. Do you need anything while I'm out?"

"You okay to drive? You want me to take them?" His voice sounds distant, as if he's stuck inside the paper bag.

"I'm good. I don't have too much on the agenda for today, besides decluttering, vacuuming, you know. I have a few things I want to do for work, but—"

"Okay. Then I'll see you back here."

What's with people cutting me off today? First Mindy, and now Ethan. Do I speak slowly? Usually, Nika is the one in the rush, not Ethan. *Whatever.* She shakes her head and rises from the table. Another cup of coffee sounds good, so she'll have one when she gets back from chauffeur duty. These days, the more caffeine, the better.

Nika thinks about taking a page from Rainey's playbook and adding some Bailey's to the cup.

Interior: Guardian Angels Catholic High School,
Eleventh Grade Chemistry Class, 1994

The sun streams through the windows of the chemistry classroom. NIKA and her lab partner, SAMANTHA, open their lab notebooks. SAMANTHA reads aloud the instructions, and NIKA stands to fill the graduated cylinder with distilled water.

SAMANTHA
(looking down at NIKA'S seat and whispering)
Nika! Oh no. You need to go to the restroom.

NIKA'S face flushes crimson, and she stares at the chair, covered in a matching smear of bright red blood. She clenches her jaw.

NIKA
Why today? It wasn't supposed to be here until this weekend. Oh shit. What am I going to do?

SAMANTHA whispers something into NIKA'S ear, then grabs the wastebasket. NIKA wipes the chair, places the paper towels in the wastebasket, and walks to the front of the room. SAMANTHA follows close behind, basket in hand, trying to shield the back of NIKA'S stained skirt. A classmate, JASON PETERS, notices.

JASON
(sneering)
What'd you do back there, Washington? Oh, wait. Is that why you've been so bitchy? I thought I smelled something fishy today!

NIKA blushes, grabs the hall pass, and rushes out
the door.

                         JASON
               (calling out behind NIKA)
        I guess this means you're not pregnant though,
            right? Which is a good thing, isn't it?

The class laughs, and SAMANTHA punches JASON'S arm
before following NIKA out the classroom door.

chapter twenty-one

Driving isn't Nika's favorite task, especially in Ethan's compact car, but they live in such a small community, kid drop-off doesn't take much more than twenty minutes total. Neither child told Nika a pick-up time—Cora's dad said Lila could even stay through dinner—and Nika realizes how old the kids are getting . . . They don't have as many family dinners anymore, and spending quality time with either of them? She might need to make appointments with Alex and Lila soon. Forget a vacation *day*—they haven't all had a true vacation in a while.

"Maybe our next day off, I'll plan something fun," Nika says to herself. If she gives Ethan enough warning, he can take the day too. "We need to do that before the kids—" Nika's thoughts skip to the future, when first Alex and then Lila will go off to college. Her eyes mist, and she sniffs, thinking of her babies out in the sometimes-scary world, thinking of the big, blubbering mess she'll be when they fly away from the nest. She's done a pretty good job raising them, took plenty of time with them, and maybe . . . Are they *too* close?

There's no time for Nika to ruminate as she pulls into the driveway. The thought of more coffee lures her, directs her to the kitchen. The house is quiet, which means Ethan is napping, or maybe he's doing something out back. He couldn't have gone far without a car. A quick glance at the calendar reveals nothing for him, but Dad has an appointment today, maybe NA? Has he left for it yet?

Dad's not in the kitchen, so Nika heads through the living room to her father's space; it's empty, at least of people. She'll have to wait for his update, but she hopes he behaves himself. Listens to the leader, doesn't try to push his own thoughts on everyone else. Cleans up after himself. Nika chuckles as she reaches for the sweater her father wears every other weekend and folds it neatly, placing it on the bed. *Sometimes it feels like I have three kids.*

As she heads out of the room back toward the living room, she stops. A line of turquoise rose petals leads up the stairs. Only one person would use a tactic like this on a weekend morning, and his name begins with an *E*. Nika snorts and shakes her head, leans down to grasp a petal in her fingers. A softness like this should soothe her edges, but this time, it unnerves and amuses her; she follows the petal trail up the stairs.

"I think I know what you're doing!" Nika calls out as she reaches the landing.

The path leads to their bedroom, and Ethan doesn't respond.

"Okay, I'm heading in. But I don't know what you're

expecting!"

But of course, she does. And a Saturday morning after passing out in a therapist's office is *not* the time to be getting intimate, but honestly, since no time is right, there probably is no better time. How's that for strange logic? As she enters the room, a soft breeze hits her in the face; the window must be open. "You know I'll be cold, right?"

Still no answer.

"And what is *that smell?*" She walks farther into the room and sniffs. "Peanut butter?"

Nika's mind whirls with the trappings of an awful erotic novel and how peanut butter can be involved. She loves peanut butter. On sandwiches and celery, in ice cream, pies; she even likes peanuts in her noodles. But the thought of peanut butter on her skin and other regions—

"I can hear you thinking, Nika. You need to stop."

Nika laughs. She can't see Ethan yet because he's probably under the enormous blanket pile on the bed.

"I'm not—"

"You are."

"Okay, maybe I am, but why can't anyone let me finish a sentence today. I mean—"

"I'll let you." A rustle of sheets.

"You did that on purpose, didn't you?"

"May-be." Ethan draws out the word like Lila might.

She's standing at the bedside now, still rubbing the petal between her fingers, thinking. Of love languages and how Ethan's seems to involve touching and kissing and all things sexual. Hers does not. Nika sighs and pulls back the covers. There's Ethan in . . . his T-shirt and pajama pants? He has rosy cheeks, as if he's too warm under the covers.

"Okay," Nika says. "I have to be honest—I expected you

to be naked, like maybe you were asking for something since everyone is out of the house."

"I'm not going to lie—I might have, had this been a regular Saturday, but I get the sense the morning has been extra stressful for you."

Grateful he noticed, Nika places the petal on the side table, settles on the mattress, pulls the covers over her legs and feet. "It has." Saying more might be the right decision— tell him why it was stressful, why she fainted, why she was there, in Susan's office, not that she really understands herself—but she can't. Not yet. So she places her head on the pillow and stares at the ceiling, at the tiny indentation in the drywall right above her side of the bed. The mark has been there since they bought the house; they've done nothing to repair it. Nika crosses her arms over her chest. "If you're not trying to get me naked, what's your plan? What's with the peanut butter?" She turns her gaze toward Ethan, who is looking directly at her.

"It's in case we need snacks." Ethan raises his eyebrows. "I have many plans for the next few hours."

Nika considers her husband, what he's trying to say. She reaches under the covers to his crotch, certain she'll encounter an erection.

He bats her hand away, saying, "Snacks because I have a movie lined up for you, for us, and no, it's not porn." He sits up, grabs the remote, and turns on *Anatomy of a Fall*, a movie she's heard a lot about.

He'd be so disappointed if she said no, and really, why should she? She already told him what she did or didn't have scheduled for the day, and clearly, he has the time. The kids are gone, Dad too. If she says no to spending time with him when he's trying so hard, he'll be hurt—*deeply hurt*—and Nika never intends that for this man. Plus, didn't she once read about repeated exposure? Could the approach work here? Expose herself to him—no pun intended, or maybe completely intended—in all ways, repeatedly, and perhaps the drive, the desire will come back. Ethan would be happy to try that method. Maybe it begins with spending more time together, snuggling with a movie, sharing some beloved snacks.

She nods, then says, "Okay. Give me a sec," and she heads to the bathroom. There, she throws her hair on top of her head, uses the toilet, and washes her hands. Then she grabs a comfortable pair of sweatpants and changes into those before sliding into bed beside Ethan.

When the movie is over, Ethan leans in and kisses Nika, his lips gentle against her own, once again asking nothing. Still, she pulls away and burrows her head against his shoulder. His warmth penetrates some of her angst, and her body settles against his. "It's been a bad day, a bad couple of weeks."

His lips shift against her hair. "Hugs are especially good for dispelling bad days, bad weeks, you know." He adjusts his arm around her side and pulls her even closer, silently communicating his intention, how he tries to make things better. Always has, always will.

Nika's heart lurches, and she thinks of the idea of exposure again. One hug and kiss down, how many to go? "I know I push you away. I push everyone away when I'm upset or stressed. Turning inward has always been my go-to response. I *know* this." She sighs.

"You know what they say, though, Nik—knowing is half the battle. We all have our *things*, for lack of a better word."

Nika reminds herself she's taking those first steps, being

active about making a change. The appointment with Susan, spending time with him now. "Yes." She squeezes him, lifts her head up, and presses her lips to his.

As if he'd been in her head, Ethan doesn't push Nika—he relaxes into the kiss, and this time, he pulls away before she does. "Thanks," he says.

Nika nods, her mind on both what just happened and the intake forms she needs to fill out, one more thing to deal with in her already overloaded schedule. Then, for some unknown reason, she thinks of her mother's favorite song, "Perhaps Love." She'd always play it at high volume while dusting the furniture and washing windows, sometimes warbling at the top of her lungs as she repeated the lyrics that resonated most with her—all the things love is like: a resting place, a shelter, a window, a door. A cloud, a storm. Nika, on the other hand, concentrated on different lyrics, those about losing yourself and being unsure of what to do. Isn't that what she feels like now? *Hopefully, the universe will throw in a pinch hitter for me over the next couple of weeks,* she thinks. *I'm going to need all the help I can get.* "You're welcome," she finally says, extricating herself from Ethan's hold and adjusting the covers back over him. "The peanut butter and crackers were great, but I think I need something sweet right now. Like ice cream." She heads toward the door, then stops. "Don't worry, I'll bring two spoons."

"Some things never change, I see," Ethan says, a smile in his voice.

That's what I'm afraid of, Nika thinks, and she heads down the stairs.

chapter twenty-two

Rainey floats in on Monday morning with mischief in her eyes. "So," she says and leers at Nika. "How was the weekend? Any progress?"

"You do realize I *just* went to see Susan. She didn't give me any tips. She sent me home with intake forms and told me she'd see me in two weeks. How would I make any progress?"

Rainey's shoulders slump. "I don't know. Maybe I thought she was a miracle worker. Like she'd give you the forms, you'd open your mind, and you'd have fabulous sex all in one fell swoop." She falls onto the revolving stool the kids love and almost tips it over, then rights herself with a quick "dammit" and "don't blame the kids—these are death traps." She shakes her hair out of her face and stares at Nika.

"What?" Nika wipes her cheek, adjusts her shirt, brushes away a stray thread on her forearm. *Why is Rainey staring?*

"I'm waiting. I want to hear *all* about it."

Nika leans back against her chair. "As much as I wish the intake forms were magic, they're not. I filled them out, don't get me wrong. They asked about any positive or negative experiences about sex early on in life, whether I've experienced sexual abuse, and where and from whom I learned about sex, among other things. By the end, I was slightly depressed, and in no mood at all to get it on with Ethan."

"In general, or specifically?"

"In general, I think. Those questions got me thinking, which is probably what Susan Harris intends, right? We can have an honest chat at our next meeting. But get this—Ethan had a plan for the day. A big plan. Ginormous. One involving peanut butter."

"Get out. How was it?"

"Actually, the peanut butter was for the crackers he brought into our bedroom for sustenance. His plan involved hours of tantric sex, whips, chains, you name it. I told you— big plans."

"What?"

"I'm kidding, but I had you there for a moment, didn't I? Actually, we watched a movie and snuggled. The most action he got was a kiss, though I'm sure he'd have done more had I given the green light."

"Well, that's progress, isn't it?"

Being alone on Saturday would have been her preference, but Nika understands part of the draw to being alone is habitual, a default action she performs to rebalance a world tilted dangerously on its axis. Instead, she stayed with Ethan, so . . . "Maybe, but it doesn't feel like it, you know?"

Rainey waves a hand in the air. "Think of it this way—

Ethan provided what you needed, a low-key afternoon with zero pressure from him, and you let him do that."

"You have a point. I never thought of it—"

Alanna pokes her head into the room. Her mom and dad both work, and she takes advantage of the before-school care. Because she's always so well behaved, the early morning attendant often gives her little errands to run throughout the school.

"Good morning, Alanna. Please, come in. Ms. Delaney and I are chatting before the day begins. Did you know we're best friends?"

Alanna shakes her head as she comes into the room, a slip of paper in her little hand. She's one of the most petite children in the school, but her maturity more than makes up for her small stature.

"Yep, we are," says Rainey. "Been friends for a while. It's fun to work where your best friend works."

"That sounds like a good idea. Maybe someday Gwendolyn and I will work together."

A complete, grammatical sentence every time Alanna speaks, and she even got the subject of the sentence correct there. Nika should keep feeding her more books over the next five years or so. Perhaps she can mold her own little librarian!

"What can I help you with, honey?"

"Miss Trudy sent me down to collect a stack of books for Ms. Cremeans. Miss Trudy says something about," she looks at the paper and then back up at Nika, "on reserve."

"*Reserve* is a big word for your age. Do you know what it means?"

Alanna shakes her head again and raises her eyebrows, an expectant face like no other. This kid is a sponge and reminds

Nika of her own children at times. Maybe that's why she's so drawn to her.

"*On reserve* means Ms. Cremeans set books aside so she could come back later and get them. Of course, you're going to take them *to* her. But she didn't take them right away. I held them for her. Does that make sense?"

"Yes," she says as she nods. "It does."

"You'll hear the phrase more as you get older and go through Evergreen. I let the older students do the same, and I call it putting the books *on hold*. Sometimes, the books technically *on reserve* mean they're behind the desk—they can be looked at, but they can't be checked out."

"Why not?"

"Well," Nika says. "When I was in college, which was a long time ago, we had a set of textbooks in the library for a class. Because there were only eight books and sixteen students, we could borrow a book for two hours at a time, in the library only. So we took them and looked at them and then gave them back. They were *on reserve*. A way of letting all the people use the books, sort of like a fairness thing. Share the goodness, you know?"

Alanna furrows her brow.

"You know what?" Nika smiles. "That's a lot for today. Let's get you the books, and we'll have Ms. Delaney walk you down to Ms. Cremeans's classroom. What do you say?"

After they leave, Nika remembers she and Rainey haven't talked about the ruined books or the pamphlet. Has Rainey made any headway on finding the miscreant? Nika texts her before the morning rush. *Quick question. Are you still processing clues in my library?*

Rainey: *I just laughed out loud, and a few students looked at me like I was nuts, but that's to be expected. Yes, I'm still thinking. Don't rush the process.*

Nika: *Not rushing you. I wonder who and what and whether I should talk to Cole again, see if he knows who might— Hold on. He's at the edge of the office and made eye contact with me. Maybe he's coming this way. I'll get back to you. Have a good morning.*

Rainey signs off as she often does: **kissy face emoji**

Nika shoves her phone into its little cubby on the desk, continues to shuffle a few papers, and waits to see if Cole comes in. Her patience is rewarded.

Cole enters the library, hands in pockets. He seems disheveled for today, and Nika wonders about him and Danielle. Something about them strikes a chord—a minor one. Like the whole world comes to a screeching halt and stares at them. Not because of their beauty and elegance, but because even though they seem right for one another, everything about their coupling also seems so, so wrong.

"Nika," Cole says. "Can I speak with you?" He knows the library is empty, so why is he asking? Out of courtesy? That's more than some people give these days.

"Sure. I don't have a class until eight thirty." Nika glances at the clock. It's a bit past eight right now. If he doesn't stay too long, she can work on cataloging, something she's always behind on.

"I want to see how everything is going. With you, your dad, Alex . . ."

What does his trailing off mean, and how does he know about Alex? *Damn, this town!* So far, no one has said anything to Nika, but there's still time. There's *always* time for the rumor mill to spread its arms far and wide.

Cole waves his hand in front of her face. "Earth to Nika. Are you okay?"

"Oh, I'm fine. Sorry. Just distracted. Dad is fine. He's

going to meetings, I think, and remember, he might have a problem with weed, but he could have a much worse problem, you know. Weed isn't—"

"That's fine." He plunges his hands back into his pockets and rocks back on his heels, his gaze landing anywhere but on Nika, like he's uncomfortable being in a school he's so familiar with. "I . . . I've had a few more calls from concerned parents. They want to know what we're doing as far as changing the play."

"Your intel didn't tell you?" Nika huffs.

"My intel? No. Are you making changes?"

Nika refrains from spitting on the ground before saying, "No, sir, I am not making changes. *Once Upon a Fairy Tale* is a story about a princess, yes. Does she fall in love with another girl? Yes, she does, but the play isn't so superficial. It's layered and deep, a story of belonging, family, knowing who you are and who your friends are. It's about being accepted no matter what and learning to love yourself. This play," Nika pauses, proud of her former student for writing it, proud of all the Evergreen students for taking on the challenge, "sends a message to everyone, a message we all should embrace."

Placing a hand to his cheek, Cole digs at a scab there, then frowns. "Do you actually think that, or does the message only apply to you?"

Ouch. Did Cole Hannon show some balls? Nika ignores the jab. "Question: Do you know why the police were at my house looking for Alex?"

A flush moves across Cole's cheeks, and he shakes his head. "Not really. If I were the high school principal, probably, but I heard they wanted to speak to him about some possible drugs and then your dad, well, weed was an issue."

"You're right, mostly, and I'm not surprised because news goes hell for leather through this town, like people don't have anything more important to do besides sit, gawk, and talk. You forgot one major detail, which is: the police came to talk to *my son* because a student in this district—*not my son*—was accused of spiking someone's drink. Yup, some kid—again, a student in this district—had drugs, and he used them in an attempt to assault someone else—another student in this district. That's who this community—the parents, the teachers, the staff, the school board—should be worried about. Not my son, who did nothing. Not my dad, a seventy-two-year-old adult. Not my play, which celebrates love in all its forms. If you think we should be worried about any of those last three things . . ." Nika pauses. Cole is still her boss. She has to be careful how she words this next phrase if she wants to keep her job. "I guess you aren't the person I thought you were."

Nika's real intention was to call Cole narrow-minded and self-focused, a typical ball buster who doesn't do much himself. An at-times pompous, frat-boy boss. She's glad she chose to step away from that course of action. Hurtling abusive words isn't something she strives for on the regular—at least not out loud.

Cole nods, and a phone rings in the background. "No, I get it." He rubs his hand over his almost bald head and then puts his chin in his hand. "Well, keep doing what you're doing then."

What? "That's it? Why did you come here? We've made no further progress than the last time we spoke. Is there something you're *not* telling me?" Nika runs the conversation over again in her head, like an old VHS tape, searching for subtext, clues, but nothing stands out.

Cole hesitates, and Nika's heartbeat increases in her chest, the *thrum* reverberating in her ears like the rumble of thunder. She knows the look—of not wanting to say something to someone. Cole might be a pompous ass who doesn't always know where his head is or how to deal with the situation correctly, but he's also never been one to intentionally hurt anyone, at least as far as Nika is aware. Is he thinking about how to phrase his words too?

"Be forewarned," he leans closer and whispers, "I don't want you to have to attend a disciplinary hearing with the board."

Nika places a hand to her heart. "Me? Because of the play? Let me say it one more time for the people in the back—the play *they* approved?"

"I guess that remains to be seen."

Two beats pass in silence as Nika lets Cole's words sink in. She takes a breath, inhaling through her nose. Cole's cologne is subtle, but there, neither attractive nor unattractive. She lets out her breath. "And do they know what I found in my library?"

"They do."

Well then. "Do they care?"

"Whoever did what they did didn't hurt school property."

A class bell rings over the PA. "That's what it's come down to, hasn't it? They don't care about me . . . It's all about the school. The decimated books weren't the district's, so they don't matter, and the people who are *concerned* about the play will be loud about it until—"

"I think—"

"Please let me finish. I want to go on record and state my

displeasure. If I weren't standing inside an elementary school library at this moment, in the vicinity of little ears"— footsteps slap against the tile outside the door—"I'd say much more. But I will say this: If the school district is looking for a reason to get rid of me, and they're using this play as an excuse, then I have no way of winning. Simply firing me would have been preferable. But if that's not it, then answer this: What is the district's agenda? Am I too outspoken? Am I teaching these precious children something they don't want me to teach? Is the Dewey Decimal System outlawed in this state now? Do they want to make a lesson out of me?"

Cole shakes his head and touches her arm. "Nika, please. I don't want you getting upset over this—"

"Upset?" Nika throws her arms wide. "I already am! This is my job, my career, my calling! And my family—my students are my family." Nika places her hands on her hips and glares at Cole, a stout burning in her gut. In the distance, footsteps trail off as the students enter classrooms. Soon, the school will be starting another day with some of the district's most energetic youngsters.

"Listen," Cole whispers, "I understand everything you said, and I don't know what they're thinking. I'm warning you because I know how this district works."

"And what . . . You're being kind? I'm sorry if this sounds harsh, but when have you just been kind to me?" Nika taps her foot like her students do, an immature and petulant gesture.

Cole extends his hand again and places it on Nika's shoulder. "You're right. I deserved that. But I've been on the receiving end of the rumor mill around here." His eyes widen for a moment—*he's talking about his relationship with Danielle.* "People can be cruel, but I never hear you say anything bad about me, and I respect that about you."

Nika has no reason to think Cole is lying, so she dismisses him and shakes her head. With everything going on in her life, is it any wonder why her libido is as closed as the minds of the community?

Interior: Pius X Elementary School, Seventh Grade
Hallway, 1990

It's class exchange time, and NIKA stands at her
locker. She switches her English book for her
science notebook, then closes the door and turns.
JASON PETERS stands next to her, and she gasps.

NIKA
Jason! You scared me. What do you need?

JASON
Just wanted to tell you I like your red T-shirt.

NIKA
(looking down at her ringer tee)
Uh, thanks? It's my new favorite.

JASON
(smirking)
It's my new favorite too. Want to know why?

NIKA
(blushing)
...

JASON
(throwing a glance to a group of boys next to him)
I'll tell you. It's easy to see those tits of yours!
When did that happen? Over the vacation? You
know, I visited Pike's Peak once. That might be
your new nickname.

JASON taps the locker next to hers and laughs, then

strides away, looking back once to tip his chin at NIKA before high-fiving one of the other boys in the group.

Tears form in NIKA'S eyes, but she refuses to cry. Instead, she opens her locker, takes out her sweatshirt, and pulls it over her head.

chapter twenty-three

Mindy's kittens lend some variety to Nika's long, monotonous days, but her life is almost at a standstill as so many distasteful issues stagnate, foul and unmoving around her; she's not making progress on any of them, just spinning her wheels. In the school library, where she questions her value. At the police department, where Alex is in the clear, but the investigation is "still pending." With her father, who really "doesn't want to talk about it." One of the only avenues she's truly moving forward on is the play—the set looks great, and the props are as realistic as anything she's seen on Broadway, or so Rainey says.

After her chat with Cole, Nika vowed to be more available to the children involved in the play and their parents. Hoping to find out which families have an issue with the play and which do not, she calls two short meetings: one each for said children and families.

The students' session is easy: homemade treats, fruit, and juice before play practice means the kids are focused. "Fifteen, twenty minutes tops," she tells them. "We'll have some snacks and then we'll practice. I want to be sure we're all on the same page."

"The same page!" The actor playing the knight's attendant doubles over in laughter. "Funny, Ms. Stewart."

Nika doesn't find as much humor in her inadvertent pun as he does, but her heart swells with pride. These kids have fun with these productions. They learn about cooperation, teamwork, time management, and self-confidence. With the set issues they've had this year, the lessons also include adaptability and creative problem-solving. Why can't all the parents see this?

Because they're jaded. Indoctrinated. Subscribing to a belief that some are worthier than others. Worried about power and lack thereof. What's—

Don't go there now, girl, Nika thinks, and she focuses on the kids in front of her. They all sit on the floor, juice in one hand, snack in another, chatting about teachers and homework and movies and television shows. This little group is so inclusive, so close. They'd do anything for one another—she's sure of that. Nika peppers them with questions, asking how they're enjoying the experience, what they've learned, and what could work better. One stage crew member mentions they need more tools, and Nika agrees, while a second comments on costume quality.

"They're all right for a fifth-grade play," the girl says, "but they aren't as nice as the ones at the high school."

The kid speaks the truth, and Nika makes a note to contact the high school theater directors early next academic year.

"Anything else?" Nika bites into a dark chocolate chunk cookie and chews and swallows before speaking again, always aware of being a role model for these kids. For some, she's all they have. "How do you feel about the storyline? Do you like it? Anything you'd change?"

The boy playing the wizard raises his hand. He often checks out science fiction and fantasy books from the library, and Harry Potter is one of his absolute favorite series. "It's a good story," he says. "It's funny, and I like funny, and it has action! It's strange we don't have a prince though. This *is* a fairy tale."

There it is.

Not all fairy tales involve princes, Nika thinks as several twitters ripple through the room, and a tingle works its way up her back. "Strange? What do you mean? Would you prefer a prince?"

The kid crinkles his nose, like he's thinking. "Strange because . . . because fairy tales usually have princes and princesses, you know? That's who falls in love all the time."

"You know I have two moms, don't you?" The girl playing Princess Saoirse says behind him. "It's not always about princes and princesses!"

The boy's cheeks flush bright red, and he turns to face the girl. "I know. I said it was strange. Weird. Not *bad*. It's not like they kiss or anything."

Nika nods, wondering if things would be different if she had left the kiss in the script. *Once Upon a Fairy Tale* was originally written for high schoolers, but at Nika's request, the author adapted the script for the younger crowd. "I see and thank you for your feedback. Anyone else?" She scans the small group.

"Too much pink and purple," the cobbler says, "but

that's it. I know it's supposed to be royal and all, but maybe blue would be good if you do this another year."

"Duly noted," Nika says and scribbles *color, blue* on her notepad. "Any other grievances or comments you'd like to share?" The students shake their heads, and Nika's questionable frame of mind solidifies: she was right to direct *this* play, right to stand her ground. It's not the kids with the concerns; it's the parents.

After inhaling and exhaling a fortifying breath, Nika says, "That's all then. As you know, I have another meeting to attend after practice, and while I'm with your parents, I'd like you to make sure backstage is cleaned up and everything is set for scene one for the next practice. Okay?" She waits for the kids to nod. "Then let's go!"

~

Student chitchat from backstage filters to Nika's ears as she places more cookies onto the table at the side of the room. A knock sounds at the door, and someone Nika's never met before peeks their head in. The woman is tall and thin and sports cat-eyeglasses and pressed linen pants. A man stands next to her, even taller and thinner. Behind them, another couple inches forward, both dressed in Amazon delivery driver uniforms, which gets Nika wondering about Mindy, and her gut clenches. She pushes the feeling away as best she can, unwilling to consider it a bad omen. A few more folks trickle in, and Nika says hello to them all, welcoming them with the offer of cookies and coffee or juice. None of the parents partake. Instead, they sit, lined up on the folding chairs, staring straight ahead, waiting for her to begin.

So she does. "Thank you for coming. Evergreen Elementary's principal, Cole Hannon, let me know some of you have concerns about this year's play." Several people nod, but no one speaks, something Nika is grateful for. Perhaps they won't be the unruly crowd she envisioned over her morning coffee. Speaking of grateful, she would have been even more so if Cole had agreed to attend this meeting . . .

"I don't want to take up too much of your time, but I called this meeting to give you the opportunity to share your concerns with me. For those of you who don't know, I'm Nika Stewart, Evergreen's librarian. I've been here for almost fifteen years, and I've directed the play for five of those. I'm also a Five Rivers resident and district parent."

One man raises his hand. "If you've been around here that long, then you should know better."

Nika frowns. *He did not* . . . "Excuse me? Know better than what?"

"To choose a play like this."

"Like *this*?" Nika knows what he means, but she wants to hear him say it aloud, to her face. "Please . . . I'm not sure what you're trying to say."

The man rolls his eyes, a juvenile reaction for someone his age, and crosses his arms over his chest. "Come on. You know exactly what I mean. This story features two women, two princesses. That's no fairy tale, if you ask me."

Centering herself when she's angry has always proven to be a challenge, so right there, in the moment, Nika focuses on the paint on her shoes, a bright cyan they used for some of the picture frames hanging in the castle. Then, she looks up and pastes a smile on her face; it feels too tight, too forced, but she cannot say what she needs to say without some outward sign implying she doesn't feel threatened. "With all due respect, the story doesn't feature two *women*—they are girls. This play was adapted, by the author, mind you, for this age range. And while *your* fairy tale may not involve two princesses, the same can't be said for other people. Evergreen hosts a wide range of families."

A woman speaks this time. "I, for one, don't want my children to see two people kissing at all, much less two women, er, girls."

Nika holds up her hand. "There is no kissing in this play. It focuses more on friendship than anything else, on finding out who you are inside, who you surround yourself with. The messages this play sends are timely and—"

"It's not right," someone mutters, but Nika can't see who.

"Does the school board know about this?" another person asks.

Nika sighs and takes a seat, knowing the night will likely be overly long. She details her process of choosing a script, which always involves feedback from the principal, superintendent, and school board, and the steps leading from script choice to play production. Fielding answers is relatively easy, though frustrating, because Nika—always that rule follower—actually followed the district rules. At the end of the day, she did nothing wrong, regardless of what the parents may think.

As the minute hand continues its circumference and the meeting closes in on three quarters of an hour, Nika switches tactics. She pulls out information she's printed and waves the paper at the group. "I'm happy to give you a copy of this—a statement from the Office of Intellectual Freedom." A man snickers, but Nika ignores it and continues. "Three reasons are often cited for challenging materials. The material is considered 'sexually explicit,' it contains 'offensive language,' and/or it is 'unsuited to any age group.' *None* of those three apply to *Once Upon a Fairy Tale*."

The room is quiet, and Nika takes a beat for questions, comments, or some sort of retort. Nothing comes, so she nods and says, "I always appreciate airing concerns, and I thank you for coming. The kids will be bringing home a flyer with the dates and times of the play. We hope to see you there! If there's nothing else, feel free to take some snacks with you. They need a good home."

Several folks mutter thank you and shuffle out the door. Two couples take some cookies and stand at the side of the room, talking quietly while shooting Nika glares. Nika begins to stack the chairs, hoping no one bothers her as she goes through with the monotonous task. When she gets to the last row, though, she looks up to see a parent, one who sat in the far corner, arms crossed, brow furrowed, eyes narrowed. His body language put Nika on high alert, and here, as he stands next to her, she feels it even more, feels the ghost of Jason Peters. She steps away from him.

"You know," he whispers, his voice nothing like Jason's except in tone, "you can quote all the fancy freedom statistics you'd like, but it doesn't mean anyone is going to show up to your filthy gay play."

chapter twenty-four

Nika is thankful her next appointment with Susan Harris comes two days after the parent meeting since the final comment from that horrible man infused her with unease.

Lila catches her on the way out the door. "Where're you headed, Mom?"

Nika is honest with her kids, but they don't need to hear about a sex therapy appointment. Plus, she's not sure how Ethan would feel about Lila knowing. Wouldn't that change the dynamics? Between Nika and Ethan, Lila and Ethan, Lila and Nika. And, she's so young. A half truth it is then. "I'm headed to a therapy appointment."

Lila tilts her head, much like she did when she was young and trying to process what Nika said. "Therapy? Really?"

"Yes. I have some things I'd like to discuss. There's no shame in therapy, you know." Pulling open her bag, Nika checks to see if she has her phone, notebook, and pen.

"Oh, I know. My friend goes to therapy. She said it helps a lot, but if you want to make it work, you have to be honest and talk to the therapist."

Lila doesn't look up from the peanut butter and jelly sandwich she's now making for a late breakfast, so Nika isn't sure if her words are intentional or not. For a fifteen-year-old, they are far more profound than expected, but maybe she's only reporting what her friend said. Lila probably has no idea how close to the mark she is: her mother could easily lie to the therapist and not bother opening up. Or Nika could never return to the office again. If she chooses either of those options, there's no hope of solving the problem; she'll be stuffing it away in a corner to gather dust, something Nika has a lot of practice doing.

"I agree with your friend, and I should get going. There's laundry in the dryer. After you eat, find your brother, and the two of you—please fold and put away the clothes, okay?"

Asking them to do chores isn't usually an issue, but Alex can get ornery on the rare days with nothing scheduled. "And if Alex gives you trouble, go ask your dad for backup. I think he's still sleeping."

Ethan has always been a night owl, and weekend mornings for him often don't begin until well after ten o'clock. He had asked about going to this appointment, but Nika reassured him she'd report back. He could go and probably should go to a future one instead.

"Okay. See you later." Lila sits at the table with her book and sandwich in front of her. She's going to be fine.

Nika leans in, presses a kiss to Lila's forehead, and inhales her familiar scent. Soap, lotion, and a bit of sleep still linger, a potent fragrance Nika will never forget, and one she'll miss when Lila flies the coop. "See you later. Love you."

"Love you too," Lila says without looking up.

~

Like the previous visit, Susan's office is quiet, and gratitude fills Nika's heart. The last couple of weeks have been too much in so many ways. Too much stress. Too much deceit. Too much to keep track of. Nika's not sure if she's coming or going, and if she said that out loud, Rainey would say, "Well, you're certainly not *coming*—which is why you need Susan."

This week, Nika left Rainey at home, and she's still laughing at Susan's presumption of a threesome. She's probably seen everything over the years, which is why being a therapist has never entered Nika's mind. Has Susan thought about writing a book? Maybe she's written one already.

While Nika waits, she pulls up Susan's website on her phone and pokes around more than she did the other day. Susan Harris has an education section, complete with online courses one can take. *Why didn't I try that first? I might have been able to spare some embarrassment.*

Nika clicks on the course menu. She indicates her gender and what she's interested in—Susan Harris has quite a list of topics to choose from—and then two suggestions pop up at the bottom.

On the right: *Reclaiming your libido*, which will provide advice and actionable strategies to increase your sex drive. Interesting. Nika hovers over an arrow: *Want to learn the science behind why you lost your sex drive in the first place? Get a better understanding of what you want and what you desire. Reconnect with your partner and create the sex life you envision!*

Sounds like a good goal. What's on the left?

A quick shift and the screen reads: *Project Passion.* Click. *A guide for couples of all kinds to help balance mismatched sex drives and create a fulfilling sex life. We'll cover the different types of sex drive and what each type needs. Get easy-to-understand, actionable tips to bring back the fireworks.*

Does this work for perimenopausal folks? Menopausal folks? Stressed-out folks? Anxious folks? Folks who want to get horizontal *only* for sleep and nothing else?

Ack. Again, a wave of overwhelm pushes Nika under, threatening to hold her there, so she tucks her phone into her bag. A few minutes later, as the soothing waterfall noise veers toward irritation, Susan steps into the room. They head back to her office, with the soft lighting and inviting walls. The couch practically reaches for Nika and embraces her.

"I need one of these in my bedroom. A smaller version, maybe. This couch is delightful."

"Nice things in our bedroom can make all the difference. Do you like your bedroom?" Susan asks.

Nika thinks of the bedroom's size, which is more than adequate. It gives enough room for dressers, a bed, and a little sitting area, more than she could ever ask for, maybe more than she deserves. The wall color is a favorite, Argos gray, and the red and blue accent colors lend an inviting air to the space. The colors suit her (it's all about color), and the pattern (a pleasant plaid) suits Ethan. "Yes, I do like my bedroom. Ethan and I chose most of what's in it together."

"That's good. At least we know the space itself isn't the problem."

"For Ethan, space is never a problem! He complains we haven't christened all the rooms in the house!"

Susan laughs, the sound rich and hearty. "Typical of some folks I know." She leans in over her crossed legs. "Tell me—how are you feeling today?" She holds up a finger and stops Nika before she can speak. "Hold on. I'm not trying to read into anything here. I want to know how you're doing—if you're nervous, what you expect. Are you glad to be here? Would you rather leave? I want this to be a positive experience for you." She pauses. "Okay, now, you may answer."

Nika doesn't take long. "I *am* nervous, but I need to be here. It's not only about holding onto Ethan—he'll stay with me because he loves me. It's about me—understanding why I feel inadequate, what I can do to become more confident, and it's about finding . . . pleasure again, I guess." Nika shivers. "That word bothers me."

"*Pleasure*?" Susan Harris lifts an eyebrow.

"Yes. I'm not sure why. *Pleasant* is fine. *Pleasure* is not."

"Even when used in a nonsexual context?"

"No one uses it in nonsexual contexts, not anymore. Archaic usage, sure. You know, some words—ugh, they're awful. *Discharge* is another one. And of course, *moist*. Who likes that word? Even when it comes to baking, it's a little like . . . ripping a library book. I don't want to hear it."

"Okay." Susan makes note of something on the paper in front of her.

"Do you think I'm odd?"

The corners of Susan's eyes crinkle as she smiles. "Honestly, nothing seems odd. Each of us is different, and I've learned to appreciate all types. I've also learned to look at most things in life as continuums, which means I try not to use terms like *normal* or *abnormal* or *odd*."

Nika shifts in her seat, somewhat relieved, and pulls on her shirt. She could be worse and have some off-the-wall fetish . . . Nika forces her attention back to an abstract painting on Susan Harris's wall. The reds, the blues, the creams, the browns. She has no intention of letting her mind go off the rails.

"Anyway, thank you for sending back the intake forms. The information will be helpful as we go forward. For today, though, I want to hear what's been weighing on you since I saw you last."

Weighing. What an interesting word choice. That's how Nika feels, though, doesn't she? "My life is always full, and lately, it's been a little too full." Nika chuckles. "Along with sexual issues, I'm dealing with something at school." She details the particulars of the play and the parent meeting for Susan.

Susan responds at the appropriate moments, allowing Nika to vent her frustrations. A few minutes later, Susan says, "That's a lot to put on you, but I'm proud of you for standing up, for standing your ground. You've done nothing wrong—you realize that, don't you?"

"It certainly doesn't feel that way sometimes, but yes, I know, and I have to believe it to be true."

"Believing is a tough thing to do. The way we're brought up impacts our ability to see ourselves the way others see us. I think that's at stake here a little bit, but we can explore the topic further another time. Question for you—does Ethan feel the same way? Is he on your side with this?"

Nika doesn't hesitate. "Ethan's always on my side. Always. I never doubt that."

"Except when it comes to sex."

The words stop Nika cold, make her think twice before answering. "I never thought of it that way, actually."

"You have to remember—all relationships involve more than one person. That's the nature of a relationship, right? So, let's think of things this way. With these sessions, we certainly want to tackle what you need to be fully yourself—

the person you want to be—and why words like *pleasure* bother you. But we also need to think about your relationship with Ethan, and the biggest component there will be your communication. How do you two communicate? Do you feel you communicate? Is communication important to you? You don't have to answer any of those questions right now. I want you to think of this as a multi-pronged approach. Because you're not the only one in this relationship. Does that make sense?"

Nika nods. "It does—complete sense. Do a little digging into myself and who I am, and then I can address more with Ethan."

"Yes, so here in this office with me, we'll tackle you, and I'll give you some homework that will help you and Ethan. Be forewarned—I've sent this first assignment to Ethan as well. But," Susan holds up a finger, "I want you to recognize one other thing: it sounds like you've been very focused on Ethan and how *you* might not be giving *him* what he needs. Your response says a lot about you and who you are, and I admire you for it. However, these sessions are for *you*, and I want you to really think about what you want, what you need, and if Ethan is giving it to you."

What Nika needs is peace and quiet. A harmonious work and family life. A boss who trusts her. Family members who love her for the person she is. A thank you from her kids from time to time and appreciation from Ethan for everything she does. She needs to empty her mind of all the self-deprecating thoughts and feelings of inadequacy. She needs to continue these sessions.

"You're right," Nika says. "So what's next?"

Susan takes the opportunity to ask Nika about some of the answers to the intake questions, which include her thoughts on sex in general and some of her habits. By the end of the hour, Nika is tired, exhausted really, and she realizes the toll talking about her and her sexual habits takes on her.

Nika places a hand to her temple and presses the skin there. "Is it always this tiring?"

"Sex or talking about it?" Susan says. "Talking about it—usually. Sex, it can be." She winks.

Nika tries to remember back to when she and Ethan first became intimate, to recall the spark, the fireworks, the thrum of excitement and desire. Had they ever come away like they'd exerted themselves? A thumping of hearts, a tingle of electricity across her skin and low in her belly. Those, she remembered. But sex so fierce it counted as true exercise? She's not—

"It can be that way, if you want it to," Susan says. "It's a question of what *you* want."

If you want it to. Do I? A strong feeling of discomfort invades Nika, and she rubs the tight spot on her chest. Her fingers do nothing to help, but she looks at Susan, her earnest eyes and encouraging smile, and hope bubbles within her.

The feeling has been a long time coming.

chapter twenty-five

Since the kids know about the therapist, no one is surprised when Nika tells her family—after they've looked in on the kitties—she has homework to take care of. Ethan cocks his head, raises an eyebrow, and asks, "Do you need any help?" A smile tugs at his lips, but Nika is adamant. "No, but thanks. Maybe another time."

"I'll hold you to it," he says, and Lila throws him a questioning look.

"I'll be back." Nika grabs her folder, her water bottle, and her sunglasses and heads out the back door to the corner of the backyard. Set there against the cedar fence is a small teak and wrought iron bench that looks out over the lilac bushes. In May, Nika takes short rests here, inhaling the lilacs, centering herself. The corner reminds her of Indian Lake, a place she used to visit when she was little. So much peace and tranquility. Strength. She needs that the most right now.

Nika opens the folder Susan Harris gave her. The bland white paper sports bold writing, and Nika whispers the words to herself: *Welcome to your journey! This will be an exciting step in finding a new and improved sex life, a new and improved you. This is the first of many assignments that lead to a new level of contentment for you and your partner. We must start at the beginning—COMMUNICATION. Direct, effective, and open communication is essential to a vibrant, healthy partnership, and ineffective communication is the biggest obstacle to having the relationship you desire.*

While being open and honest can be incredibly difficult for all partners involved, it's essential to strive for it. These exercises will ask specific, possibly detailed, questions so I can help you widen and clear your channels of communication. And yes, even if you think you communicate well, we can always try to communicate better with one another.

First and foremost, answer these by yourself. Then, when you're feeling brave, redo the assignment with your partner. You'll be glad you did.

So here we go! Ask yourself the following questions. Give both a gut reaction and a thoughtful answer.

Nika reads the list once, laughing to herself. And then, she goes back to the list a second time.

1. When do you feel sexiest? That's easy—she doesn't. Which is part of the problem, she's sure. Ethan is up front, maybe even bold, about his admiration of her; in his eyes, she's the most beautiful woman on earth. Even the pudge around the middle, the stretch marks, the parts of Nika she's hated since she was young, which is pretty much everything. Those seem not to matter to him. Or, rather, he thinks of them as part of her beauty. But *sexy* and *Nika* in the same sentence inside her head? Not going to happen.

2. When do you feel the least sexy? Is all the time an appropriate answer? Nika imagines Susan Harris shaking her head and saying something like, "We have our work cut out for us, don't we?"

3. What do I do in bed that you really like? So many moons ago, back when Ethan and Nika were dating and had little time to spend with each other, everything was quick, done almost without thinking. *I liked everything, didn't I? And even after we got married?* Nika has trouble coming up with one thing she likes for him to do right now.

4. What do I do in bed that turns you off? Nika closes her eyes and sighs, wishing the lilacs were already in bloom, knowing Ethan wouldn't want to hear her answer. That answer, though, propelled her to see Susan Harris. *Right now, everything.*

A tear escapes from the corner of Nika's eye, and she does nothing to wipe it away. Just takes a cleansing breath, and plunges ahead.

5. If there were one thing you would like me to do when we are making love that we have not done, what would it be?

A second tear follows the first, and Nika folds the paper and turns it over as she whispers, "Just leave me alone."

Buzz. Wrong answer.

Now is not the time to tackle this again because Nika is feeling pretty shitty about herself, and she's sure that isn't Susan Harris's intention. What to do and where to go next? This task seems so pointless, like she's beyond repair. The bubble of hope from before? Shattered into a million shards. She feels like giving up, but how fair is that to Ethan, who pretty much changed his entire life when he met and married—

A knock sounds at the side of the house. Speak of the devil. Ethan silently hands Nika a piece of paper. "These are my answers to the questions. I'm supposed to give you time to read them before we discuss them together. How much do you need?"

His strength and calm demeanor have always been attractive, and he's taking Nika seriously, which gives her a lick of courage. It's almost imperceptible, but it's there. She grabs onto it and nods. "Fifteen minutes, maybe? I can text if I need more."

"I'll be back then." A genuine, warm smile passes across his face.

"Okay." The word tumbles out of her mouth in a shaky breath.

Ethan cocks his head, and his smile drops. He approaches Nika, a deep furrow on his brow now. "What's wrong?" He sits. "Oh, Nik." With a gentle caress of his thumb, Ethan wipes Nika's tears away then leans in and kisses her on the nose. "You know we don't have to do this, right?"

"I know. But we have to. Don't ask why. We just have to."

"But if you're going to get upset, it's not worth it. I love *you*, Nika. As you are. We'll figure it out—"

Nika places a hand on Ethan's knee and squeezes. "We *will* figure it out, and we'll try this way first. I'll be ready soon. Okay? Go, please."

Ethan stands, concern still etched on his face. He opens his mouth and then shuts it again before an enormous grin cracks his face open once more. "Then, cheer up! 'If you were happy every day of your life, you wouldn't be a human. You'd be a game show host.'"

Nika bursts out laughing at the quote from *Heathers*, one of her favorite movies, and she blows him a kiss as he turns and walks away. His laughter still rings in the air when the screen door claps behind him.

Time is wasting, so she opens Ethan's paper. He's written his answers in tight, black, block letters—his usual penmanship exuding potency, competence, contentment. She'd know the handwriting anywhere, a sentiment that eases her heartache a little.

1. When do you feel sexiest? When you look at me as if I'm the hottest man you've seen.

2. When do you feel least sexy? When you tell me no, or another time, or when you want to make it quick because you have things to do.

3. What do I do in bed that you really like? Everything. I like everything you do, and I'd consider doing anything with you. At least try it and see if we like it.

4. What do I do in bed that turns you off? Not being engaged. Not being present. There's not a thing you could do to turn me off, as long as you're there.

5. If there were one thing you would like me to do when we are making love that we have not done, what would it be? I don't think this is the way the question is supposed to be answered, but I'll answer it this way anyway. I would like you to enjoy what we're doing. I want you to come up to me and initiate it because it is something you want, not because you know it's something I want or I need. I want you to feel like being with me is less of an obligation, less of a debt to be paid. I want you to be with me because you want to. I want you to want me.

Ethan's answers bring more moisture to Nika's eyes, and she's not certain how she'll be able to speak to him when he comes back. She tugs at her sleeves and wipes away the tears. And then he's there, and he sweeps Nika up into his arms and lets her sob before pulling back and moving the hair away from her face.

"I didn't mean to upset you, you know."

"I know."

"But I did."

"It's not your fault. At all. I don't know what the issue is anymore. The overwhelm is sometimes too much, so I want what I want when I want it—like if I can keep the order, I'll be less overwhelmed—and most of the time, I just want to be left alone. But then, I think about how selfish I am, to want that."

He settles her on his lap, his arms still around her. "You want to know what I think?"

"I guess so. Why would I be doing this if I didn't?"

"Good point. Well, I don't think those two things are mutually exclusive. I think they're connected, and therein lies the . . . issue. I wanted to say *problem*, but that's not it. You carry a lot of the burden and always have. First dealing with your ex, then being a single mom. Now, your dad. Let's not forget about the school, either. Evergreen has your heart and soul. Those kids? They're almost like your own. You care for so many people, you care about so many things, and you care so much—maybe you're tapped out."

"So you're saying I don't have any time or energy for you?"

"Yeah, maybe I am. And while I don't like it, and I get frustrated by it, I understand it."

"You do?"

"I do. On most days. Even though we both work full-time, you definitely bear the brunt of the housework and dealing with the kids. It comes with the nature of the hours we work. Those tasks are often simple, but they add to the everyday to-do list. Part of what I love about you, Nika, is you are such an active go-getter. You get shit done." Ethan pauses, lifts another strand of hair away. "What I would like is for you to consider this relationship as a part of you and your health. Make it more of a priority."

His words hurt, but he takes the sting out with a soothing hand to her back, tracing circles over and over again.

"I hear you, I understand you, and I want to do that, but there's only so much I can give. I *am* tapped out, as you said, and so it's going to take time."

"I know it will."

"And I also want to go on record as stating you *are* a priority to me already. I think we show that in different ways."

"Like?"

Nika moves out of his arms and off his lap and sits next to him on the bench, allowing herself space to breathe. She lets her hand linger on his thigh. "Like the coffee, for instance."

"Coffee? I'm not following."

"I make your coffee every morning, and you don't have to ask. Not that you would—you'd be more likely to make your own. In the morning, you come to the kitchen and know coffee will be there. It's a priority I put on my list long ago. It might seem small to you, but to me, making coffee is important."

"It is?"

"Yes."

He thinks for a moment and smiles. "Well, knowing makes a huge difference. I never thought about it that way before."

"We probably have a lot of things we haven't thought about before, which means we—at least I—have a lot of learning to do."

"You were right the first time, Nika. *We* have a lot of learning to do." He squeezes Nika's hand, and the connection flickers to life, and she truly believes she can do this, even if it takes more help, time, and energy than she thinks she has.

~

Later that day, Nika sifts through the paper piles scattered across her dresser. Tackling the task every week would make this marathon session unnecessary, but she can't seem to muster the energy on a weekly basis. A knock sounds at the door and then a gruff, "Nika, are you in there?"

"You can come in, Dad."

He opens the door and closes it behind him. His usually straight spine seems curved today, and the typical ruddy cheeks are pale. Something is wrong, and these days, she knows it could be anything. Nika braces for the impact.

"Do you have a minute?" he says.

He's holding something in his hand, but Nika can't see what. A piece of paper.

"Have you heard more from the police? Is—"

Dad stops Nika. "Don't worry. Nothing like that. I have something else to show you." He moves closer and thrusts out some sort of statement. "Do you see this?" He points to a row of information. "I'm not sure what this charge is about."

Nika takes the paper, which is his credit card bill. The charge in question is large—well over four thousand dollars. At this point in his life, he has everything he needs. Plus, Medicare and supplemental insurance cover most of his health-care costs. Those premiums are taken out monthly, directly from his bank account.

Her dad drags the office chair from the desk and sits next to Nika. "I know what you're thinking. You're wondering what I spent that much on?"

"Yeah, I am."

"Well, I don't know, or I don't remember. My usual charges don't cost this much. Phone, insurance. I pay some doctor's office invoices with my card, but I'm not sure who this charge even came from."

Nika frowns at the paper. The transaction number and abbreviation aren't even enough to search online. Then, she looks up at her dad. Lines etch his face. He's always been strong, but conflict has never been easy for him. "Don't worry. We can call the credit card company and sort everything out. It shouldn't take long. Sound okay to you?"

"Yeah, I guess so."

Nika settles into another chair and calls the number on the bottom of the paper, then presses the speaker button. Soon, a representative greets her on the line.

"Good morning," Nika says. "This is Nika Stewart, and I'm Michael Washington's daughter. He's here on the line with me. Say hi, Dad."

Dad straightens up, leans toward the phone, quietly says hi, and then shrinks back in his seat.

"What can I do for you today?" the representative says.

"We're wondering about a certain charge on January seventeenth of this year."

"Do you want to dispute the charge?"

"No, not necessarily. Maybe. We don't know yet." Nika takes a breath, urges herself to speak slowly and clearly. "We want to know which company charged him. My dad doesn't recognize the charge, and we want to be sure someone doesn't have access to his card."

"Okay, ma'am, let me look that up. One moment please."

A slight whir and then: "I see two charges for the day in question. Which one are you wondering about?"

"Yes, I see two charges as well. We're looking at the charge for four thousand, two hundred dollars."

"I see, and it's been billed through Southside Clinic, LLC."

"Southside Clinic?" she says into the phone and turn toward Dad.

His eyes darken, like a storm moving in, and he leans back in the chair, placing his hands behind his head. Nika silently gestures, hoping to figure out what's wrong, but he turns his gaze toward the window, effectively shutting her out. He's so good at it, and Nika cringes at how similar they are.

"Can I assist you with anything else?" the call representative says as Dad shakes his head.

"No, I think we're good. We appreciate the help."

Nika and the representative exchange closing pleasantries, and then Nika ends the call, puts the phone on the table, and looks at her father. "Well, there you have it. Southside Clinic. Does the name mean something to you?" Dad has never been one to mess around with money, so her spider sense says yes, but . . . *Will he tell me?*

A beat passes. "Yeah, I guess I'd forgotten about it, but it makes sense."

"What was it for?"

He stiffens, turns to Nika, gazes directly at her and then back at the window. "Nothing. Don't worry about it. I forgot. A lot has been going on lately."

He speaks the truth, but he's not saying something. "Dad . . ."

"No, Nika. It's fine. Thank you." He stands from the chair, picks up the paper, and leaves the room, a trace of frostiness lingering in the air.

Nika isn't certain what to think of his clipped tone. Has

a lot been going on lately? Yes, but the same could be said for all of them. Would Dad spend four thousand dollars and forget about it? No . . .

Ethan pops his head in. "What's up with your dad?"

That's it. Nika could have overlooked the situation, but for Ethan to notice something too? "I have no idea. And right now, I don't have the energy to ask." Nika checks her watch. "I do have the energy to get dinner started, which will likely be quesadillas. Any hope of you heading to the store for a few ripe avocados?"

Ethan nods. "Anything else?"

"Some fresh salsa, if we need it. Please."

Nika moves to land a small kiss on Ethan's lips, something they used to do more often. Something Susan would encourage her to do more often now. Thankfully, Ethan doesn't prod her for more, and after he leaves, Nika calls Rainey. "Hey, Velma. I might have another minor case for you."

"I think I'm working overtime when it comes to doing mystery work for you. But what do you have?"

Nika tells her about her dad and his behavior.

"I'm doing a superficial search on Southside Clinic right now," Rainey says. "It looks like it's some plastic surgery center."

Nika laughs out loud, the sound echoing on the line. *Dad? Plastic surgery?* The chiseled lines, liver spots, gaunt cheeks. No Botox, filler, or surgery scars to be found. "Uh, Dad hasn't had any surgery, so I wonder what that's about."

"I'll dig as far as I can go and let you know what I find. You do the same, got it, Daphne?"

"Can I be Fred instead? I love traps."

A snort, a snicker, and then Rainey clears her throat. "As long as you wear an ascot."

chapter twenty-six

Nika is lulled into thinking life can be without its bumps as nothing major erupts over the next week. The students are ready to learn, the play is making progress, no other parents have caused a problem, Lila and Alex move along with proper speed toward their goals, Dad is in a good mood, and Nika doesn't hear from the police or the school board.

With everything else seemingly settled, Nika goes back to Susan the next Saturday with a renewed purpose. Not that she's getting anywhere with her homework exercises. Nika still feels like everything is wrong with her, and the pressure to change is mounting. But Ethan's in this for the long haul, and she reminds herself that slow and steady will win the race. She pushes herself to make physical contact with Ethan as much as she can, leaning against him while they watch television, taking his hand as they walk from the car into the house after a night out, snuggling up to him when he comes to bed.

"Welcome," Susan says. The weather is improving each day, and with sun and spring on the horizon, Nika itches to be outside. Running, walking, anything but inside this building where she's forced to reflect on her inadequacies.

"Any revelations this week?" Susan prods.

Nika isn't prepared for the question and mulls the week over in her head. Her period arrived, so any obligation she feels to Ethan's needs lessened. Doing the deed then is too messy, and Nika's nether regions can be sore, especially the first few days. But even with the reprieve there and with life in general, she hasn't really thought about anything in terms of this sexual issue, so . . . "No. No revelations. I'll be honest—the homework made me a little uncomfortable. It made me feel bad about myself. And frankly, I don't need any help in that arena."

Susan smiles, but nothing like a laughing smile. "It's not meant to do that. It's simply meant to open communication between you and your partner. Be the beginning of a long conversation."

"Well, we did talk about it, so that's a step forward."

"It is." Susan says nothing more.

"And if I'm thinking about the conversation, maybe the most revealing thing that came from it is I'm so busy sometimes that at other times, I want to be left alone."

"Ah."

"*Ah?* What do you mean?"

"Busyness can mean many things, honestly. Some people are busy because of different pathologies, such as ADHD—"

"Sorry to interrupt. I don't have ADHD, but I do need to stay busy, or I don't feel right."

"Can you sit and read a book?"

"Yes, if everything else has been accomplished. I love to read." Nika dips a thumb toward her chest. "Real live librarian, right here!"

"Okay, good. Well, other people use busyness as an excuse not to do something. Is there something you *don't* want to do?"

"Besides have sex?"

Susan takes a moment. What is she considering? Nika blurted those words out, without thinking at all. What if . . .

"Very telling," Susan says. "Do you find having sex repulsive?"

"Lately, I'm not into touching. Skin-to-skin contact bothers me, especially when it's warm or you know, during a hot flash, so sometimes I physically shrink away from someone."

"Even your kids?"

"*Never* my kids."

"Huh."

"That's not what I expected."

"Sorry. Tell me this—are you a wall constructor?"

"What?"

"Do you build a lot of walls? Keep yourself closed up?"

This woman is good, Nika thinks. "For many years, I did. I don't always let people in, especially after my first marriage ended. I allowed my ex to do a huge number on me—"

"Hold on. Don't take that one on yourself. You might have been vulnerable, and he might have taken advantage of the situation. I don't know the particulars, and right now, I don't need to. We might explore those later. Just like your relationship with Ethan, your relationship with your ex involved *two* people. We cannot, as humans, take on everyone else's garbage. It will weigh you down."

Realization dawns, and Nika looks at Susan. "I think that's the problem. I *do* take on all the garbage—mine and everyone else's. I often feel the weight of the world, sorry for the cliché, on my shoulders."

Susan extends a tissue, and Nika takes it. She's not a crier, but Nika is beginning to believe she's more of a mess than she initially thought. Susan isn't making her feel this way, but maybe the whole world is. What is it trying to tell her?

"We're going to get you through this. Don't you worry." Susan leans toward Nika, holding her gaze. "I want you to remember—you chose Ethan, and he chose you. You are partners, which means you don't have to carry any burden by yourself. If he truly is the partner you tell me he is, he'll gladly take up some of the load." Susan pauses, as if she's allowing Nika's brain time to catch up. "My guess is Ethan might not be fully aware of your burden, which is why we're working on communication. Having said that, I have some new exercises for you for this week and next. Something a little more fun."

"Are you going to tell me what they are?"

"Nope. I'll email them to you by tomorrow at the latest, meaning you will have time to anticipate them. Do me a favor, though, and *make* time for these. They should each take about an hour, and Ethan is encouraged to help. Choose a time when you won't be too tired to take on these exercises, okay? Sorry to repeat myself, but these are designed to help with communication, which, as we've discussed, is crucial here."

"Too tired?" Nika chuckles. "That describes me almost every day. Fatigue and menopause—something *no one* ever talks about."

"You're right. *Many* of my clients would say the same," Susan says. "Some of those clients have opted for bioidentical hormone replacement therapy. Have you looked into it?"

Nika has, she's still on the fence about them, and she tells Susan so.

"Enough said," Susan replies. "It's not my job to convince you to try anything you don't want to try, but if you have questions, I might have someone with answers. Now, back to the exercises—considering your fatigue, a weekend might be a good time to do them. We tend to allow ourselves some slack on those days, and I encourage you to do so as well."

"Any other tips?"

Susan winks and says, "Keep an open mind."

~

The email comes in late that night, but Nika sets aside time the next afternoon for her and Ethan. The kids will be out of the house—they want to spend more time with the kitties over at Mindy's home—and Dad will be out for the day. *Out* could be anywhere, but he's an adult, and Nika decides to let that worry go. She mentally pats herself on the back and doesn't look at the email until a few minutes before she's scheduled to meet with Ethan. Fatigue plays a part in her decision, but if Nika is truly honest with herself, so is fear—maybe even more so than fatigue.

She clicks on the email. *Welcome to this set of exercises! The primary thing to remember is you do not have to tackle all of these in one setting. Choose one and go from there. You can always come back to these later and do more! That's the fun part.*

Nika stops reading and thinks about Susan Harris. Does *she* have a fulfilling sex life? Nika doesn't want to "see" Susan and any possible sex life in her mind—that's not what she's aiming for. Instead, she wants to know: Does Susan take her own advice? Does she perform these exercises? And, does she *enjoy* sex? Should Nika keep trusting her?

For Ethan's sake and the sake of her marriage, she should.

She will.

Nika scrolls to the list of exercises and breathes out a sigh of relief. These are thinking exercises more than anything else. *I can do this.* She scans the page. *One: What actions has your partner performed to make you feel loved this week? What could they do better? What actions have you performed for your partner, and what could you do better? Two: How can you and your partner make intimacy a priority? Three: Tell your partner what you need in bed to feel pleasure, and they'll tell you.*

As usual, Nika's face warms at the use of the word *pleasure*. What is it about that word? It's embarrassing how much she detests it. She isn't even sure where or how or why, but even the thought of the word makes her insides shudder. So she taps the screen: *Skip the third question for now.*

Her gaze travels back to the top of the page, but hesitancy fills her as she again reads the first set of questions. Her mind jumps to the conversation with Ethan about the morning coffee. He understands now why she does it, so maybe he'll look at more of what she does daily as a means of showing her love. *But even if he recognizes it, is it enough?* Maybe acts of service aren't enough for him. Maybe she needs to express her love verbally. *Or physically.*

"Let's go to the next one," Nika says, quickly scanning the question about prioritizing intimacy. It will take more time to think it through, so she moves to the third. This time, as much as she wants to, she doesn't skip it, instead closing her eyes and thinking about a cozy room, comfortable bed, a worn paperback, a eucalyptus candle. A cup of peppermint tea sits on the nightstand next to a warm chocolate chip cookie the size of her hand. The only thing missing? Ethan.

Nika's gut clenches and tears prick at her eyelids. Damn those tears again. When did she get so weepy? And why is it any time she thinks about what she needs to feel *pleasure*, an image of her, *alone*, comes to mind? How worried should she be? Nika takes in a shaky breath and channels Susan, who would probably tell her not to worry. "We've just started," she'd say, a sympathetic smile on her face. "There's room to grow here, Nika. I know it, so trust the process."

Hasn't Nika always had trouble trusting the process?

Nika glances at the second set of exercises, and she stifles a laugh. The instructions talk about role playing, something Ethan would be ready to tackle, and a giggle escapes when she reaches the bottom of the list, where it talks about extra credit. *I can't even imagine what Ethan would say if—*

Speaking of which. He's at the door. In worn blue jeans circled by a leather belt, chaps, scuffed cowboy boots, and a ten-gallon hat on his head.

More giggles emerge, and he tries to straighten his own face, which has broken into an enormous, mischievous smile. "Don't laugh, pardner," he says. "Maybe this will do it for you?"

Nika wipes away tears, happy this time, and she leans back in her chair, clutching her stomach. "I'm sorry, no. I mean, the chaps look great—accentuate the butt and all— which is of course still nice, but no."

"What do you mean by *still* and *nice?* No one wants to hear the word *nice* used in reference to them." He mock frowns.

"I mean . . . We're getting older. Nothing bad. It's still firm, but if you're anything like me, your rump will be sagging soon."

"Cut the qualifiers, Stewart, and I like your butt. It's not sagging. And I'm messing with you. Figured we'd start with a nice full-body massage, if you're up for it."

Full-body massage? Despite Nika's aversion to touching, a massage sounds divine. She's been tense for months, and no amount of walking or hot showers has done the trick. "Right now?"

"Why not?" Ethan says and moves into the room. "Lie down wherever you want, and let's go." He rubs his hands together in preparation.

Nika is surprised. To be honest, she expected Cowboy Ethan to go full throttle on her, propose they try being frisky with him dressed as John Wayne, and he hasn't. He so hasn't. In fact, he's making this moment more about her than him, and her heart swells. With love, gratitude, optimism. Optimism that *her* baby steps will amount to something, that *his* baby steps will amount to something.

She lies on the bed, hands at her sides, and closes her eyes, relishing the quilted softness at her back. Rarely does Nika stop to appreciate little things like this.

Ethan takes her foot in his hands and begins with soft circles against her arch. When Nika lets out a little moan, she opens her eyes, laughing at Ethan's raised eyebrows. He says nothing and tips his hat toward her, his lips curling at the edges before he continues his ministrations. One foot, then the other. Then her calves, her thighs. Ethan reaches her hands, and Nika closes her eyes again, thinking about her reaction. Her heart should be double-timing it inside her rib cage, leaping at the idea of quality time with her husband while the rest of the family is away. Yet . . .

"So, a cowboy isn't it?"

"No. Any more costumes up your sleeve?"

"Why yes. But first—"

Ethan moves forward, takes Nika's face in his hands, and before she knows what he's doing, he dives for her mouth, as if he hasn't kissed her in years. Nika's hands go to his shoulders, and instead of leaning back, as she's inclined to do, she leans in. *Lean in. Isn't that the name of—*

"Now is a time to do, not think," he says against her lips.

Damn, he knows me well.

She concentrates on his mouth, soft and firm at the same time, gentle yet demanding. *When was the last time we kissed like this?* Soon, the pressure leads to more, and he teases Nika with his tongue against her mouth, a simple whisper of an action, coaxing her lips apart and allowing his breath to mingle with hers. His hands move from Nika's face to her hips to her butt, and he lifts Nika against him—

"Mom? Dad? I need— *Oh.*" It's Lila, and her face blazes red.

Of course it does. She's not that *naive to not know what was happening.* Nika shifts her weight so she and Ethan fall onto the bed, laughing. Her body covers his erection, and she'd like to keep it that way. "What do you need, honey? I thought you were with Alex at Mindy's," Nika says as she tosses Ethan a blanket near the bed to cover what won't be covered once she gets up.

"I wanted . . ." Lila says, a hopeful expression on her face. "It can wait—"

Nika pats Ethan's leg and rises from his lap. "It's okay, honey. We're just being silly here. Let's go."

As she and her daughter cross the threshold of the bedroom, Lila turns back once and smirks. "Nice hat, Dad."

chapter twenty-seven

Nika straightens her shirt and pats her hair as she follows Lila into the kitchen. Her usual frizz, something she's complained about since elementary school, will help cover any mussing from her interlude with Ethan. "Where's your brother?" Nika asks. "Is something wrong?" She glances around the kitchen, looking for Alex. The two had taken their bikes to Mindy's house. The ride is short, safe, and on early spring days, quiet, but Nika's not sure why Lila is here by herself.

"Well, Mindy comes back tomorrow morning, and we're trying to get the last of the mail out of her box."

"And?" Nika is missing something.

"Her mailbox is stuck. Jammed or whatever. We could leave the mail and let her know, but she asked us to do a job, and well, you know. I want to *do* the job."

Lila has to complete a job in her own way, or she won't

be satisfied. It's another tendency that pokes through often, her own brand of meticulousness that makes Lila who she is.

"What do you need from me? And why didn't you call?"

Lila's cheeks once again erupt with color. "I did, but you didn't answer. So can you come back with me and look at it? Maybe you can figure something out about the box. If not, we can leave Mindy a note. It was fine yesterday, so I'm not sure what happened between then and now." Lila often anticipates what Nika is going to ask next.

Nika smiles and nods, marveling at Lila's maturity again. The divorce impacted the kids, but it's good to see they're doing all right. Nika has Ethan to thank for his part in that. *I am so, so lucky*, Nika thinks. "You know what? Grandpa's out for the day. Let's go grab your dad, and we'll jump in the car. We'll figure it out and then maybe get ice cream or something, depending on what time it is."

"What about Bell Pepper Pizza? Can we go there?" It's their favorite pizza place, and the family hasn't been in a while.

"Let's see what time it is when we're finished, and I'll say maybe. Let me go get your dad."

"Tell him I said to giddyap!" Holding onto imaginary reins, Lila trots away.

~

Ethan is lying on the bed when Nika enters the room, and she sits next to him, stretching her hand out to his calf and rubbing it. On one of their first dates after the dance class, they'd decided to play tennis. Nika had been struck by the solid definition of his calf muscles, so different from her own softness. She squeezes her fingers against him, and he contracts his muscles in return. Years on, they still have so much strength.

"Why do I have the feeling you're going to tell me we're finished for now?" He's lived with them long enough to know interruptions are common occurrences, even with older kids.

Nika tells Ethan about the mailbox. "And you know Lila—in her head, the mail cannot stay there until Mindy gets back. It just can't."

Ethan draws in a breath, then gazes at Nika. "I love you, Lila, and Alex, and I'd do anything for you, but are you pushing me away again? A mailbox? Couldn't a mailbox wait?"

It could. But couldn't he, for once, not make everything about sex? Nika knows better than to be on the defensive, knows better than to answer a question with a question. She loves this man and wants to get through this part of their lives with an intact relationship.

"You're right," Nika says. "I can see how it looks that way to you, and I'm sorry. All I wanted was a massage, and we got a little off track there, didn't we?" Ethan doesn't argue, so Nika adds, "I have to admit, I might have stopped you anyway. I'm not *there* yet, but I hope to be."

Ethan must trust her and her words. Instead of showing anger or annoyance or impatience, he changes direction saying, "Lila is an interesting kid." He smiles and props himself up on his elbows, the cowboy hat askew on his head.

He could be one of those middle-aged men in a cowboy calendar, Nika thinks but keeps the thought to herself. "Don't I know it."

"She reminds me of someone I know," Ethan quips, and he winks.

Nika blows out a large breath. "Let's hope she has all my good qualities and none of the bad." If only they could be so lucky. "Seeing how she *needs* to get this mail, my guess is she has the bad too."

Ethan shakes his head, placing his hand on Nika's. "You can't look at them as *bad*. We all have issues or quirks or eccentricities. We all have ways of doing things. You accept them in Lila without question, so accept them in yourself, okay? Let's concentrate less on the issues or whatever you want to call them and vow to have more fun. What do you say?"

God, I could cry sometimes with this man, his generosity of spirit, his intuitiveness. Nika nods and sighs. "I'll try. Now, can you come with us? Bell Pepper Pizza might be involved." Nika narrows her eyes and smiles.

Ethan rubs his stomach. "I'll do anything for a pizza."

"Ahhh. I'll have to call Rainey. I found my Shaggy."

"What? What does he have to do with Rainey?"

"Never mind, and maybe I'll explain later."

"In costume? I'll be Shaggy, and you can be Daphne, but you'll have to wear a shorter skirt."

Nika turns, leaves the room, and calls over her shoulder, "We'll meet you in the car! By the way, I'm already Fred!"

~

As Nika, Lila, and Ethan enter Mindy's house, the kitties scamper to them, one tumbling over the next. Alex is stretched out on his back in the middle of the living room, a cat toy in his hand. He swings the long wand back and forth like a metronome over his stomach, and the kittens alternate attacking it. Cheetah runs as fast as she can from the trio back to Alex and pounces on his chest. He laughs until Olaf gets him directly in the crotch. "Ugh!" He rolls over to his side, clutching his groin. Lila and Nika laugh, but Ethan says, "Bad luck there, bud. You should have seen it coming."

Alex doesn't say anything, a grimace still graces his face, but his eyes glow with a happiness Nika hasn't seen in the last few weeks. Mabel is no longer a puppy, and there's something magical about fluffy kittens like these two. *Maybe a new pet, or two, is exactly what we need.* That's a subject she'll bring up with Ethan later. Alex and Lila are both summer babies, so maybe for their birthdays . . .

"Okay, on to the task at hand. Let's look at the mailbox," Ethan says.

Alex stumbles as he rises and gives the evil eye to the kitties. "My fault. Totally my fault." Then he points a finger at the cats and whispers, "You're both little monsters."

The little monsters look up at him, then plop down and roll over to their sides, front legs outstretched, exposing their soft, pink bellies. Lila squats to scratch each kitten one more time before she rises and marches past Nika with a satisfied grin on her face.

Nika admits they probably look ridiculous as they head to the mailbox. Four determined people getting mail at a house they don't reside in. The scenario would bother Mindy, if she were there to see it. Something to make Mindy curl her lip, toss out some snarky "happy family" comment.

But she's not there, and when they reach the end of the driveway, Nika understands why Lila came to get them. "Looks like a rust problem," Nika says. "Or . . . See?" She points to a paper at the top under the clasp. "Maybe this is jamming the box."

Ethan tugs on the handle, but nothing happens.

"We didn't want to break the thing," says Alex. "That's all I need—Aunt Mindy to be mad at me, at us."

Nika frowns. "What do you mean?"

Alex's eyes widen. "Nothing, but with everything going

on around here, I didn't want to make one more misstep."

Nika's heart hurts for her son, but his grin, a little shaky but genuine and all Alex, reassures her. He'll be okay, regardless of what the future brings.

Ethan pats Alex on the back and whips a screwdriver from his pocket. "I have just the thing." He holds up the tool like he's conducting an orchestra. "Stand back," he says, "and let the master do the work."

Nika turns her head and raises an eyebrow at the kids, who both roll their eyes before leaning in to watch Ethan. He drags the screwdriver across two rust patches at the hinges, then stabs the area underneath the clasp, pushing back the paper. One pull and then—

The box pops open, and Nika reaches in for the mail. Then she shuts the door—twice. It moves easily. "Write Mindy a note about the mailbox. She can choose to get another one if she wants."

"Can we stay a little longer and play with the kitties?" Lila asks.

"Maybe. Anything else you need to do? Scoop the litter? Water the plants?" Nika pushes open the front door, then holds it for everyone else. "Where's the rest of the mail?" she asks as she glances around the small foyer. It screams Mindy: bare white walls, brown trim, spare dark table with a vase of dusty dried flowers.

"On the kitchen table," Alex says with a kitten in his hands. "We've done everything else so . . . a few more minutes?" He tucks his nose into Cheetah's fur and nuzzles the cat, who headbutts his face. Alex hasn't been this engaged in something that doesn't involve Minecraft, Fortnite, or Discord in ages.

By the look on Ethan's face, he knows it. "A few more

minutes," he says. "Your mom and I will be in the other room."

The kids' coos follow Ethan and Nika into the kitchen, where Nika adds the envelopes from the mailbox to the growing pile. It leans to the right, so she places her hands around the stack, then pats the side, straightening it. Her gaze lands on the top envelope, which has the return address of Southside Clinic.

"What the hell?" Nika whispers and looks up at Ethan.

"What's wrong?" He furrows his brow as he glances at the stack of mail.

Nika taps her finger on the envelope. "This says Southside Clinic, and I just had a conversation with Dad." In as few words as possible, Nika details what she and her father learned from the credit card representative. "Dad had no intention of revealing what the charge meant to him. But now . . ."

"You're thinking maybe he paid for something for Mindy?"

"Yes, but to the tune of four thousand dollars?"

Ethan's jaw drops open. "What the fuck?" Swearing like a sailor is more in Nika's wheelhouse than Ethan's, and the words sound bizarre coming from him.

Nika snorts. "Exactly." She plops into the kitchen chair and puts her head into her hands. "I can't open this bill. It would be so wrong." But she snags it and holds it up to the light. Nothing. She checks the seal, which is solidly shut. "The only way I can get more information on this is by asking my dad. And I will. Because he shouldn't be paying that much money for anything that doesn't concern him. I'll do it as soon as I can."

"Do you think he'll tell you anything?" Ethan understands her father. He's pretty tight-lipped, but occasionally, he reveals something.

"I'm not sure. I think it depends on the day, but he's living in our house now, and in truth, I'm a little tired of what's happening with him lately. Too much drama. What happened to our peaceful little life?"

Ethan nods. "Evaporated, I guess. I know this all affects you more."

"Then let's leave the bikes here and go eat pizza. We'll figure everything out later."

chapter twenty-eight

Bell Pepper Pizza is a little slice of New York right there in the Midwest. Black and white tiles on the floor, small booths with red laminate tables, grated cheese and dried hot peppers in the center of said tables. A warm burst of tantalizing aromas like cheese, yeast, vegetables, and meats hits Nika when she opens the door. Nika's mouth waters every time she visits, and she imagines Ethan dressed as a pizza instead of a cowboy.

"You know," Nika leans into him as they're standing at the high counter waiting to place their order. "Maybe you should find a pizza costume."

"Anything for you, babe," he says, nudging Nika with his elbow. Then he whispers into her ear, "As long as you order the sausage, we'll be fine."

She slaps his arm, and his eyes twinkle. Ethan's mind is *always* in the gutter, and it's getting worse the older he gets.

Of course, Nika's homework from Susan could very well exacerbate everything in that arena, but she doesn't want to think about it now, in her favorite pizza place with three of her favorite people. "What do you want, kids?"

They go for the usual order—pepperoni for Alex and black olive for Lila. Nika prefers a little more spice on her pizza, but she's willing to give it up for the kids. She imagines she'll be doing that for years to come, compromising where it doesn't really matter to her to put a smile on their faces, to show them she cares. It's the least she can do for the two people who give her more joy than they'll ever know. Nika squeezes Lila's elbow lightly as they slide into their regular booth and wait for the pizza to arrive. The kids chatter while Nika and Ethan listen, and times like this remind Nika how content she can be, happy even.

All's right with the world . . . at least for now.

The boy who places their breadstick order in front of them tips his head in Alex's direction as he leaves.

"Do you know him?" Nika asks.

"Yeah. I go to school with him." Alex helps himself to two breadsticks and takes a large bite of one.

"Do you know him well?" Ethan asks.

Mumbling around his full mouth, Alex says, "Not really. I've seen him at a couple of parties."

Nika wonders what Ethan is getting at, if anything, with his question, but the sports announcer from one of the ceiling-mounted televisions gets their attention. Aziaha James of NC State's women's basketball team hits a three pointer late in the game, and teammate River Baldwin extends the lead over the Texas Longhorns. Nika isn't much for March Madness, but even she can appreciate the beauty of a clean basket. Suddenly, a hand lands on Nika's shoulder:

Detective Brine.

"Are you here for one of us or for pizza?" Nika places the breadstick she's chosen on the plate and wipes her fingers on a napkin.

"I'm here for pizza, but I thought I'd come over. Check in. See how your dad is doing—and Alex."

"As far as I know, Dad is fine. Do you know differently?" Graduate school taught her to think wisely, to critically question what's around her. Actually, graduate school might have made her a tad skeptical too.

"Really, I'm just asking how he's doing, and that's all."

"Can you not bother us anymore?" Alex says, which is surprising. He doesn't usually talk back to authority, and Nika sends a scowl his way. "Come on, Mom. This is ridiculous. Grandpa is an adult. If he wants to smoke weed, let him. He literally did *nothing* wrong."

Brine places his hands on his hips and shakes his head. His voice is deep as he says, "Weed can lead to even greater problems down the line, son. I don't think you know—"

"I don't think *you* know everything!" Alex stands up, throws his napkin onto the table, and rushes toward the door. He wrenches it so hard and quickly the glass windows on either side of it shake.

"Shit," Ethan says. "I'll go after him."

Detective Brine sits next to Lila, whose eyes are wide, but she stays silent, like she knows better than to talk at the moment.

Nika isn't sure what to say. She doesn't understand why Alex ran off, but she's also curious why Brine, who is only here to order pizza, is wasting his time with them. "Do you need to go after Alex too?" she asks.

"He's not a criminal, so no. And I know a thing or two

about teenagers. It's better for your husband to go after him."

Relief courses through Nika, and she releases her breath. "That's right—he's not a criminal, and you know this, so has anything changed?"

Brine holds her gaze for a moment before speaking. "I shouldn't be saying this here because then I'm not going through the proper channels, but he's good. Alex is good. Without saying too much, we have our suspect."

"Was it someone from the party? Do you know why they chose to involve Alex?"

"No. I think it was a coincidence. A crime of proximity. Alex was in the right place at the right time, and the kid had no idea about your father."

"Really? Because you know how news travels in this town." Nika doesn't mention anything about the library or what Cole said about the play or the school board. There's no point.

"Yeah, I do, but this time, it might have been a random series of events."

Nika checks her watch. Ethan and Alex have been gone for four minutes. No text, no calls. Nothing. The view outside the window doesn't include them, either, and she mulls over Brine's words. Random series of events? Coincidence? This isn't a Scooby-Doo episode, and because of the library incident, Nika wonders if Brine could be wrong. "Detective Brine, may I ask you a question—off the record?"

He hesitates. "Yes, but if I think we need to go on record with it, I'll tell you. How's that?"

"Fair, I guess." Nika ruminates on what to say and how to say it. And then, much to her surprise, she blurts everything out. She tells him about the day she went into the library and the books. Her theory of a disgruntled parent being behind them. She lets him know when it happened, in the context of her dad, Alex, and the party. She tells him about the parent meeting but doesn't say anything about the school board.

He furrows his brow and rubs his chin. "Do you think it's all related?"

"Honestly, none of it makes sense. Okay, maybe my dad smoking . . . No, that doesn't make sense either, but he's an adult, so I have no business telling him what to do. Simply put, I want to know who messed up those books. Why not approach me like a sensible adult?"

He laughs. "Criminals aren't so smart—you know how it goes. But off the record, I don't like vandals, and I don't like the idea of someone being on school grounds after hours— that's a safety issue. I'll see what I can find and get back to you."

"Great. I'll let Rainey know."

"Rainey? Rainey Delaney?" He smiles and lifts his eyebrows. "I haven't seen her in a while. How's she doing?"

Holy crap this town really is ridiculously small, Nika thinks. "You two know each other?"

"Who doesn't know Rainey? A buddy of mine dated her a while back. I never met her officially, but we've circled each other."

Nika's not shocked by Brine's answer, and though she feels like asking him how his buddy fared or how long the relationship lasted, she doesn't. "Rainey is my best friend, and she's my own personal Velma. I should check in to see where she stands on this mystery, but I've been a little busy." Nika's phone buzzes on the table, and she turns it over. "Speak of the devil. It's Rainey. Hold on."

Rainey: *Where are you?*

Nika: *Bell Pepper Pizza.*

Rainey: *I thought we were going for pedicures???* Texting according to Rainey: the more terminal punctuation, the better the point gets across.

Nika: *Shit! I forgot. It's been an afternoon. Can I cancel and call you in a few? I'm talking to Detective Brine.*

Rainey: *What a hottie!*

Nika: *Good to know how you feel. I might use it for leverage later. Gotta go.*

"Hope all is okay," Brine says. "Look, I should get going. If I find anything out, I'll let you know."

"Thanks, and maybe you should call Rainey. To, you know, see what she knows and all. She *is* a great amateur sleuth."

He clears his throat, and his cheeks turn a warm pink, then he stands and salutes Nika. "Maybe I will. Thanks. I'll check for your husband and Alex on the way out."

Nika nods, then stares after Brine as he holds the door open for an elderly couple holding hands. He tips his head to them, chats for a moment, and recommends the spinach calzone. With a wave and a smile to the owner, Detective Brine leaves. Rainey could certainly do worse—

The server brings the pies over and places them in the center of the table. "Be careful, these are hot," he says.

Nika thanks him and turns to Lila, who grins and says, "That's what she said," causing both to burst out laughing. The tension of the last couple of minutes disappears, and Nika serves Lila a slice of pizza and then slides one onto her own plate. As they each take a bite, Ethan and Alex walk through the door, one of Ethan's arms slung across Alex's shoulder. Alex looks at the tiled floor and listens to Ethan as they walk, but Ethan glances at Nika and gives her a thumbs-up. She takes another bite of the hot, cheesy pizza and savors its perfection.

243

Interior: Evelyn Washington's Kitchen, 1982

Evelyn Washington pours melted wax into bee-themed silicone molds set out on the laminate kitchen table. She is making candles again this year, hoping to sell a few at the school's fall bazaar. NIKA, age four, enters the kitchen, a scowl on her face.

NIKA
Mama, what's the difference between girls and boys?

EVELYN'S eyebrows rise, but she continues to pour the wax. A drop spills onto the table, and she swipes at it with a towel. Messes always get cleaned up in Evelyn's kitchen.

EVELYN
What do you mean?

NIKA
Jackie said boys have penises and girls have vaginas. I know what a vagina is, but what's a, a, a penis?

EVELYN wants to hold off on the conversation but knows she has to tell her daughter something. She wipes her hands on her apron, then pushes the container of hot wax toward the center of the table so it won't fall. She approaches her daughter and kneels in front of her.

EVELYN

That's nothing you need to know about right now,
honey. Girls and boys have different parts, and
those parts are private. We don't touch them or
allow anyone else to touch them, you hear?

NIKA opens her mouth to speak, to ask about
touching that area in the bathtub. Her mother had
always said she needed to clean her pits and parts,
but if she's not supposed to touch them, then how
will she get clean?

EVELYN
(holding up her hand)
No one should touch you, and you don't touch them,
and we only touch our private parts when we
bathe or shower. Now, come help me with these
candles. I need more than two hands to make sure
these look better than Farrah Lee's.

chapter twenty-nine

The day after the encounter at Bell Pepper Pizza, Detective Brine leaves Nika a voicemail. Something about a family emergency and personal leave. "Hang tight," he says. If there's anything Nika has developed over her years as an elementary school librarian and a parent, it's patience. She can wait things out like the Chicago Cubs, who endured 108 years between pennant wins, or so her dad always liked to remind her.

So Nika tackles the never-ending cycle of duties: library, play, chauffeur, parent, cook, and more. She leaves two messages for Mindy, who, conveniently, isn't calling her back, and she heads to Susan's office, twice in five days. At the first meeting, they delve into more of Nika's backstory, unearthing long dormant feelings about her mother's absence and father's attempts to fill the void. They also chat about self-confidence, something Nika woefully lacks, and the ability to "be ourselves, to let go, to enjoy what should be fun."

At the second meeting, Susan brings up the idea of Sensate Focus, a sex therapy technique created in the sixties.

"It's been around that long?" Nika asks.

"Yes, and it's been well received. It helps people overcome obstacles in the way of finding sexual satisfaction, and it can deepen the sexual experience. It involves touch," Susan winks at Nika, "your favorite, I know, but it's mindful touch, purposeful touch. We want to try to get away from the idea of expectations. Take those off the table, so to speak, and when we do, we hope to lessen any anxiety around intimacy and sex. We want to replace the idea of achieving orgasm with something less demanding. Touch because you're curious—about yourself and your partner. That's it. Sensate Focus encourages you to explore your partner's body as well as your own."

Nika is silent for a beat, waiting for Susan to continue, but she says nothing. "Are you looking for a reaction?" Nika finally says.

"Yes. Do you think it's something you want to tackle?"

"Well, I'm here, and I trust you, so yes, I guess I do." Nika closes her eyes, thinks back to when she and Ethan first got together, how she craved moments with him snuggled against her, when he wasn't demanding sex or anything else. Maybe demand did have something to do with it. Too many demands in one day, and he was supposed to be her safe space. Hmmm. She might be onto something here.

"I think you can do this, Nika. You've already said you're prioritizing communication and Ethan seems to be responding. The only way this approach will work is if you keep communicating. Also, and this is paramount and something we've touched on before—the idea of mutual responsibility. You and Ethan are partners, a couple. Two of you are in the relationship, so this issue or whatever you want to call it involves you both. It's not your problem or his problem. It's yours, as a couple."

The exercises Susan provides for the week fall into two camps: a set involving simple touching and following the Sensate Focus guidelines and another featuring role-playing in the form of screenplays. "If time is of the essence, concentrate on the first set. The second set can be more for fun than anything, as I'm sure Ethan will agree," Susan says as she hands over a stack of papers.

Nika must look skeptical because Susan is adamant as she continues, "Sometimes, we think we're going to hate something, but once we allow ourselves the opportunity to become a different person, we find we enjoy what we're doing. I'm not saying you need to become someone else to enjoy sex. I actually want *you*, the genuine Nika, to enjoy sex. But a fun, flirty side of you might exist, and maybe we haven't met her yet."

Susan's voice reverberates in Nika's head as she pulls out the papers later that day, her fingers agitated and shaking. Ethan is finishing the dishes while she's in the bedroom sitting area. Everyone else is gone, so interruptions should be at a minimum, but something roils in Nika's gut, strong and urgent. Can she do this? Feeling ridiculous never appeals to Nika, but then her mind jumps to Ethan and the damned cowboy hat and chaps. Ridiculous? Yes. Funny? Also, yes. And they'd moved past that episode with nary an issue. *Plus*, Nika reminds herself. *You're doing this for you, and for Ethan. Something needs to change.*

Nika sighs, lifts her legs onto the ottoman, and looks at

the pages of Sensate Focus instruction. She and Ethan are supposed to take turns touching one another—kissing allowed—anywhere on the body *except for* the genitals and breasts. When both partners are comfortable, they should repeat the process, still alternating turns, this time *including* the genitals and breasts. Simultaneous touching occurs in the third phase, and in phase four they should move into a position *mimicking* intercourse—they don't have it. Nika looks again at the paper, zeroing in on the words of the fourth phase again: *Move against each other but avoid intercourse or orgasm until you've completed this two times.*

She chuckles, imagining what that looks like—

"Nika, are you ready?" Ethan says from the doorway. His brown eyes are warm and earnest. They always have been. And he's always been an attractive man.

Nika waves the pages at him. "Ready? I'm not sure. This honestly makes me want to laugh. Hysterically. It's like—"

"There's nothing wrong with laughing."

"Except when you're having sex. Sex and laughing—do they go together?" she says.

"It depends." He takes a seat next to her on the oversize chair and places his arm behind her.

"On what?" Nika cocks her head, trying to come up with a time when laughing during sex would be okay.

"Well," he says. "If I strip my shorts off and you laugh, I guess I'd be a little annoyed. But if we're going at it, and we roll off the bed, or I hit my head or whatever? That could be funny. The appropriate response is to laugh, which would be sexy. Of course, you're sexy in general, Nika."

She bats him with the pages. "Yes, yes, I'm glad you feel that way, and I see the distinction. This, though, I don't know." Nika hands him the papers and cocks an eyebrow, curious as to what he'll say about this exercise.

Ethan reads to himself. "Well, it's a start. Let's think of it that way. And if you giggle, then I'll deal with it since you've given me the heads up. What do you say?"

The right answer is yes because she wants to hang onto this man and have a fruitful, happy life with him. She takes the papers, places them on the ottoman, and moves to the bed, where she lies on her back.

Ethan steps into her line of view. "Uh, are we supposed to be naked for this?"

Nika holds his gaze. "I'm sure that's the unwritten rule but go with me for now. Can we start slow, please? I only have one layer on today anyway." One layer instead of her usual three.

Ethan laughs and lies down next to her, placing a chaste kiss on her lips. "I love you, Nika, and that's my turn. So now, you go."

Nika feels a little ridiculous, like Masters and Johnson are looking at her beyond the grave, frowning at her inability to take on this exercise in the expected manner. She shoots the ceiling a glance, as if they hover there, glowering at her, then she turns and looks at her husband. His scruffy chin, dark eyes, straight nose. At the nick on his cheek where he cut himself shaving two days before and the chicken pox scar near his lower right eyelid. She focuses on the silver at his temples and his full lower lip. If she doesn't at least put a modicum of effort into this exercise, then she's willfully looking away, ignoring the problem, right?

Nika leans over, drags her fingers up and down Ethan's arm, watching as goosebumps rise on his skin. He sighs, and she smiles, and then he's moving his hand back and forth over her leg. She responds with a hand inside his shirt, where she tickles his stomach, and he moves his attention to her cheek. They continue like this for a few minutes, and when Ethan asks about moving forward, Nika has only one request: "Breasts are okay, but genitals are not." Ethan doesn't argue, and her mind begins to quiet. It feels so incredibly good, she decides to linger there for a while.

~

"Do you want to at least look at the other exercises today?" Ethan holds up his watch to check the time. "No one is home, and I think that went rather well, didn't it?"

Nika agrees. *Maybe Masters and Johnson really knew what they were talking about.* "Yeah, let's take a look." She gets up from the bed, grabs the papers from the ottoman, and heads back to Ethan.

The first scene takes place in a school gymnasium. *Well shit.* Nika pushes the bad memories back into their tidy box and focuses on the screenplay, which involves an art teacher and a track coach. She glances at Ethan and wrinkles her nose.

"Yeah, something about the school. The gym part doesn't matter, and thank god these are two consenting adults, but . . ."

"And the sweat. The sweat doesn't do it for me."

"I'm sure you're not surprised to know sweat doesn't bother me." Ethan leans in, inhales deeply right next to the space at the back of Nika's right ear. "Sometimes the sweatier the better, you know?"

Nika's imagination conjures images of two faceless people, beads of sweat dotting their foreheads, droplets coursing down the space between the woman's breasts. She's happy to sweat when she's working out, but too much heat during intimacy? Not her thing anymore. She shudders. *Damn*

251

menopause.

"I know what you're thinking," Ethan says, "so let's go to the next one. What else have we got?"

Interior: Coffee shop in a big city, on a late afternoon in autumn. A fire crackles in the corner, patrons chat at tables, and customers stand in line. A petite woman is at the front of the line with a large, hulking man standing behind her.

WOMAN
May I please have a caramel macchiato?

BARISTA
Do you want whip with that?

"Whip it good!" Ethan says and bursts out laughing, most likely proud of his own humor.

Nika slaps his arm. "See? I'm not the only one. These are ridiculous!"

"Yes, but let's read more. I want to see what happens. This is a public place, so it can't be too bad, can it?"

MAN
(whispers something suggestive into WOMAN'S ear)

WOMAN
(gasps and turns)
Why I never . . .

Her POV: She takes in the tall, dark-haired man, his tousled hair and his fancy shoes. He's dressed impeccably, in a light wool sweater with a collared shirt beneath. His hands scream billionaire. But the thought of money isn't what makes the woman want to lean in. It's his lips, full and inviting, and his scent, crisp and woodsy.

MAN
You *never?*

His POV: The woman is breathtaking. The set of her eyes, her fruity scent, the heat emanating from her. His gaze focuses on the pulse at the base of the woman's throat, which beats wildly. Her breathing matches his, jagged and heaving. He moves into her orbit, and she curves her spine backward, her head and neck extended. Slowly, he makes contact, licking the right side of her neck and then the left, and his eyes lock with the barista's as she fans herself with her hand.

"Okay, I think I'm done here," Nika says. "No one needs to see this. The whole voyeur thing. Not quite my bag."

"You don't want to watch me do my thing, and you don't want to watch others, and you don't want to do those things either?"

"Do we have to have this conversation right now?"

Ethan frowns and narrows his eyes. "Yes, I think we do. We're supposed to be doing these exercises, and it feels like you're finding a way to get out of them. So what if we feel foolish and silly with respect to these scenes? We need to let that go. *You* need to let that go. We're married—I chose you, and you chose me. If you can't be foolish and silly with me, then who can you be those things with?"

Ethan's tone annoys Nika, as if he's telling her what to do, something she never reacts well to. Her hackles raise, like hair on the back of a cat, and she clenches her jaw. "A way to get out of it? Have you lived my life? Do you see what's happening right now? With Dad? With my job? With Alex, whatever that is?" Standing from the chair, Nika turns to Ethan, heat blazing across her skin, hot oil in a pan. "Do you know how much each of those weighs on my mind? Even when I'm not thinking of them, I'm thinking of them! Just let it go? Do you think it's so simple?"

Ethan shakes his head, saying nothing, and Rainey's words leap into Nika's mind: *What's to say Ethan won't make his own change and walk away?* Salt in a wound. A knife to the back. Everyone has their breaking point. Has Ethan reached his?

In her mind, Nika hums, willing her anger to recede, and as she looks at her husband, she recognizes what else lurked behind his words—hurt, maybe heartache, a little distant but present. Ethan is wounded that she can't be free with him, her husband. A man she willingly chose and would choose again. And if Nika can't be vulnerable with him, what does it mean for them? She's always valued honesty in a relationship. That's partly why things with her ex took such a turn for the worse; he didn't have the capacity to communicate openly and honestly with anyone, especially Nika. "Okay, you're right—some of that can wait until later. Though I do wonder if I can *not* want to have sex."

A beat or two passes where neither of them speak, and the dripping bathroom faucet catches Nika's attention. She'll have to remember to add it to the list of tasks to address this week. Ethan is the family plumber, so it's probably something he can take care of—

Ethan extends a hand to Nika's. Warm, heavy. "You *can* not want to have sex, but all the time? You don't want to have sex at all?" he says, his voice uncharacteristically sharp. "I guess I don't understand—that seems a bit extreme."

Extreme? Maybe, but menopause seems to mess with her body in ways she can't even understand, and maybe she values a different sort of connection than Ethan. Maybe when they first met, the idea of new love and lust enhanced her libido, and now, her body is getting back to the way it was meant to be. Did everyone have to be having joyous, fantastic sex all the time? *Did* everyone have sex like that anyway?

Nika breathes in through her nose, concentrates again on the dripping faucet, the wafting fragrance of the potpourri on the desk, the warmth of Ethan's hand. She wanted an honest conversation, but it feels like ants are crawling up and down her spine. She recognizes what's happening: anger and discomfort are trying to extrude any honesty she's willing to put forth. The response, one that harkens back to childhood, has only compounded as she's gotten older. Usually she clams up, walks away, pushes the problem to the back of her mind until she's ready to take it on. Though she's not ready now, especially as a fierce heat—most likely a hot flash—joins the ants, Nika knows better than to walk away. What is it Susan suggested—the 333 rule? It might work here too.

Nika finds three things—a piece of paper, the carpet, the bookshelf—then moves to three sounds and three body movements. After stretching her ankles, the ants aren't as noticeable, the fire seems banked, and she sits next to Ethan. "Fine. Let's move to the next scene. However, if it involves butt plugs, we're done."

chapter thirty

"This one is a little different," Ethan says, reading from the page. "Imagine yourself in whatever way you feel is appropriate. As a third-party observer on the edge of the room"—he pauses and waggles his eyebrows, and Nika wrinkles her nose in return— "as the man, the woman, as the bed even, if you feel the need."

"The bed?" Nika laughs and shakes her head, images of an anthropomorphized bed in her mind, complete with face and limbs, waving arms, a smiling mouth. What would the bed say? How would it feel? No, just no. "I'm a little worried. Maybe more than a little."

"We'll be fine. Trust the process, right? We didn't get far anyway, so we aren't really in the scene, you know. Let's give it a shot."

Again, Ethan is right. If she balks too much here, it's the third strike. Not that he's said as much, but in her head, she'll have failed. Nika detests failing. "How are we going to do this? Read it all together and then enact it? The approach doesn't hold much charm, but neither does reading it sentence by sentence. What say you?"

Ethan gazes into her eyes, trust written all over his face. He smiles, the slightly lopsided smile that took Nika's breath away when they first met. "Let's read it together first and see what we think afterward. How about it?"

Interior: A bedroom at night. Lighted candles sit along a windowsill, and a dim lamp illuminates the desk in the corner. Clothes cover the floor: a bra, panties, boxer shorts, a white button-down shirt. Two people, a man and a woman, frolic on the bed. A song plays in the background.

She's on him, straddling his chest, and she leans in, letting her breasts graze his heated skin. When she pushes back, he smiles and cups her breasts, then places a gentle kiss on each nipple. The woman leans down, kissing him with passion.

The man breaks the kiss, then reaches up and flips the woman so she's on her back. His body is now nestled between her legs, but he leans toward her face and feathers kisses along her jaw and lips. He licks her bottom lip, coaxing her mouth to open, and he plunges his tongue in her mouth. She moans and begins to tremble.

"Is it getting hot in here?" Ethan says and fans himself with the papers.

Nika glances at his pants, which are tented. "Are you

serious?"

"Yeah. What's wrong with that? I'm into this homework. I was trying to see and feel everything. What about you?"

Great question. Nika feels *something*. A pitter patter inside her chest, maybe a warmth low in her belly. Arousal? It's been so long since Nika felt anything similar she almost missed it. But . . . but what? "I don't know."

Ethan narrows his eyes at her and cocks his head, assessing her fully. "You know what?" He reaches out a hand and moves that ever-present stray piece of hair away from her face. "I think this is too much right now for you. Too much pressure maybe. What if I surprise you someday, and you go along with the plan? How does that sound?"

Delightful, as Rainey would say, and a relief settles over Nika, warm and comforting, like being wrapped in her favorite fleece blanket.

~

Ethan proposes a movie that night, his way of offering something low pressure *and* low stakes. While Nika is extremely grateful, she also knows they can't always default to a movie when she doesn't feel like being intimate. The knowledge bolsters her, helps her commit to the task at hand. Ethan is compromising here, and she needs to do the same. *Which means sessions with Susan must continue.*

The movie—an award-winning period piece they've both been meaning to see but haven't taken the time to do so— moves a little slower than Nika expected. The main actor's accent reminds her of her high school theater teacher, the one who tried so hard to convince everyone he was from the UK. Turns out he was born and raised in Charleston, South Carolina, and had moved to the Dayton, Ohio, area after graduate school. As a high schooler, Nika couldn't understand his desire to be someone else, but she gets it now. Sometimes she wishes she were someone else, someone more confident, someone more interested in sex, someone more *everything*. Other times, she wonders if she could at least *pretend* to be someone else, this issue with sex might resolve itself.

Ethan slings an arm around Nika's shoulder and pulls her close. Despite her attempts to keep her thoughts on the movie, they wander, and Nika grapples to remember the last time they sat entwined together like this. *It's probably been years, Nika thinks, and how sad is that?* They make time with the kids and with Dad, but what about with each other? Their dates constitute going to the grocery store or walking in the park or to the library. But spending any other time together? It doesn't happen. To be fair, it's not like he's asking her to the movies or a bar or a ballgame. He's as busy as she is. Which makes Nika realize that despite her issue with a low libido or lack of interest in sex, like Susan said, they're in this together. Any disconnect she's feeling *isn't* all her fault.

Still with her snug against him, Ethan places a hand on Nika's knee and squeezes it. He doesn't look over, and she's not even sure he realizes he's touching her, but it feels good. Nonthreatening, platonic. A simple move to say he cares. Nika lifts her legs onto the couch and burrows into him. Soon, his warmth makes her sleepy, and her eyelids droop. It's impossible to keep them open, and she gives herself over to sleep.

A light mist settles over the streets as Nika walks home, and it's cool enough that she pulls her coat tighter around her body. A breeze slips under the garment, and something feels off, strange, as if she's not wearing her usual clothing. Glancing down, she sees bare legs peeking out of the long, wool coat. Is she . . .? Yes, indeed, she's naked under it, and surprisingly, the scenario doesn't bother her.

A tingle spreads from her chest outward, and her hips sway, a levity in her steps, as she approaches the house. The lights are on, and someone stands in the foyer, looking at her through the door. His face is obscured, but he's tall and broad, and a shiver runs through her entire body, tunneling from her scalp to her little toe. Something about the man propels her forward, and her steps slow as a thrum vibrates under her skin. Who is this man, and what is he doing in her house? For some reason, she's not scared.

The door opens without a touch from her, and the man beckons her forward with a gentle wave. She still can't make out his features, but the bulge in his pants speaks volumes. Her breath hitches, and she stops, waiting. Time slows, and a whisper caresses her ear. He's behind her now, pressed up against her body, his fingers trailing underneath her coat, over her breasts, to her belly . . . A clench, a gasp, a rush of warmth again. Both uncertainty and lust overtake her, and she turns to the man, places her fingers on his cheeks, and pulls his face toward hers. Their lips meet, and there, in the foyer, their clothes melt away as their bodies come together. Soon, she's reaching the highest crest, tumbling over, fireworks exploding behind her eyes . . .

Ethan's voice sounds in Nika's ear. "Are you okay?" His fingers move gently across her cheek and then through her hair.

Nika shakes the sleep out of her eyes and ignores the pulsing between her legs. "What? What do you mean, am I okay?" She extends her arms above her head and looks at the television, the light of which illuminates the dark room. They're still on the couch, but holy crap . . . "I had a dream."

"Apparently. I'm not sure what you were saying, but a lot of interesting breathing patterns were going on. In fact, you sounded like Mabel when she's dreaming."

Nika covers her mouth as she busts out laughing. "Well,

that's attractive, isn't it?" Should she tell Ethan the truth? In the context of open communication . . . "Would you believe I dreamed I was naked under a coat, and I came home to find a man in the foyer?"

"A man?" Ethan snorts. "Some random man? Anyone you know?"

"I couldn't see who he was, but all of a sudden, he was behind me, and then, well, let's just say . . . things got a little out of hand."

"Huh," Ethan says and turns back to the television. He stares at it for a moment and then looks at Nika, interest in his eyes, maybe even concern. "What do you think it means?"

Dreams have always intrigued Nika, and when time permits, she looks up their meanings, what they might signify in the context of her life. Many of her dreams involve feeling lost, not knowing where she's going, being behind or late for something—all her daytime anxieties boiled into a handful of nighttime vignettes repeating like an Instagram reel. "I'm not sure," Nika says, "but with as much as I'm thinking about sex these days, it makes sense, you know? The more you immerse yourself in something, the more your brain focuses on it."

"And did you *feel* anything?" Ethan's gaze turns hopeful.

Nika's cheeks grow warm since the slight hum still zips along her nerves. "Oh, it was a hot dream all right. Let's leave it at that."

Ethan nods and places his hand on Nika's cheek once more, then leans in and deposits a soft kiss there. He avoids her lips and goes back to watching television. A few minutes later, Ethan tucks her once again under his arm.

Nika had been sure—*so sure*—he'd press her to hear more about the dream. To tell him exactly what happened. To reveal the sexy details as a means of foreplay. He doesn't, and the lack of pressure is like coming up for air after diving deep into the vast, dark ocean.

chapter thirty-one

Lila and Alex's presence the next morning reminds Nika to check in with Mindy. She calls her, but of course, Mindy puts Nika off—something about being at the store?—and Nika's annoyance grows. She's not the confrontational kind but getting to the bottom of the charge sticks in her mind like a stubborn label. Why was Dad paying for something for Mindy at the Southside Clinic, and would it happen again? Nika's nerves are heightened and will likely remain that way until Mindy calls back, which, thankfully, happens within the half hour while Nika washes dishes. She wipes her wet hands on the dish towel and swipes the screen and says hello.

"It's me," Mindy says. "Sorry—I was getting cat food and litter, and I can't talk and do that at the same time. The litter weighs too much. What did you need?" she asks.

Mindy and Nika don't speak much about anything other

than Dad, or now, the cats, and maybe that would be the best approach here. Bring up something innocuous and unrelated and then launch into the true interrogation. Nika should have asked Ethan his opinion before he left to take photos with Alex—he sees things in a different light than she does. So, she asks herself, *What would Ethan do?* The answer quickly comes to her.

"I don't need anything," Nika says. "I have a question about Dad."

"What about him?"

Mindy isn't physically in the room with Nika, which minimizes the perceived threat. Taking a deep breath, Nika plunges ahead. "Well, he came to me the other day about a bill he wasn't sure of. Did you have anything done at the Southside Clinic?"

The heavy pause on Mindy's end confirms Nika's suspicions. Then, Mindy speaks quietly. "Yes, I did." Her words are short, clipped. An authoritative tone she's taken in the past when she feels cornered.

"Well then, why did Dad pay for it?"

Again, a hesitation, enough time for Mindy to weave one of her usual stories. "He told me he'd help me. He knew I'd been struggling with low self-esteem, and I'd been looking at lip augmentation and Coolsculpting."

Struggling with low self-esteem? Doesn't everyone? "And he agreed to pay over four thousand dollars?"

"He did. If you have any questions about it, go ask him."

Nika wills back the pulsing anger, pushes it behind the resentment toward her mother and her annoyance with Cole. Mindy's tone, her words. Everything about the conversation screeches like nails on the chalkboard, and Nika is tired of dealing with her stepsister. Two teenagers, a job, a second marriage, a dog, a father, a reason to see the therapist. Isn't that enough? "Yeah, I did already. He seemed confused about it."

This time, Mindy responds quickly. "Of course he did. He's a *stoner*, Nika. Who knows what he's done to his brain? Pretty soon, you're going to need to take him to a doctor to see what's wrong with him. Have you thought about a neurologist?"

A neurologist? Seriously? "Where is this coming from? I live with him. He doesn't seem like he needs a neurologist. And I'm not sure he's a stoner." Dad watches at least one game a week with Ethan, and her husband would have said something if he'd noticed, wouldn't he?

"I'm just saying. Keep an eye on him, okay? He might need more help than you think. Listen, I have to go. I'll talk to you later."

Mindy hangs up without another word, and Nika gazes at the phone, amazed at Mindy's ability to play the master manipulator and deflect the conversation away from her and onto Dad. How did she always do it, and why did Nika always let her get away with it? And a final question roars through Nika's mind: If Mindy took advantage of Dad this time, has she done it before?

Nika slips her phone into her pocket and walks toward her father's part of the house. The light streaming in from the window highlights a stack of statements on his desk, like she's supposed to look at it. Hmmm. She texts her father about checking on his financials, and Michael grants permission, telling her where the correct stack should be. Said stack is thick and unorganized, full of papers for checking and savings accounts, a trust account, life insurance, and an annuity, among other things like car insurance,

Medicare, and the like. She stares at the annuity. *How much money does this guy have?* Also included is the credit card statement they looked at previously. Does he have more of these available? She glances around the room. It's clean and tidy, with a large wooden bookshelf to the left. Each shelf has an unmarked binder, one of which, she finds, houses credit card statements. She sits and flips open the binder, which goes back several years. He seems to have every single credit card statement, plus the annual "year at a glance" overview they provide. Ethan and Nika switched to paperless billing a long time ago, but there's something to having the paper right in front of you. Concrete proof of existence, a connection to the world, things Nika has always appreciated.

The February statement is the one with Southside Clinic on it, so Nika searches for the months prior. Most of the charges seem legit. Applebee's. Health care. CVS. Trader Joe's. His January statement looks a lot like Nika and Ethan's, and she laughs at a sudden thought. Does he have any weed charges on here? A line later, she sees it: Weed Emporium. *Well, I guess there's something about being honest in all aspects of life.* She chuckles and flips the page, and nothing else draws her attention, so she moves onto December. That was a slow month for Dad, as evidenced by the minimal entries on the statement, and Nika remembers he'd gone on an all-inclusive cruise then. Some holiday crap for seniors, something she'd been so shocked to hear he'd been attending. Since he paid up front, he didn't have as many charges—

Wait. Two odd numbers stand out: $4,782 to Grace and Camille Designs and over $3,000 to Home Depot. If Dad was cruising the ocean, why would he charge something to Home Depot? There's no way he'd shop online there when he could run up the street. Plus, he'd never go to Grace and

Camille. They stopped there on their quest for a few new pieces for his rooms at the house, but he only wanted something "quick and cheap and sturdy."

Did Mindy charge these amounts to his account, or did someone else?

No sooner does Nina think of her dad again and he's next to her. "You're as bad as the kids," she says. "Why didn't I hear you?"

"I guess you were concentrating. What are you looking for?"

"Sit for a minute." Nika gestures to the chair, then spreads the paper in front of him. "Remember when you went on that cruise in December?"

"Sure do. Best vacation I've had in a long time. Nice crew. Nice ladies." He winks at Nika, a mischievous smile on his face.

Nika groans. Her father has always been a bit of a dirty old man. In fact, she would have been less shocked to see a prostitute in his bedroom than weed, but that's for another therapy session with a different therapist. "Great to hear, and I've heard it already. What I want to know is, what did you buy at Home Depot that month, and what about Grace and Camille Designs?"

"Who are Grace and Camille?"

"My point exactly."

"Well, I don't know what I would have bought at Home Depot, although—" His shoulders stiffen, and he crosses his arms across his chest, pursing his lips before casting his gaze to his lap.

A distinct impression that something is wrong settles on Nika. Will he tell her? She and her father have a pretty honest relationship, but not as open as Nika wants with her own children. "What is it, Dad? What did Mindy do?" Images bombard Nika's brain. Mindy and a new kitchen. Mindy and a new garage. Mindy and new windows—

Dad snaps his head up. "How did you—? Never mind. She asked if I'd help her with the basement finishing project. I said I would, but I never gave her my credit card. I *know* I didn't. How did she get the number? I also don't know for sure it *would* be her, but the timeline fits."

Nika thinks back to December and January. Mabel needed ACL surgery, which meant Nika spent evenings helping her recuperate, Ethan traveled for work, and the teachers were thinking about the new semester, spilling their anxieties onto Nika's already overworked brain. A snowstorm blanketed the region with over twelve inches of snow and ice, knocking everyone on their asses. Nika wouldn't have been paying much attention to anyone other than herself and her own family, and with Dad being warm and snug on a cruise, anything could have been going on with Mindy.

"That completely makes sense. If her basement is completed, I think she used your card to help with it."

Dad's lips turn into a frown. "How?"

Nika taps her chin in thought. As jumbled as most of it is, her father's paperwork is all accounted for, but he often leaves his wallet on a chair here or a table there. "Maybe she took it and then replaced it, or even more likely—she copied the number down and ordered everything online. These days, you don't have to step into a store if you don't want to."

Dad slumps onto the bed and puts his head in his hands, then he groans.

"Are you okay?" Nika reaches out and slides her hand up and down her father's back. She's never been demonstrative, but she can see what this is doing to him. Dad always backed Mindy, defended her when no one else would. Nika had asked him about it once. He'd said her mother—his ex-wife, Kathleen—had never treated Mindy right. Mindy was the way she was because of Kathleen, and the world needed to give her a break. He tried to *be* that break. "If someone teaches her to love, Nika," he once said, "then maybe she can become the person I know she can be."

Nika thinks of that now, in the space it takes for her dad to answer. Does he feel like a failure too? Maybe it explains the weed.

Dad shrugs off Nika's hand from his back but takes her fingers in his. "Yeah. I'm just tired. I offered to help, but I never said I'd buy all those things. That's a lot of money at one time."

"Then we have to confront her, don't you think?"

He doesn't say anything, and Nika understands his silence: he doesn't *want* to confront Mindy. He never has. Probably because of the guilt he feels. For what Mindy's mother did to her. For what he *couldn't do* for her. No amount of convincing him Mindy is an adult will help the situation; it's something her dad will have to deal with on his own.

Nika thinks back over the years, the offhand comments Mindy threw around about bills and money, about Dad's penchant for finding good stocks and knowing how to invest. How many times did Dad ask if she needed help, and how many times has Mindy siphoned money from him?

"Dad?" Nika squeezes his fingers. "I know you don't want to say anything right now, and I respect your decision, but we need to look at your accounts and figure out if she's taken any more. Okay? Also, does your weed use have anything to do with this?"

He shakes his head. "You can look at my statements if you want. And no . . ." His gaze—deep, dark, troubled—holds Nika's briefly. "I needed an outlet. To let go of some stress, some bad memories. That's why I started smoking. Now, I stopped back here to grab a few things, but I'm going to the library. Have a meeting I need to attend."

"Okay, Dad. Go ahead and do what you need to do. I'll take a quick look."

"You won't find anything, you know," he says as he heads toward the door, his footsteps heavy on the carpet. "She might have had me pay for those few things, but I'm sure that's all."

"Well, it can't hurt to check. You have a long life ahead of you, and we want to be sure finances aren't something you need to worry about."

Her dad stops and turns, his gaze gentle and loving. "I'm proud of you, honey. You, your family, Ethan, the kids. I don't say it enough, but I am. I also don't say thanks enough, so thank you. For everything." He doesn't wait for a reply, just exits the room, and a minute later, the sound of the back door closing echoes across the house.

chapter thirty-two

"Ethan," Nika speaks into the phone, which she's put on speaker. "I'm going to need you to come home. Where are you?"

"We're still taking photos, but I think we're almost finished. What's wrong?"

"No emergency, and I'll show you when you get here, but I don't want Alex to know. Meet me in my dad's room when you get back."

"O-kay." His voice is hesitant and unsure.

"I can at least tell you it is *not* any of Susan's homework." Nika ends the call before Ethan recovers from laughing.

Dad's papers, all in disarray now, cover the table, so Nika tries to sort them by account and date. It looks like the perpetrator wasn't stupid enough to take directly from Dad's standard bank account, so she digs a little further, unearthing papers from Dad's files spanning years. Old receipts, user manuals, electric bills from a house he no longer lives in. Finally, a folder with TRUST on the label comes into view, and Nika pulls it out, opening it on her lap—

What the hell? Several card charges and multiple checks written from his trust account don't make sense. Nika quickly does the math in her head. Holy hell.

A scuffing of feet occurs as Ethan hustles into the room, hair mussed, eyes bright. "What's this all about?" he says as he pulls out a chair, sits down, and looks at Nika with an unnerving intensity. Thank goodness this doesn't have anything to do with them as a couple.

In a quiet voice, Nika reminds Ethan of the credit card charge to the Southside Clinic and informs him of the other charges on Dad's account.

"By the look on your face," he says, "I suspect you found something else."

"I sure did." She holds up the trust statements. "These show almost forty-five thousand dollars have been taken out of his account for various purposes over the last fifteen months."

Ethan startles, as if the amount surprises him, which it should. "You don't think your dad is spending the money?"

Placing a finger against the top paper, Nika points at one line, then taps it. "He doesn't have a Mastercard, and the trust account is paying off one each time. Look." She places the statements in front of Ethan, highlighting the card payments in various denominations. Some low, some high. Checks have been written from his account, too, to people who don't make sense. "This guy here—I don't know why a one-thousand-dollar check was written to him, but he's connected to Mindy. That's the only way I recognize his name."

"Does your dad know this?"

"I asked him if he thought she was taking more, and he said no. But this is proof, isn't it?"

"Circumstantial maybe, but yes. We need to tell him."

"I will. I just, I can't believe this. Who the hell does she think she is?"

Ethan shakes his head and rubs his neck, saying nothing. And at that moment, Alex peeks his head in. "What's for dinner?"

"A reminder to get back to the real world. Thanks, honey," Nika says. "Pull out what you want, and I'll get dinner started as soon as I put these away. Maybe you can help."

~

After dinner, Ethan sneaks up behind Nika and threads his arms around her waist. His solid, broad chest pulls her in, a balm after the aggravating afternoon revelations, and soon, she's against him from top to bottom. Then she feels him, the hard length of him nudging her backside.

"Are you serious?" Nika says and twists her neck as she leans away from him to rinse the last dish. Coming down to a clean and tidy kitchen in the morning is the best way for Nika to begin her day.

"Aren't I always?"

Nika snorts. "We just finished dinner. Is that *all* you think about all day long?"

Ethan turns Nika around, places his hands on her shoulders, and looks deeply into her eyes. "If you haven't noticed, I think you're hot. I don't care if you're standing here in old jeans and a ratty T-shirt or if you haven't done your hair since this morning. I wouldn't care if you'd just come back from a walk or a run. You. I like you. An awful lot. And I can't help it that this," he gestures to his crotch, "happens to agree with me." He crosses his arms over his chest, leans back, and arranges his features into a determined line. The look is funny, like a little kid taking an extreme stance, but it's apparent he's not a little kid, and he expects a more mature answer from Nika.

She grabs her favorite hand towel from next to the sink, the rainbow-striped one Lila and Alex gave to her for her last birthday, dries her hands, then twists it between her fingers. She's had enough sessions with Susan to know communication in the here and now is crucial to how the rest of the night will go. "Great to hear. Now, what I want you to know is I was always a good student, and despite what you may think, I'm keeping my appointments with Susan and speaking honestly to her. I'm making progress, even though I still have a hard time slowing my brain down and letting go of my responsibilities—"

Ethan stops Nika with a wave of his hand, which he gently places against her cheek before cupping her chin. "Didn't we go through this already the other day? What are your responsibilities right now? This minute, this second."

Realization descends on Nika, and she knows what Ethan is doing—leading her to the conclusion before giving his own take on the situation. It's a tactic he's been using for years. While it doesn't bother her, she knows she needs to spend more time considering that conclusion, but there's only so many minutes. "Whatever I want them to be."

"Right." Ethan moves his hand, lovingly strokes the side of her face. "We don't need to *worry* about any of those responsibilities, and even if we did, we'd get to them. We're a good team, Nika. At the end of the day, you and I both know that. We'll get to everything in time, today, tomorrow, or the day after. And there's something I want you to know—

I'm not sure you understand this, so I'm going to say it now, and I'll say it any time I need to in the future. My body will react to you each and every time, but that doesn't mean we have to be intimate or have sex each and every time."

"But—"

Ethan laughs and he scowls. "No buts."

Nika's mind flashes to the last romance novel she read, where the dark and mysterious sex-club owner whispers to the curious new member, dressed only in a sheer bra and panty set and high heels. "No buts," the man says, then growls and pounces, eyes flashing, heat almost radiating off the page. *Ethan would love that book*, Nika thinks, *or at least a reenactment of it.*

"Let me finish, please," she says. "You want *it* a lot, and I know it, even if it's not every time. And I think," she sips in a breath, hoping her words land gently, just like she means them to, "that puts pressure on me."

Ethan looks at her, his gaze thoughtful, and then he nods. "I'll admit I never thought of it that way, but I get it, so what now?"

Great question, Nika thinks, but something eases inside her like a loosened corset, and she says, "I have some homework for this evening."

Ethan's eyes light up, and he pumps his fist in the air. The behavior is both so ridiculous and so Ethan that Nika can't help but chortle, the action releasing the last of the negative energy swirling inside her gut. "Here's the deal. Let me go look at it by myself for a few, and then I'll let you know if I need any help."

"What are the kids doing this evening?" Ethan arches a brow. "You know what? It doesn't matter. I'll figure out something to give them. Or they can drown themselves in

Netflix." Ethan winks and points at Nika. "Because my bet is, or maybe my hope is, you're going to need help with your homework."

~

Ethan's constant enthusiasm for Nika's homework is somewhat overwhelming, but she'd rather have a caring, ardent participant. A husband with an interest in anyone but her? Nika shed one of those like a snakeskin years ago, and she has no intention of sticking with another one. Ethan has always been different; Nika knew this from the moment she met him, when the look on his face served as a warning she could fall again. *Hard.* But lately, the stress of everything gets to her, and a few nights prior, her normally placid dreams had turned nightmarish. In the dream, she was in a hotel and had told Ethan she couldn't marry him. After she'd turned him down—and Nika still isn't sure why she did—her old pseudo boyfriend popped the question.

"Why don't you marry me?" he said after he materialized from thin air. Despite the heaviness in her gut, the blaring foghorns pulsing in her ears, Nika said yes. Even in a dream state, Nika understood nothing made sense, but the dream continued, fast forwarding to a few days before the supposed wedding. In a haze, Nika found herself, again, in a hotel room, this time with the intent of getting naked with the man. What stood out then was the cool breeze on her skin, which prickled her arms and made her teeth chatter. The heat in the man's eyes unnerved her because nothing felt right at all, like a dress two sizes too big. "This isn't right," Nika said. "I can't do this!" Then, she willed herself to wake up.

Of course, the next morning over coffee, Nika told Ethan about the dream. At the time, he'd laughed, but now, she wonders what the dream means and if whatever it's trying to tell her applies to her. To Ethan. To her *and* Ethan.

Nika shudders at the thought and opens her homework. The paper is filled with words, and at the top a few invite fear into Nika: *Kama Sutra.* The sexual positions book? She reads on, learning that while the book dedicates at least one chapter to sexual positions, the book itself is so much more. Apparently—and why no one ever told Nika this, she's not sure—the book focuses on the relationship between two people: *Introducing a thorough and serious investigation, the text not only provides a deep reader with the ability to know a true meaning of love between two people but also opens the mind to a better understanding of human nature along with his or her partner.*

Her eyes zero in on the words *better understanding.* Isn't that what most couples need? As for opening the mind, well, Nika could probably use a little, at least in these circumstances.

Nika glances at her watch, unsure how much time Ethan is going to give her. In an odd way, she's excited, and by *excited*, she means *hopeful*, a word that keeps reappearing like the strand of gray hair on her head. *Better than dread*, she thinks and continues with the reading. The instructions tell her to go to an article on Cosmopolitan.com, and Nika scoffs. *Are you kidding me? The sex therapist quoting Cosmo?* Susan anticipates her scoffing, though, for next up in the reading is one sentence: "Don't judge me for citing articles from *Cosmopolitan*; the illustrations are tasteful and the explanations simple."

Clearly Susan has enough experience to know people like Nika exist, but it's eerie how accurately Susan has pegged her. Nika grabs the laptop. As she keys in the URL, she can only imagine what someone might think about her search history. Ethan would be amused, as would the kids. Rainey? She'd pull up the pages, settle in with a drink or two, and lean in close to the screen, not letting a single word get by her. Nika wonders what Rainey is up to, then lassos her mind back to the task at hand.

The page takes longer than normal to load, but then a crisp, clear page appears. *Nonthreatening. Clean lines. Appealing.* The byline reads Jill Hamilton, who, Nika sees, also writes a blog entitled "In Bed with Married Women." She's tempted to scroll over to the blog, but she only has so much energy and needs most of it for this homework. She looks back at the title: "5 Dildo Sex Positions to Get You Aaaall the D." Four *a*'s, not one. In her head, she draws out the word like she's pulling taffy.

No. Dildos aren't my thing.

Nika clicks on the next link: "5 Butt Plug Sex Positions That'll Open Up a Hole New World for You."

Clever, but butt plugs aren't either; that's been established.

The third link points Nika to an intriguing article. "Everything You Need to Know About the Wanton Wheelbarrow," which, apparently, is for those who enjoy a "from-behind ride." From behind has always been more palatable for Nika. Her hips don't ache the whole time, and Ethan can't see the lack of desire in her eyes if she's not fully there. Which is often. Which is why she's doing this in the first place.

She snaps the lasso again.

Nika skims the page, taking in the details of the maneuver, one that requires flexibility. She cocks her head as she tries to imagine keeping one leg on the ground while bending over at the waist so Ethan can stand behind her. He's supposed to grab an ankle, lift the leg up, and enter from behind.

Oh my god. Nika's shoulders shake with laughter. The vibrant vision in her head is not good. Nika's lack of flexibility, lack of confidence, lack of enthusiasm—all will likely cause a muscle strain or worse. What would—

Ethan walks in the door. "You ready?"

Nika blurts out, "Homework involves Kama sutra investigation."

"Oh goody," he says, smiling and rubbing his hands together as he plops down next to Nika. "I'm ready."

Of course, he means that in multiple ways, and the telltale bulge in his pants confirms the truth. She grazes it with her fingers. "I'm amazed by your willingness all the time. I really am."

Ethan smirks, an adorable look that hits Nika square in the chest. "Any time, any place," he says. "Well, maybe mostly any time, mostly any place." In the past, a virus or work obligation has interfered, but on most days, he's ready to go.

"Okay, I haven't gotten far, but . . ." Nika glances at the papers again. "It looks like we're supposed to experiment with a few positions. I'm game, but I draw the line at sex toys or vegetables." Nika doesn't have anything against sex toys, but she's intent on taking baby steps.

He pouts. "We have a perfectly good cucumber out there—"

Nika doesn't let him finish. "This is *my* homework. I set the stage. See this here?"

He leans in and looks at the computer, the screen's glow highlighting his face.

She taps the screen. "These have to do with Kegels. My muscles are shot after two pregnancies and two vaginal births. Let's try these."

He's already up and taking off his shirt.

"No foreplay?" she asks. At her age, it takes time for her to be ready. Vaginal dryness is no joke. Hell, menopause itself is no joke.

"No. That's not it. I'm enthusiastic, as always." He flings himself on the bed, takes the rest of his clothes off, and slides under the covers. I'll warm it up for you." He flashes a Cheshire cat grin.

Afterward, Nika lays on the bed, reflecting on what happened. Physically, she felt more. Not desire, necessarily, because she was still too much in her head, too clinical and thinking too much, but her parts responded more than in the past, like those Magic Grow capsules she used to play with. Was it because she opened her mind to the possibility of what could be? And if so, is Nika's mind blocking her ability to feel, to be present? Ethan always says, "Don't think, just do." Could he be right?

In his sleep, Ethan rolls over and drapes an arm over Nika's chest. It's too early to go to bed, but at this moment, she snuggles into him and luxuriates in his touch.

chapter thirty-three

Nika's next meeting with Susan Harris goes well. She unabashedly tells her about her and Ethan's last round of intimacy, how she wonders if living inside her head is part of the problem.

"That's very astute of you," Susan says. "Introspective. I'm not surprised. We haven't known each other long, but you're a thinker through and through."

"An overthinker," Nika adds.

Susan smiles. "Maybe, but we can always think less or spend less time in our heads. I personally believe it would be a more arduous task to help someone learn how to think more, to be more introspective. In my experience, it's the introspective ones, those who are self-aware, who contact me and grace my couch." Her voice is soft and kind in the near silence, a sort of absolution.

"So," Nika says, adjusting the edge of her shirt. "Progress

is good, but it's slow. I realize this. What I'm afraid of is slipping back into the same patterns because they're easy, because there's no conflict in the status quo. Which, for me, is putting off my husband or going ahead and doing it because I'm supposed to."

Again, Susan smiles, this time nodding. "You'd have made a good therapist. Since you're aware of the possibility, you'll be less likely to fall back into bad habits, but let's revisit something we spoke about before—you tend to keep busy. Why?"

Nika mulls the question over, an image of her day planner popping into her head. Each square is littered with tasks, both work related and personal, and she also keeps track of tasks by the week and by the month. Doctor and vet appointments, music lessons, soccer practice, library clean-out days, staff meetings, set design, and prop deadlines. When she's not attending to one of those tasks, she's emptying the dishwasher, loading laundry, vacuuming, weeding, helping with homework, taking walks, or offering assistance to friends and neighbors. "Fuck yes, I keep busy!" Nika slaps a hand over her mouth. "I am so, so sorry! Just then, it felt right."

Susan waves off the gaffe. "No worries. My guess is you need to do more of that."

"What—more swearing?" Nika asks.

"Not exactly. More living in the moment. Doing what feels right."

"You sound like Ethan. Or Rainey."

"Is that a bad thing?" Susan lifts a brow.

In another lifetime—or even last year—Nika would have bristled at the idea of Ethan and Rainey being right. Not because she always needs to be right but because their being right would be like holding up a mirror to her behavior. Nika does that to herself at each session with Susan, and now, she knows one thing: she wants to make more progress, which means getting down to brass tacks. "It's not a bad thing, but . . ."

Nika stops. She ruminates on Susan's question, tossing it over in her mind. She isn't sure why she stays busy. She's always *been* busy, even as an adolescent and teenager, and staying busy is another habit she holds onto. Tenaciously. *Damn that word.* "Are you going to tell me *why* I stay busy? Because I don't know."

Susan blinks and crosses one leg over the other, highlighting her pedicure. A bright teal graces her toes.

Nika's never taken to a pedicure. Something about people handling her overly ticklish feet doesn't sit well with her. But now, she wonders if she should stay in the moment the next time an opportunity for a pedicure arises. Try something new and different, live a little.

Susan's voice overrides Nika's thoughts. "I can't be sure, but we've talked enough about you, who you are, your background, and what your present is like to say you experience anxiety. I'd group you as high functioning, but it's anxiety, nonetheless. An anxious state is all you know, so it seems normal to you. The anxiety doesn't cripple you the way it might some, but you stay busy to control your surroundings, to harness what would be an anxious situation."

Susan's words are slow, deliberate, and they hit Nika right in the solar plexus. She doesn't have time to dwell, though, as Susan continues, "Let's talk more about what's going on at home aside from your relationship with Ethan. How's your dad? The kids? Work?"

After indulging Susan and giving her the updates on what's happening, she suggests Nika eliminate as much stress as she can. "Yes, Mindy and your father and the library and play are all sources of stress, and no, you can't walk away from them. But you can do two things. One, I want you to remember a whole cast of characters exists in your life, people who will help lighten the load, if you let them." Susan's kind tone is perfect for the personal reminder. "Two, you can shift your perspective. Keep in mind—your father still has money, Mindy will be handled, the library is in good shape, the play will be performed. There's an old saying people throw out—*it's all about perspective*. Nika, it's not *all* about it, but if you shift your mindset, frame life events and reactions and conversations in more positive ways, you'll be amazed at how your life changes."

~

Life has been so hectic that Nika and Rainey haven't had much time to catch up with each other in person. Their communication has been limited to texts and emails and short chats in the hallway at school, surrounded by children like sardines in a can. Rainey has been spending her lunch hour with two students who need extra help, and Nika took the opportunity to listen to a highly recommended audiobook while munching on a salad in the library. Now, on a whim, Nika sends a text to Rainey as she leaves Susan's office, asking if she has time for a quick bite.

Rainey wraps her arms around Nika when she enters the chosen meeting place, a quaint little deli close to both their houses. They have decadent vegetarian options and meat sandwiches so thick you can feed at least three people with one order. "It's been too long!" Rainey says. "Thank you for texting."

They settle at a table for two, and Nika slings her bag on the chair, shaking her head. "It has been too long, and I'm sorry. You know how family life can be." Nika has kept Rainey up to date on all things—Dad, Alex, and Mindy. She's tired, plain and simple, and though she didn't mention it to Susan, Nika wonders if she should have. Sure, she might have anxiety—no, she probably does—but she also has so many things on her agenda. Can Susan make the sheer number of responsibilities disappear? Can she help Nika learn to say no more often? The answer is probably yes to the latter . . .

"You're a saint, Nika. I wouldn't be able to handle everything you do. You know that, right?"

"Well, I'm not a saint, but I appreciate your confidence. Also, thank you for making me meet you at Wine Bar. Susan thinks we're making progress, and I might be. I'm certainly more open to talking about the issue, and Ethan and I have had more meaningful conversations lately regarding sex. Spending more time with him has been helpful."

"You're welcome. You're my best friend, and I want to see you happy."

Nika has never been an emotional person, always ready to maintain distance. This time, though, with a safe person like Rainey, someone she trusts with her life, Nika's throat goes dry, and she tries to swallow the lump in it. *Am I becoming soft?* She sniffs. "You're the best—do you know that?"

Rainey is quick with a response. "Right back at you. By the way, I know you're not into gossip, but I have some news." She flashes an enormous, white-toothed grin.

Nika leans in and raises her eyebrows. "The secret is safe with me, as you know, but I'm not going to turn away from hot gossip. Anything to draw the curtain on my own life for a little while. Though if anyone is hurt, I don't want to hear about it. Only gossipy gossip today. Nothing awful."

Rainey twirls her hair around a finger and winks. "It's

good you're sitting." She pauses, increasing the tension. "Cole and Danielle are . . . expecting . . . twins!"

Nika's eyes go wide, and for a moment, she's speechless. "What? How did you find out?" A stark vision swims to her mind's surface: tall, lanky, dark-haired-but-almost-bald Cole and petite, light-haired Danielle, adorable twins in their arms, surrounded by the children they both brought into the union. "Is he excited about it? I mean, go big or go home, right? I guess that's going big!"

Rainey taps the table's edge with a freshly painted nail. Reddish-orange, glossy. A hue called Canadian Maple, one of Rainey's favorite colors. "Yes, yes! He's excited. I caught a glimpse of the ultrasound when he was in the copy room. He swore me to secrecy, but he had to know I'd tell *you*." She sits back against her chair. "I'm happy for him. He seems . . . content. More than content. Like he's looking forward to it."

Nika nods, remembering the square black-and-white images of Alex and Lila, how with each pregnancy she carefully counted fingers and toes, squinted to see if the nose was hers or her ex's. Despite the pain the man caused, he'd given her the two best gifts she could ever have, better than anything she could imagine. "Me too. He's not my favorite person in terms of managing everyone, but at his core, Cole is okay. I certainly wouldn't wish ill on him. How will this change things going forward at school? Speaking of, any news? Have you solved the mystery, Velma?"

Rainey rummages in her purse and comes up with a vintage key on a rubber band. "Do you know what this is?"

The restaurant lights glint off the key's bronze surface. "It looks like one of the keys from the play." Nika pulls the object close to her face and inspects it.

"Well, I found it outside *your* library. What is it doing

there? Maybe it's the perpetrator's, maybe not. Want me to give it to Ben—Detective Brine, if I see him?" A flush steals over Rainey's cheeks.

"Detective Brine? Did you almost call him Bennett? Have you been texting with him?" Nika cocks her head and glares at Rainey, daring her to make a rebuttal.

Rainey flushes again. "Maybe."

"Is someone smitten?"

"Maybe."

Nika hands the key back to Rainey. "If something good comes out of this for you, then I don't care if we don't find out who destroyed those books. Whoever it was hasn't been back, and I guess, no harm done."

"I'll keep you posted then, and now, switching gears, how's your dad?"

"Honestly, even though he's living in my house, I feel like it's not my business. I have no right to any information unless he's willing to share it. I'm pretty sure he's attending meetings and has been, for the most part, but he won't tell me anything—" Nika's phone buzzes.

It's Mindy, asking if the kids can watch the cats again the next week: *I'll be gone Wednesday through Saturday.*

Nika: *Let me double check with them, but probably. Where are you going this time?*

Mindy: *Phoenix. Quick trip. Found some great airfare and using hotel points.*

"Probably another trip financed by Dad," Nika says to Rainey as she places her phone back on her lap after signing off. "Didn't she just get back from a trip? My kids took care of her cats. I'm not losing it, am I?"

Rainey gasps. "You're not, no, and what do you mean about your dad and financing the trip?"

Nika hasn't told Rainey about her suspicions that Mindy is taking and has taken a good amount of her father's money. In hushed tones, Nika lays it on the line, and in true best friend form, Rainey offers to help.

Susan's voice reverberates in Nika's ears: A whole cast of characters exists in your life, people who will help lighten the load, if you let them.

Interior: Glenn State University, Frat House, 1996

NIKA and CUTE GUY sit on the bed in the dark frat-house bedroom, chatting quietly about politics and the patriarchy. Music from somewhere thumps and echoes off the walls. CUTE GUY leans in and moves a piece of hair away from NIKA'S face.

CUTE GUY
(staring at NIKA)
So, the patriarchy? I can show you how powerful it is.

NIKA
(wrinkling her nose)
What?

CUTE GUY pushes NIKA back against the mattress, trapping her with his weight. He kisses her neck and nibbles her ear as she tries to push him away.

NIKA
Stop! Please, stop!

CUTE GUY
I don't think you mean it.

CUTE GUY shoves his hand into NIKA'S underwear and gropes at her crotch. NIKA pushes against him. CUTE GUY kisses her neck again, ignoring NIKA'S protests, and shoves a finger into her.

NIKA
Yeah, I mean it, dammit! And fuck the patriarchy!

NIKA raises her knee, catching CUTE GUY'S groin, and he doubles over, coughing. NIKA leaps off the bed, grabs a book from the nightstand, and hits CUTE GUY on the head, then yanks the door open. She weaves down the stairs, finds the front door, and leaves, her legs shaking, teeth chattering, cheeks blazing with shame.

chapter thirty-four

Nika has always relished time alone in the car. Like walking and running, sitting with her thoughts while moving in a steel box is good for her; it allows her to sift through the scrambled mess, spread it out like puzzle pieces that must be separated before putting them into a cohesive unit. Sometimes she comes to an understanding about issues, other times, she problem-solves obstacles. Susan might call those occasions Nika's *Zen interludes*, and Rainey would tell her she's crazy to spend time in silence and should be busting out the tunes—loudly. But Nika is content in knowing that the time she spends in the car is all hers.

Usually, anyway. Today, though, as she passes the drugstore on the corner, Nika's mind swings to Alex, to Dad, to summer's approach, and how great it would be if all the rigamarole was behind them soon. If they could abandon the drugs and the play and Mindy and the overall threatening weight as smoothly and easily as her ex left her and the kids. A sign in the tree lawn at the vacuum store catches Nika's eye, and she idles, staring at it and reading it aloud: "Freud never figured out what a woman wanted, but we did! Head in now for some fabulous deals on all vacuums!"

Nika blinks, frozen. Misogynistic bullshit apparently never gets old, but somehow, having it show up on the heels of her thoughts about some significant life issues—far more important than a clean house—ignites a fire inside her. "Fuck you, vacuum store. Fuck you and your outdated ideals. Fuck you and the men who staff the counter. Fuck you and the men who repair the vacuums. Sure, I like a good vacuum, but you know who does the vacuuming in our house, fuckers? Ethan!" She flips up her right middle finger, waves it at the store and the offensive sign, then presses the accelerator and peels away, mumbling under her breath as she does so. "Fuck you, Cole Hannon. Fuck you, Detective Brine. Fuck you, whoever damaged those books. Fuck you, ex-husband. Fuck you, frat boy from freshman year."

By the time Nika gets home, her ire has waned. Alex lounges on the sectional, legs crossed and thrown over Nika's favorite pillow, wiry arm behind his head. His eyes are closed, and he seems to be listening to some video on his phone through his earbuds. Purple moons linger under his eyes— the tell-tale sign that his world is off-balance. Lila sits to the left of him, legs tucked under her, a smile on her face as she devours yet another novel.

"What is it this time, sweet cheeks?" Nika glances at the heart on the book's spine. "Teen romance? Is there a ship name for the protagonists?" A few years ago, Nika couldn't say what the term *ship* meant, at least in terms of characters, but Lila stopped in her tracks, threw two hands on her hips, and slowly, patiently walked Nika through the process of combining two characters' names into their *ship* name. "You know, Fierrochase for Alex Fierro and Magnus Chase or Snowbaz for Simon and Baz? Do *any* of those ring a bell?"

"No, and more importantly, why?" Nika asked. "What is the point? Why not call the couple by their given names?"

Pure Lila emerged then, and she rolled her eyes and walked away, a stomp to her normally light steps.

Now, Lila purses her lips and says nothing, clearly ignoring her mother on purpose, so Nika ruffles her hair and kisses the top of her head. Then she turns to Alex: "Can you come with me to the kitchen?" She waits for him to open his eyes and acknowledge her request, which he does slowly. Alex has two settings: warp speed and slow as the honey he pours on his pancakes. Nika understands where they are today—there's nothing urgent about any of Alex's actions—but she raises her eyebrows and cocks her head in the direction of the kitchen.

Alex follows her and tumbles into the dining chair, his spider-like legs splayed away from the weathered cushion, earbuds hooked in his ears. Nika fills two water glasses and extends one to him, then tugs on the earbud, requesting he take it out. He does, but he won't meet Nika's eyes.

"Spill it, kid. I can read you, and something's wrong. Does it have to do with school? With everything happening, I can—"

Alex straightens in the chair, tugs the other earbud out, and takes a breath, his face pale. "You can't do *anything*, Mom. Swear you won't. It will all blow over soon. I know you'll keep asking, so . . . Some kids accused me of being a rat since I talked to the cops, and a few others yammer on about Grandpa. I've been teased before, but this is like, like, what does Lila say? Like it's all too much."

A gut punch to Nika. She's been in an all-too-much place before, and there's nothing enjoyable about it. Alex's mental state has always seemed robust and sturdy, but now? "Do you want to speak to someone about it? A therapist? A school counselor?"

Blotchy spots of red color Alex's cheeks and neck. "We can't talk everything out, Mom. Not all problems can be solved with therapy!" He springs up and lunges away from the kitchen, his water glass still full, shaking on the table like a pond during a small earthquake.

Nika should follow him, but Alex does better with a little space, so she'll give it to him this time—

"Would now be a good time to tell you we need a new washer and dryer?" Ethan steps into the kitchen, his shirt covered in dust and his hands black with, what? Grease? Oil?

"Why did I think you were working today?" Nika hands him a wet paper towel.

Ethan nods his thanks, then wipes his hands and holds them up to her. "I am working, but yeah, not in the way you think. I figured I'd check out what was wrong with the units. To be fair, the washer is okay, but the dryer? Alex told me it stopped the last few times he's used it. Didn't he tell you?"

A familiar deflated feeling fills Nika. Drugs, parties, school issues, normal everyday activities like laundry. Why is Alex not sharing things with her? Does she need to be worried, or is he being a fickle seventeen-year-old boy? "I don't think so. Then again, I barely know if I'm coming or going these days, you know?"

Ethan nods. "I do, which is why I'm happy to take this one on. Any requests? Large capacity or extra-large? Front loader or top? Top, hmmm, maybe—"

He's trying to lighten your burden, girl, Nika thinks, which reminds her to be honest, keep communication open. "Thank you, but don't go there right now. I just had a nice session with Susan, and remember what I said about comments? Even comments like these—which are, admittedly, funny—put the pressure on." Nika's gaze darts from Ethan to the water glass still sitting on the table to the oak sapling outside the kitchen window, its thin branches swaying in the breeze. Then she looks at her husband again.

He places a hand over his heart. "Thank you for the reminder. Now, do you want to go with me to get a new washer and dryer?"

Nika has an itemized list requiring her attention: some paperwork for the library, canned goods for a play-sponsored food drive, overgrown weeds threatening the life out of the rest of the plants poking up in the flower beds. But this—an ordinary outing with her love to choose a washer and dryer—sounds enticing. Just the thing to bring her back from the edge of her anxieties, the thing to show her husband that yes, she *does* still have an interest in spending time with him. Furthermore, she'd communicated her needs, and he heard her. *That counts for a lot, doesn't it?*

"Sure. Alex isn't going to open up to me right now anyway. Let me grab my shoes, and we should tell the kids where we're going. Then, I'll be ready."

An enormous smile fills Ethan's face, like his only wish has been granted, and Nika's heart swells in her chest.

When she moves to the front door to grab her favorite sneakers, the area rug draws Nika's attention. It's full of Mabel's hair, dirt from the front walk, and . . . is that still salt from winter? Didn't she sweep the rug three days ago? She leans down, grabs a tuft of dog hair entwined with what looks to be Lila's, and rolls it between her fingers. *Damn, the men at the vacuum store might have been right.* As she slips her feet into her sneakers, she pushes the silly thought of yet another task on her to-do list to the back of her brain but makes a mental note to check out new vacuums while she and Ethan are at the store.

chapter thirty-five

The next day, while Ethan waits for the appliance installers, Nika moves the old vacuum to the basement and hauls out the new one. It's exquisite: bagless, lightweight, and easy to use, with a serpentine cord that extends for miles, a vacuum unlike every other she's ever owned, and she's energized to see what it can do. No, she's ecstatic, almost overjoyed. Earbuds in, The Killers blaring, Nika shimmies and shakes and vacuums the accused area rug, the family room, her dad's living room, and the stairs. Only their bedroom has carpet, and she tackles it with abandon, ducking into corners and under the bed, behind the bookshelves and under the chair cushions, emptying the container repeatedly and marveling at the amount of hair, pet dander, and dried skin cells she collects. The act of vacuuming is wholly satisfying: her efforts leave little patches of almost perfection, and she trusts her habitat is getting cleaner, improving.

Concrete proof of better days ahead.

The vigor from the chore stays with Nika through the week and into the following Monday as she goes to work, a renewed spring in her step. She chats with the usual morning suspects—Cole, Rainey, and her favorite crossing guard—then begins her day with the students, effectively leaving thoughts of the books, the play, and the school board behind. If the five power-hungry souls sitting in the ivory tower haven't contacted her yet, then maybe there's no issue.

Alanna rushes into the library, takes her seat, and folds her hands on her lap. The rest of her classmates enter, most of them whispering to one another about what they did for the weekend or what they might do for summer vacation, which will be here before they know it. When Nika was young, she never even whispered in the library—voices were verboten to her. Messed with the vibe, the sacredness of the space. But she's taught these wee ones that speaking is okay. By using your voice and asking questions, you'll learn more, grow your brain, become your authentic self.

Use your voice.

Become your authentic self.

Nika tables the thoughts as Reggie almost spins off the rotating chair, a sheepish look on his heated face. She raises her eyebrows but says nothing; a stern look usually serves its purpose. A few other children scuff their shoes against the carpet, then touch their neighbor, causing an electric zap to tether them. Three kids giggle, and Nika can't help but grin. Sometimes Mondays are hard to take, but today, so far, everything is looking up.

Then Gwendolyn raises her hand, a big step for such a shy girl, and Nika kneels in front of her. "What do you need, honey?"

Gwendolyn swallows, then looks away like a skittish cat.

"Are you okay? Can I help you with something?"

The girl opens her mouth to speak, then tips her chin down before looking up once more, eyes wide and alarmed as vomit projects from her mouth and spills over Nika's knees.

The vigor Nika felt before plummets like an anvil from a tree.

Alanna escorts Gwendolyn to the nurse, and Nika makes an emergency request to the front office for some extra recess time for the class. "The smell alone is going to bother some of these kids," she whispers into the phone as she cranks a window open.

"Enough said," the administrative assistant says before hanging up, and she rushes into the room less than fifteen seconds later, her eyes wide, brows crumpled, most likely at the stench. "Whoa. Let's go, kids!"

Alanna, who is back and closest to the door, forms the line, a broad smile on her face, and everyone falls in, even Reggie, who normally hangs near his chair, tearing erasers into small pieces and scattering them onto the desktops. Not today. Today, his hands are empty, and he moves so fast, he's tenth in line; Nika sighs a breath of relief and calls the custodian.

~

After having cleaned her knees and shoes in the restroom, Nika enters the uncharacteristically quiet library. At this time of the day, little hands should be turning pages, and young voices should be sounding out unfamiliar words. Instead, the warm breeze trickles in through the open window, lifting next week's schedule and play-poster template from the desk; they float to the floor, tracing graceful *z*'s in the air. Nika is reminded of when Lila danced ballet, the way her tiny legs moved back and forth as they formed letters on the floor.

"Nika?" a voice sounds behind her. "Can I have a minute?"

She looks around the room and gestures at the mess. "I'm a little busy, as you can see."

Cole tips up his chin. "We have folks who can handle the mess. It's what the district pays them for, and I need to speak with you. In my office. Now."

"Okay," Nika says to Cole, and follows him down the hall.

Cole's office is cool and stench-free, and Nika closes her eyes and inhales deeply through her nose, imagining the air molecules as they move through her nasal passages, down the pharynx, and into her lungs. She rejoices in the unsoiled air. "Can I stay here as long as I want? I don't know what Gwendolyn had for breakfast, but that was the worst case I've ever—" She opens her eyes and slaps her hand over her mouth. "I'm so sorry for being unprofessional. Poor Gwendolyn."

"You're not wrong, Nika," Cole says, inviting her to sit with a wave of his hand.

It's then that she sees the superintendent sitting in the corner of the office. *Shit.* Nika nods at Blakely Balfour, takes a seat, and discreetly takes two more breaths. Breathing deeply, she realizes, is for more than cleansing her respiratory tract of all the odors; it should calm her, too, as her heart races inside her chest. *Book, desk, lamp. Vent, voices, footsteps. Finger wave, wrist roll, neck bend.* Why is Nika here, and what does the superintendent want with her?

Cole steeples his fingers in front of him. "I've gotten

word the school board would like for you to do something for them." He stops, lets his gaze hold Nika's for a moment, then tips his head toward the superintendent.

"And that's why I'm here." The woman stands. She's tall, much taller than Nika expected. Blakely Balfour has only been in the district for four years, and because Nika keeps to herself in a typical academic year, as do her children, she's rarely been in the same room with her.

Here, now, sitting below Blakely's level puts Nika at a disadvantage, but standing would seem deferential in the wrong way, so . . . "What can I do for you?"

Blakely leans against Cole's desk and purses her lips, like what she's about to say is sour, rancid. Thoughts of forced retirement or sabbaticals or movement within the district flood Nika's mind. She wishes for the woman to get on with it, but Cole's phone rings, and the administrative assistant pops her head in the doorway before popping back out again, nervousness splayed across her features. It's like a bad dramedy, one Nika would never watch.

"With all due respect, Ms. Balfour, I have a library to get back to, so please say what you're here to say."

The superintendent nods. "That you do. And I'll let you do it, if you prepare to do two things: One, come to a school board meeting and speak about why you chose *Once Upon a Fairy Tale*, and two, don't do the play. Choose another one more . . . appropriate."

Nika steps out of herself for a moment, looks down on the office, the three of them in a triangle. Smoke curls from her ears, and she's clenching her teeth and flaring her nostrils, like an archaic cartoon character. Blakely can't do anything without board approval, so Nika stands and glares at her. "Answer one question for me," she says.

"Sure. What is it?" Blakely replies.

"Why are you asking me to do these things?"

Blakley smiles, one lip curled at the corner almost like a sneer, her coffee-stained teeth highlighted under the fluorescent lights. "Someone has to be accountable, don't they?"

Accountability again. Cole says nothing, and Nika inwardly seethes, contemplating what to say and how to say it. Communication is key—Susan says so—and effective communication now, when anger ripples through Nika's entire body like a hurricane, will be impossible. She moves past Cole and Blakely, only turning to look over her shoulder at the door. "I'll be in touch," she says, not agreeing to anything at all.

chapter thirty-six

Someone has to be accountable. The phrase echoes in Nika's skull as she returns to the library and sends a text to Rainey letting her know she's taking the day off, as she calls in her favorite sub, as she leaves a voicemail for Mindy informing her they need to talk, as she checks with Susan Harris's receptionist and squeezes in an appointment for late that afternoon, as she texts the kids and Ethan and tells them she'll be home late and to eat the leftovers in the fridge for dinner. *I'll explain later,* she says to them all, *but I'm fine. No, not fine, I'm good.*

And she is good. It's a gorgeous spring day, all blue skies and cottony white clouds, the sort of day that makes Nika optimistic about the future and grateful to be alive. The kind that calls to her with a soft voice, inviting her to walk through the breeze, gaze at the new life, and take a moment to just be. So, she heads to the duck pond near the music pavilion. The path surrounding the pond isn't very long, but scattered along the edges are the newest residents of the area: two families of ducks, fuzzy ducklings included, and three families of geese. Most folks can spare the sight of the Canada geese calling this pond home, but Nika has always loved them, and when they hiss at her as she gets too near the young goslings, she hisses right back. "Rough day," she says to what looks to be the leader of the group, a female she has named Ruth Bader Geeseburg, before laughing at herself.

Her phone alarm rings, and Nika heads for the car. It's time to see Susan Harris, and something inside Nika almost hums with anticipation as she buckles her seat belt. For once, she's looking forward to the appointment, and even though Nika's not where she probably should be in terms of progress, she knows—*truly believes*—it doesn't matter. Actively making an appointment and being ready to speak fully means she's moving forward. "That's what I'm telling myself anyway," she shouts out the window to Ruth, who only hisses once again, before pulling away. On the drive to Susan Harris's office, she opens the windows and lets the spring air upend her already wild hair.

~

Susan welcomes Nika in with her usual manner, cheery and bright, offering a bottle of water and other refreshments. If she's curious about the last-minute appointment, she doesn't say anything, just waits for Nika to get settled into her seat and speak.

Nika snuggles into the couch cushions and places her hands in her lap. "I'm here because I need to talk. Not about Ethan and me or about my lack of libido or the horrors of menopause or anything else. I need to get something off my chest, and this is a safe space to do so."

Susan nods and gestures for Nika to continue.

Nika closes her eyes, thinks about what she wants to say, and then gives Susan the rundown on her impromptu meeting with Cole and Blakely Balfour. Susan listens intently, and then, when Nika finishes, remains quiet. The ticking clock and whirring fan are the only noises Nika focuses on, and she thinks about lingering in this moment, this bubble, this cocoon, for a little while longer. Silence, sometimes, is not overrated.

Susan leans in, asking, "You've told me what happened, but now I want to know how you *feel*. If you hadn't been sitting in the school office, what would you have said to the administrators?"

A frown crosses Nika's face as she allows her true feelings to bubble to the surface and color her words. "I'd tell them the district is using me as an excuse, a scapegoat. I've done nothing wrong—they're the wrong ones."

"And what else?" Susan asks astutely as she taps her chest. "Inside, you must have more feelings. Don't you?"

Nika nods, licks her lips, carefully chooses her words. Not because she's afraid Susan will judge her but because she only wants to say this once in this space, and she wants to use the proper, most accurate words. "If I can speak freely, and I know I can here, I'd tell them that times have changed, attitudes have changed, families have changed. Kids have two moms or two dads or even two moms and a dad, all under one roof. The idea of the nuclear family is so antiquated and frankly, it's not applicable in all cases anymore and probably never was. Furthermore, by offering a play like *Once Upon a Fairy Tale*, we're being inclusive, thinking of all children, servicing all children, and allowing children to see themselves." She pauses and tugs at the end of her shirt.

More words surface, and she plunges ahead. "You know what else? I'd ask them about all the other shit going on in the district—the things they refuse to acknowledge. The nepotism, the subs who mooch off the school instead of teaching, the predator subs—yeah, we know about the teacher who was jailed for inappropriate relations with students. *Those* are the people they should be worried about. And the racism, the ableism? The lack of equality for the LGBTQIA+ crowd? For the people of color? Did you know a friend's husband, a generous community member and longtime parent in the district, was stopped at the arena door because he was Black? White people all around him were allowed to enter, and he wasn't. Not until he agreed to show identification. Either we all show ID or no one does! *Those* are the issues they should be paying more attention to, dammit! Talk about being accountable—when has the district ever been accountable for anything?" Nika's hands shake with her last words, and heat trickles across every inch of skin, and yet, deep inside, bonds begin snapping, and she feels light and free.

Susan takes a beat, probably waiting to be certain Nika is finished, and raises her eyebrows. "You had a lot to say, didn't you? I'm proud of you for being willing to share what you did. Now," she directs her gaze right at Nika and holds it, "I want you to say what you said to me to the district. What's the worst that can happen?"

"I could lose my job."

Susan shakes her head. "I don't think you will, and I think what you said needs to be shared. And I think you need to find the same level of honesty and share your thoughts with Ethan. Doing so will help you make more progress. Total honesty with your partner. Because, again, what's the worst that can happen with him?"

"He could leave me."

Susan shakes her head once more. "I don't think that will happen either. Be accountable for you, your life, your choices, your actions. And hold others to the same standard of accountability too. You've got this, Nika. Trust yourself."

~

Nika pulls out of Susan Harris's parking lot with a renewed sense of self. She knows she and her family are not the district's real problem, and while she may be the real problem for Ethan and her, she's only one component of the issue. She needs to be as honest with him as she was with Susan. All the homework, all the questions—they're useful, but they also distract from what is truly important: open communication and transparency with her husband. It's what they lack, it's what the school district lacks. It's what Nika and Mindy lack and Mindy and Dad. As much as Nika hates to admit it, Blakely Balfour is correct: someone needs to be accountable.

Nika can do that, and there's no better time like the present, so she heads over to the board office, pulls into the closest parking space, and turns off the car. Checking her face in the mirror—if she's going to do this, she doesn't want to go into battle against the superintendent with smudged lipstick—she pinches her cheeks, grabs her keys, and rushes out of the car.

The quiet hallways contrast with Evergreen's bustling ones, and Nika wonders what it would be like to work in this environment. Would the quiet be welcomed, or would it drain her energy? Right now, it's adding a layer of unease, but Nika stops, takes a breath, and pulls up her metaphorical big girl panties before continuing around the corner and pushing on the superintendent's outer office door.

The administrative assistant looks up, startled. "Do you have an appointment?" She taps her pen against the wood desk and drags the mouse over her mouse pad.

"As a matter of fact, I do not, but I'm certain Ms. Balfour will be happy to see me." Nika rushes past the surprised admin and her weak protest and opens the inner office door. "Here's how things are going to go," Nika says to the superintendent before pulling the door closed behind her.

Blakely stands, eyebrows furrowed as she gestures to Nika to sit. Nika waves off the invitation. Standing is what she needs to maintain her current courage level. "Since your board had every opportunity to peruse the script and they approved it, we're going to perform the play as written, as scheduled. You will show up on opening night, which will showcase your support of me, your support of Evergreen, and your support of every family that doesn't match the school board's idea of what a family should look like."

"Ms. Stewart, I think—"

Nika points a finger at Blakely Balfour, effectively interrupting her. "Then, you and I will go to the May board meeting and report what a success the play was. Because it will be, and my guess is you'll have families and children patting you on the back for being so open-minded about what family and friendship look like. Will you have your share of naysayers? Yes, you will. But it's time for this district to join the twenty-first century, and furthermore, why not worry about the real issues. I'll have a detailed list of those in your Dropbox by tomorrow morning."

Nika doesn't give Blakely even a second to react. She thanks her for her time, exits the office, tips her head to the admin, and walks tall on her way out of the building.

That night, after a late-afternoon trip to the secondhand bookstore, a stop for hot cocoa at Brewed Bliss, and a solo picnic in the park, Nika goes home, climbs on top of Ethan, pushes him back against the mattress, and gives him a night to remember.

chapter thirty-seven

Nika rises extra early, places a light kiss on Ethan's lips as he continues to sleep, and drives to Mindy's house. Her knock rattles the door, and from inside, a shout surfaces.

"Hold on! I'm getting there."

Mindy has never been patient, and her shout makes Nika consider that texting first might have been a good idea. On the other hand, doing so would have allowed Nika time to think things over, talk herself out of the confrontation, and there is to be none of that today. The door swings open, and Mindy stands there, her eyes wide, mouth open.

"Just me," Nika says and pushes her way in, clutching the bag with Dad's paperwork. "Sorry it's so early.

Mindy sighs, then shuts the door with a thud. "What do you want, Nika?" Placing her hands on her hips, she almost snarls. "Listen, I'm busy here, and I'm leaving tomorrow. I don't have time for whatever it is you need to say at five forty-five in the morning."

The reply doesn't surprise Nika in the least. Day-to-day living with Mindy has always involved giving every excuse under the sun to *not* partake in Nika's life and schedule. But this isn't about Nika—it's about Mindy taking what's not hers. Though transparency is high on Nika's list these days, she chooses not to use it right now; she's lived long enough to know not to ignore any hunches and that sometimes, a little trap won't do much harm. After all, she might be able to use the appearance of knowledge to her advantage. "Listen, I don't need to take up much of your time," she sniffs, "but I want you to know . . . I know, Mindy."

Mindy's face blanches, and she backs away from Nika. "Know what?" She stands rigid, a defensive posture, a default reaction Nika knows so well.

See Rainey? Nika thinks. *I get to be Fred after all, no ascot needed.* Skirting the truth, Nika says, "Everything," and holds up the bag, then moves toward the small table against the living room wall. She lets the paperwork fall onto the scuffed tabletop and rummages through it, pointing to some highlighted lines. "Including this." She taps her finger against the page. "You have to stop doing it. It's not right."

Mindy falls into the chair and places her head in her hands. "You don't know anything, Nika. In fact, you don't know anything at all."

Nika takes a seat in the chair opposite Mindy and extends her hand toward her stepsister, who pulls her own hand away. "I do know some things," Nika says. "And I want to understand why, so can you help me do that?"

A growl escapes Mindy's mouth, and she snaps her head up, glaring at Nika with anger swirling in her eyes. "Help you *understand?* Can't you see it? You have everything. Michael has everything. And what do I have?"

Thoughts bombard Nika, memories that trip over one another, again and again. Dad taking Nika and Mindy shopping for prom and middle school dance dresses, respectively, helping them with homework, hanging their high school graduation photos on the living room wall. Dad offering to cosign Mindy's first apartment and pay for part of her college education and cleaning up after so many messes Mindy had made with school, her jobs, the neighbors. Her father had shown nothing but kindness to a kid who wasn't biologically his, one he gratefully accepted as part of his life, and *this* was how Mindy repaid him—by taking exorbitant amounts of money without his knowledge *and* having no remorse?

A waterfall of anger whooshes through Nika, but Mindy has never responded to a harsh approach, so Nika softens her tone. "You have Dad, and you always have. Since the moment you stepped into our lives, you've had him. Granted, I took a little longer to come around, but you have me too. If there's something I can help you with—"

"You can't fix everything, Nika! People like you think you can, but you can't!" Leaping up from the chair, Mindy stomps out of the room, her footsteps echoing across the tile.

Mindy's words gouge Nika like a thousand paper cuts. Is she trying to fix everything? Sure, Nika is a doer, especially when it comes to her family, her life, but has she overstepped with Mindy? Is that how her stepsister interpreted her actions all these years? Regardless, now isn't the time to dwell on that thought. Mindy has always been a master at diverting Nika's attention, and this time, Nika won't stand for it.

Nika rises from the chair, strides across the room, and enters the outdated kitchen. If she doesn't put a stop to

Mindy's nonsense, Dad might be financing a renovation in this room too. She drags her gaze from the pocked floor to Mindy, who leans against the counter, joint in hand, blowing smoke circles at the ceiling.

"You too?" Nika says. "Am I the only one who doesn't smoke these days?"

"You always were a goody-goody, so I'm not surprised in the least," Mindy says, one thin eyebrow arched.

Again, the words make Nika bristle. What did she ever do to deserve Mindy's ire? "Listen, that wasn't a judgment, just a question, and while I would love to talk about fixing *everything*, I need you to fix *something*, and that's with Dad. In the interest of time, let's cut to the chase. Why'd you do it?"

Mindy's eyes darken like they used to when they were young, when Dad would catch her in a lie she didn't want to acknowledge. Dad always made sure to hold the conversation as privately as possible, but Nika, as curious as ever, lurked in the dark hallway, feet planted on the cold linoleum, eyes wide and ears open. Maybe Mindy knew about Nika's hallway behavior, and maybe it made her feel like the judge and jury were against her. Who knew?

"You know what?" Mindy says, lifting one side of her mouth in a sneer. "I'll tell you why I did it. Michael owes me. He chased my mother away, and if he hadn't, I might be somewhere else in life. Somewhere bigger, better. But no, instead, I'm here, asking my stepsister's kids to help with cats, moving from job to job, boyfriend to boyfriend . . ."

"And traveling on Dad's dime. Furnishing your home on Dad's dime. Probably buying weed on Dad's dime. How fair is that? Don't you think if you'd asked, he would have helped you?"

Mindy's focus is on the fingerprint-covered fridge, which

has seen better days and is in only slightly better condition than the nicotine-stained walls. "Maybe, maybe not. Tough love is real, not that you'd know anything about it." She flips her middle finger up at Nika.

Nika resists the urge to throw the bird back at Mindy. "I'm not going there today. This isn't about me, it's about you. So, what are you going to do about it?"

Mindy takes another drag from the joint and releases the smoke slowly, her gaze slanting toward Nika. "The money?"

And there it is—official confirmation of her involvement. "Listen," Nika treads carefully now, as she wants to understand the whole debacle, "tell me everything, and we'll figure out what you can or cannot do about any of it."

"And why would I listen to you?" Mindy asks, taking another long drag.

Those words might have flustered a teenage Nika. The Nika from a year ago would have thought about them for months, always ruminating, casting the blame on herself. The Nika from a few months ago would have backed down from them. The Nika of now, though far from where she wants to be, sees the words for what they are: products of a hurt person. And hurt people can, and do, hurt people. Nika's father used to say it often, almost as an excuse for Mindy and her behavior, but then he'd do his best to soothe his stepdaughter's hurt, to help her realize her full potential. He tried so hard for so long; he still tries to help. That's what covering up Mindy's stealing is all about.

Nika smiles and whispers, "Because I care, Mindy. You might not think so, but I do. My life hasn't always been easy either. Maybe we need to sit and chat about that sometime, communicate for a change instead of slinging verbal arrows at one another. Aside from Ethan and the kids, you and Dad are all the family I have. So come hell or high water, I'll do what I can to hold onto you, all of you."

Mindy stares at Nika, then scratches her eyebrow and presses the joint's lit end to a dish resting on the counter. She wipes her hands on her shirt and tips her chin toward a bench near the window. "Sit down," she says. "It's time I told you everything."

Nika takes a seat, looks around the quiet kitchen, her gaze landing on a refrigerator magnet. *I am a winner*, it reads, and it's a cousin of the one Nika has plastered to her whiteboard: *It takes a team*. "You know what?" Nika says, "I have an idea."

~

As requested, Dad, Lila, Alex, and Ethan are assembled at the kitchen table when Nika and Mindy arrive at the house. As usual, Alex sports earbuds, his hair is a rumpled mess, and lavender circles hover under his eyes, while Lila, only slightly more awake, sketches on a notepad. Dad's leg moves up and down under the table, and Ethan? Despite the early hour, he's grinning at Nika, his essence as calm as a gentle ocean wave, like it's any other typical, ordinary day in their lives.

And it *is* a typical, ordinary day in their lives; these *are* their typical ordinary days, full of small family dramas, grumpy children, backstabbing, and embezzlement. Maybe a good round of sex allows Ethan to take on the world with a positive attitude. Hell, who is she kidding? *Of course* a good round does that to him. Now, if she could apply the concept to herself . . . She offers him her own unsteady smile.

"Why are we here?" Dad asks, looking at Ethan as Nika and Mindy each take a seat.

Nika clears her throat. "Ethan had nothing to do with this. It's all me. I think we need to clear the air, get to the bottom of what's going on and how everyone is involved."

Dad stares at Nika, his brow furrowed, and then a knock sounds at the door as Nika's phone buzzes.

It's Rainey, responding to Nika's SOS: *Can I come in? I'm at your front door.*

"Hold on," Nika says as she waits for the front door to open and close.

A shuffle of footsteps, and Rainey appears in the kitchen, eyes bright. "Who scheduled an early-morning party without me?" she says and winks at Lila, who smiles from ear to ear.

Alex barely glances up at Rainey but removes his earbuds from his ears and straightens in his chair, his only attempt at making a good impression on anyone. At times like this, he reminds Nika of her ex.

Rainey leans against the kitchen counter and zeroes in on Nika. "Uh, this does seem like an odd group of people to be convening at this hour on a weekday morning. Care to share what's happening?"

Mindy stands. "I don't think it's your business, so why don't you go on your way, Rainey?"

"It *is* her business." Nika chooses her words carefully, conscious of how Mindy will take them. "She's like another sister to me, and she's been through just about everything in my life at this point." Nika raises her eyebrows at Rainey. "I'm glad she's here." She turns to Rainey and nods. "I'm glad you're here."

Dad sharply raps the table with his knuckles. "Will someone tell me what's going on? I'm lost."

"You are?" Mindy says, a sneer in her low voice. "It's probably thanks to the dead brain cells filling up your head."

Rainey sucks in a breath, Alex's eyes go wide, Lila shakes her head, and Dad frowns, clearly bruised by the words. He says nothing as his gaze drops to the table.

Sorrow fills Nika's chest, pressing against her ribcage. Her father hasn't always done everything right, but he certainly doesn't deserve treatment like this from Mindy. She places a hand on Dad's back and rubs it, warming the spot, hoping touch can soothe the burn of what Mindy said but knowing the action probably doesn't come anywhere close.

Ethan stands and slices a hand through the air, raising his voice a measure. "I'm not entirely certain what's happening here, either, but this is *our* house, Nika's and mine, and we will all be respectful in this space. Do you think you can do that, *Mindy*?" Ethan's tone, authoritative and nonnegotiable, fills the kitchen.

A flush rises on Mindy's cheeks. "Yes. Let's get on with it."

Nika lets out a large breath, willing herself to stay calm, collected. *She can do this.* "Fine. I'm going to lay it on the line. Mindy, you took money from Dad, and you shouldn't have—"

"You did what?" Alex says, a stricken look on his face as he sits straight up in his chair. "You took money from Grandpa? Why?"

Mindy gives Alex the side-eye. "I needed the money. Why else would I take it?"

"So why didn't you ask him for help?" Alex says. "Or take on another job? That's what other people do. They don't *steal* money. From a family member." He stands, moves to the window, and directs his gaze outside.

Nika allows her attention to roam there too. The sun is beginning to peek over the trees in the backyard, and she yearns to move outside, soak up the sunny goodness, escape the negative veil draped across the room. "I think she did ask, didn't she, Dad?" Nika looks at her father.

Dad nods. "Yes, she did, and I gave her some money. I

gave her what I could afford." He hangs his head once more and shakes it, closing his eyes.

This time, Alex moves to pat Dad's arm. Then he looks at Mindy. "You know what Mom always says to us?" His voice is strong but quiet. "She always says we're supposed to be honest. She might be disappointed by our actions, or she might not like what we did, but she'll be far angrier if we lie about it."

"Your point?" Mindy says.

Alex rolls his eyes. "You know my point. Just tell us the truth of what happened. That's all we're asking of you. My guess is—Grandpa might not even ask you to pay him back because of the kind of person he is. You took advantage of him. That's not hard to see, Mindy."

Nika is sure Alex will bolt from the room, but he takes his seat and crosses his arms over his chest, almost like he's proud of himself. And he should be; he speaks the truth— that *is* all they're asking of Mindy.

"You're not going to let me go until I spill it all, are you?" Mindy says.

"I can't. I was going to leave this little discussion between you and me, but it seems to involve more than just you and me, so . . ."

Mindy shrugs. "I needed money, and Dad had it. Slip a little out here, a little there, and he'd never know it. I figured you, Saint Nika, would be too busy to figure it out."

"You don't need to say anything else, Mindy," Dad says, anger in his tone. "I bet you thought I'd be distracted too— by my traveling, the weed. Is that right?" Dad says.

Mindy shrugs.

Dad stands and strokes his beard, taking in the entire group, his glare finally landing on Mindy. "Then that's all I need to know. You don't have to pay me back, but you cannot take any more, and I won't be offering ever again. And Nika," he points at her, "We'll talk about where to go from here later. Now," he allows his glance to stop on everyone. "I'm going back to bed before I head to my meeting. I never meant for any of my transgressions to get out of hand, and I'm no longer smoking." He bows his head and backs out of the kitchen.

A liquid rush of emotion simmers inside Nika's chest. She's proud of her dad, not just for going to the meeting but for standing up to Mindy too. Parental guilt is real—she recognizes that as much as the next parent—but sometimes it doesn't matter how much you try to love someone. If they don't allow themselves to be loved, there is nothing you can do.

Rainey claps her hands. "So—one mystery solved." She digs around in her purse, coming up with the vintage key. "And guess who this belongs to?"

The key sparkles under the kitchen lights. "Me?" Nika says. "Or the district. I mean, those keys are part of the costumes, you know that."

"Are you sure it's not Mindy's?" Alex says and stares at her.

Mindy flips the group the bird, then opens the kitchen door and steps onto the deck, quickly lighting a cigarette.

Rainey shrugs. "You'll like this, Nika. It's Reggie's, well, not Reggie's, but his brother Jared's. He's playing the key keeper, right?" She doesn't wait for confirmation, just swings the key back and forth. "Apparently Jared's dad came to pick him up from play practice and got a whiff of the storyline. The next night after pickup, they stopped by the library, and you all know what happened then."

Lila raises her hand. "Why was the key there? It's too early to put this all together."

"Because Jared dropped it. And yes, I know what you're going to ask—how did I find all this out? Yours truly, being the best teacher ever, overheard Jared asking about the key, and when I pulled the key out of my bag, he caved like a house of cards. Sad, really, but he's a kid, so I'll take pity on him."

Everyone looked at one another then burst out laughing. "You know what?" Ethan said. They would have gotten away with it, too, if it weren't for that meddling teacher."

The tension in the air lightens, and Alex asks, "Have any Scooby snacks?"

Interior: Guardian Angels Catholic High School,
Ninth Grade Gym Class, 1992

NIKA runs around the indoor track. MALE GYM
TEACHER tells the kids to go faster. NIKA loves
running, but she feels something in her underwear,
asks to use the restroom, and heads to the locker
room, where she enters a stall.

NIKA
(mumbling to self as she pulls down underwear)
What the hell? This is too much.

NIKA wipes her underwear, cringing at the globby
white mass on the fabric. She makes a note to ask
her friend about it. Then she finishes, washes her
hands, and goes back to the gym to complete her laps.

MALE GYM TEACHER
Move it! I don't want to see you running like a
girl.

SAMANTHA
Ever heard of Flo-Jo, teach?

NIKA
(laughing)
Good one!

MALE GYM TEACHER
Two more laps for you, girls! Top speed!

NIKA and SAMANTHA increase their speed, run the
laps, then walk off the track, surreptitiously

throwing MALE GYM TEACHER the bird.

A few minutes later, NIKA leaves the locker room, backpack slung over her shoulder. MALE GYM TEACHER taps on her shoulder.

MALE GYM TEACHER
(gesturing to NIKA'S chest)
Be sure to wear the proper bra, Washington. You got quite the rack there. We don't need any of the boys looking at it and getting distracted, you hear me?

chapter thirty-eight

Nika stands at the kitchen counter later in the week sipping tea when Ethan sneaks up behind her and threads his arms around her waist. His skin is still damp from his morning shower, and he smells like soap and clean laundry. Nika has always appreciated his scent, and she leans back against him and inhales deeply.

"Hey, I've been meaning to ask—what *was* that the other night?" Ethan says as he nuzzles Nika's neck. "I'm not complaining. If you need to be gone late and we eat leftovers for dinner every night—fine with me." He places a kiss on her shoulder, then removes his hold and opens the cabinet above the coffee pot to grab a mug. "No pressure intended and thank you for making me coffee."

They sit at the kitchen table, hands curled around their respective mugs. It's still early, and the kids are asleep, but Mabel slumbers under the table, her snores barely audible, and the birds outside the kitchen window fanatically chirp their morning song as the sun crawls out of bed.

They should have had this conversation before now, after the showdown with Mindy, Ethan had taken off for a conference and Nika pushed forward with play production.

"I'm not sure what it was." She recounts her conversation with Cole and Blakely, then the one with Susan, and finally, what she'd said to the superintendent in the confines of her office. "I should have told you before, but it's like I had to take time and figure out the why behind my actions. I refuse to do their bidding, Ethan, and I don't know . . . I felt like I was finally saying what I meant, and I meant what I said. To Cole, to Blakely, to Susan. I felt empowered and powerful. Like I was in control."

"And you felt like having sex?" he says, then takes another sip of coffee and encourages her to speak with a lifting of his eyebrows. "Again, not complaining." He smirks.

"I felt like doing something reckless, or . . . Maybe *reckless* isn't the right word. Something where I did what I wanted when I wanted to do it, regardless of what was happening around me. Like being caught up in the moment, and I figured, why not?"

Ethan says nothing, just taps his chin with his finger.

"I don't want you to think it will always be that way. It's not like everything has been solved. But I recognize I haven't always been honest with you. Even though we say we communicate well, we don't. We really don't."

Ethan's face pales, and he furrows his eyebrows. "What? What do you mean you haven't been honest?"

The look on her husband's face pains her, and Nika wonders what he's thinking. She covers her hand with his and squeezes his fingers. "Don't look so scared, honey. You're it for me, and I'm sorry if I don't do a very good job of making you aware. But all this shit with the school and Dad and Mindy reaffirms you deserve transparency."

"I'll be honest—that still doesn't make me feel better."

"I mean, you need to hear it like it is. I'm a woman approaching menopause. My libido is low. My responsibilities are great. My main needs right now are food, exercise, shelter, and love, but my preferred form of love is companyionship. I like walking with you, grocery shopping with you, spending time with the kids, and watching movies with you. I have always enjoyed those things. And yes, years ago, I enjoyed sex, too, but probably not as much as you'd like to think."

Ethan swallows and looks away, hesitancy and fear still palpable in his expression.

"My baggage, as I've discovered, is *enormous*. Susan has helped me discover a lot, actually." Nika pours Ethan another cup of coffee and then goes into all the events that have colored her perspective. "I've never felt good about my body, and the attached shame is massive. It doesn't matter if you tell me how much you love to look at me, how you like my hips and my legs, the jiggly parts of my breasts, and the saggy parts of my stomach." She breathes in, trying to capture the precise words. "When you do that, my subconscious groups you with those who came before, those who made me feel bad about breasts, periods, and sex, bad about myself."

"But I do like those."

Nika lets loose a quiet laugh. "Yes, but what else? What *else* do you like?"

Ethan leans back against his chair and crosses his arms over his chest. "Well, that's easy. I like that you put an exact teaspoon of sugar in your coffee each morning, that you still read the labels on the food you buy even though you've been buying the same brands since I've known you. I like that you have the nuttiest best friend who cares for you more than anything. I like that you like waffles without butter and syrup and that the kids at school bring a smile to your face every day, even on days when they throw up on you." Ethan pauses, closing his eyes. "I like that you snore softly at night even though you won't admit it, that you hog the covers, and that you find my clean shirts even when I can't find them. Every time, Nika. *Every time.* Same goes for my wallet and keys.

"I like that your toothbrush is always right next to mine in the cupboard and that I'll trip over your shoes at the garage entrance. That the timer on the microwave will always be left with a few seconds on it, and your scarf will almost always be on the hook near the garage door. I like that if anyone needs anything at any time, they can come to you, no questions asked. Please know, too, that when I say *like*, I mean *love*. Most importantly," Ethan opens his eyes, moisture pooling in them, and holds Nika's gaze, "I love that when I'm on my way home from work, I know, without a doubt, that I'll walk into the best home I could have imagined. Ever. The day I met you, Nika, was the first day of my life. Maybe it sounds sappy, but it's true. You and Lila and Alex brought something new and unexpected to my world, something unimaginable."

Hot tears rush down Nika's cheeks, and she's so damn proud of herself for choosing so wisely the second time around, for choosing to love this man, so wrapped up in goodness and grace. She rises from her chair, sits on Ethan's lap, and hugs him, his heart beating rapidly under her cheek. "That," she whispers into the front of her shirt. "I need to feel that. Appreciated for more than my boobs and my legs and my body. I need to feel cherished for *who* I am, not *what* I am—"

"But—"

"No, please let me finish. I know that's what you thought you were doing by telling me you like my parts, but that's not what I *need*. I need you, of course. And I choose you, will choose you every day. But this is where transparency comes in. I need something other than appreciation the way you show it. If you appreciate and love me, then lighten my load. Put my shoes away, turn the microwave timer off. Offer to fold the clothes. Yes, I know you'll do it if I ask, but if you *offer*—that shows me you love me, appreciate me. It's like the coffee. Me making you coffee says I love you. You doing something without me asking is the same thing. Now, I'm not saying I'm going to be all in for sex every day, but I think little by little, I can overcome some of my baggage, begin to see the good parts of myself. And when I'm happy with myself, I'll be happier to share myself with you. But—"

"Am I going to like this but?"

"Probably not. I'm still almost menopausal. So having sex sometimes feels like my flesh is roasting on a spit, and other times, the roughness of it all—vaginal dryness is the bane of my existence right now, and no amount of Astroglide compares to physiological secretions. No amount!" Ethan laughs, his chest vibrating under Nika's cheek. "While we're at it . . ." Nika places every card out there for Ethan. "Please know I need you to communicate as openly as this. All the time. I probably needed to tell you this well before now."

"Yes, I think you did."

"I also need you to listen. In my head, I *was* telling you this, though I wasn't using the words. Maybe I thought you were a mind reader." Nika pulls away from his chest, then places her lips against his. The kiss is soft, gentle, unhurried. Exactly what she needs. She leans back and rubs his cheek, the stubble there rough against her palm. "And you know what else? I used to think I had a happy place or two, and I do, but what I know now is it's not a place, it's a person. The happy place is where the person is. So thank *you*, Ethan, for being a happy place. Thank you for your patience, your support, your love."

Ethan smiles, one tear now making the trek down his cheek, then lightly kisses her nose. "And thank you, Nika, for your patience, your support, your love." He gazes at her for a few beats, eyes and smile wide. "Are we good now? I mean, I know there's more work to be done, but . . . we're on the right track? You're on the right track?"

"I think so. Don't you?"

"I do, but what now?"

Nika slides off his lap and adjusts her shirt, then smoothes back her hair. "Today is my day to be optimistic. Honesty and transparency worked so well here. I have always valued that everywhere, except with myself, I think. And clearly, with you, at least in some respects." She reaches a hand to Ethan's face and cups his palm, running her fingers over the light scruff there before placing her lips to the same spot. "And optimism is good. Rainey has always said so. Therefore, I'm going to head to work and do what I do best. Help the kids appreciate books, be sure the play is ready to go, and then come back here and be home with the kids. Revel in my life, even its ridiculousness at times, and snuggle up with you and a movie. And maybe, if you're lucky . . ."

Ethan raises his eyebrows and tilts his head, the kitchen light reflecting in his eyes.

"If you're lucky, I might let you rub my feet *and* choose

the movie!" Nika smiles and runs out of the room before Ethan can swat her behind.

329

chapter thirty-nine

"I heard what went down in the superintendent's office," Cole says. "I never took you as one to go up against authority, but, good for you. It's about time."

Nika hasn't seen Cole since that day thanks to an extended GI virus on his end. "Why am I not surprised at how news travels? That was last Monday. What time did you hear about it? The same afternoon?"

Cole doesn't say anything, just holds up his hands, palms outward in surrender.

"Well, I appreciate your kind words. I didn't want to take the fall for anything, especially when this district has far more to worry about than a play about friendship."

Cole nods. "Got it. I wanted to tell you I'm proud of you, and I don't mean to be patronizing. Keep up the good work, here and, well, with life in general, I guess. It's good to have people like you in the building."

The compliment causes a lump to form in Nika's throat; Cole is stingy with kind words, and while she wasn't actively reaching for his approval, it's always good to be appreciated. She thinks back to the open conversation she had with Ethan about appreciation, and she crosses the metaphorical distance to Cole. No need to be at odds with a man she sees every day. "Thank you, Cole. I enjoy my job, and I can't imagine being anywhere else. Now, do you have five minutes?"

~

After telling Cole what she learned about the key, Nika closes the library, tapes a sign to the door, and walks to the auditorium. It's the afternoon of the dress rehearsal; she's confident the kids will do fine, no, spectacular. She just hopes any props reinforced with duct tape will hold steady for the entirety of the play's run.

The auditorium door opens, and Lila and Alex peek their heads out. The kids have taken the afternoon off from school to help corral the actors between scenes. "Mom! Everything looks awesome," Lila says. "Come on!"

Lila is right. The soft, purple lighting spills over the wood and foam castle, and the bricks sparkle, transporting the soon-to-be audience into the fairy tale life. The verdant meadow grass almost looks real, and the actors, all fifth graders, stand proud and tall.

"This play is going to be great!" Nika says, just as Rainey taps her on the shoulder.

"Hey, you." Rainey says. "This looks amazing. You did a fantastic job." She cranes her neck, looking over one shoulder and then the other. "You haven't . . . you haven't seen Detective Brine, have you?"

Nika snorts. "You know he's not our resource officer,

right? That's Officer Jenkins. Brine is probably *at work. At the precinct.*"

Rainey doesn't say anything, but a rosy blush spreads from the top of her boat-collared shirt, up her neck, and into her cheeks.

"Yeah, as I thought."

"Next coffee is on me, and I'll give you the deets. Now, I need to skedaddle." She blows Nika a kiss and in usual fashion, shimmies away. Right before she gets to the west auditorium door, a male figure steps in line with her. He reaches for Rainey's hand, and she takes it.

"Rainey and Brine?" Alex says. "I guess there goes my chance."

"You realize you never had one, right?"

"Somehow, I always hoped, you know?" Alex winks. "Is Grandpa here yet?"

Nika shakes her head. "He'll be coming with Dad, and they should be here soon. Hey, I know you don't want me to ask, but is everything okay?"

Alex scuffs his shoe against the wood floor. "Yeah, it's good. Someone squashed the rumor mill with actual facts, can you believe it? Everyone knows I wasn't a rat, and they know Grandpa and his weed weren't involved at all. It bothers me that Mindy was mean to Grandpa—and you. She's a cat owner, Mom. How could she be so mean?"

Seventeen years old, and sometimes, Alex still sounded so young. Nika wraps her arm around her son, leans in, and puts a kiss to his temple. "We're lucky to have you, Alex."

"I'm lucky to have you all too."

Lila zips by. "Thank goodness I missed the love fest," she says, then flips Nika and Alex the bird.

"Watch it," Nika calls after Lila. "Little minds will be

pouring through here at any moment!"

~

The dress rehearsal goes off without a hitch, except for Reggie, who needs to quickly excuse himself from the audience when the lights go up. His pale face worries Nika, and she follows him. He makes it halfway up the hallway, then stops. Thunder roars in Nika's ears. Oh no . . . Reggie vomits all over the tiled floor, but this time Nika's knees and shoes are spared.

Nika calls her dad. "I'm in the hallway. Can you come help me?"

A minute later, Michael joins Reggie and Nika. He carefully takes the boy's hand and leads him to the restroom. Nika washes her hands, calls the office, and places a clean-up request. Then she opens the library and sits in the dark. The call of the books, the smell, the feel of them. This space. Her space. She sits for a few more minutes, allowing her thoughts to stay there, in the room, refusing to let Cole or Blakely or Mindy or anything else intrude. Then Dad leans in, raising his eyebrows as if to ask if he can enter. Nika waves him in, and then Alex, Lila, and Ethan enter. They all take a seat silently, and Nika looks at each one. A warmth spreads throughout her body. Light and love and laughter and everything she's ever needed all in one spot.

Nika pulls out her phone and opens the text app, keying in a message to Susan: *Just wanted to say thank you. I'll see you in two weeks, and I wanted you to hear it before then. So, thank you. I still have work to do, but I'm on my way.*

Exterior: Emporio Acapulco Hotel, Acapulco, Mexico,
Sometime in the Future

NIKA and ETHAN lounge by the pool on chairs while
LILA, ALEX, and GRANDPA play catch in the shallow
end. RAINEY and DETECTIVE BRINE sit at the in-pool
bar, her foot wrapped around his calf.

NIKA
What are you thinking about?

ETHAN
How lucky I am.

NIKA
We are lucky, aren't we? And how is it Rainey and
Bennett are here with us? Life is odd sometimes,
you know? But Rainey looks happy. I hope she is.

ETHAN
Agreed. You know what else I'm thinking?

NIKA
That you'll love me forever?

ETHAN
(smiling)
That I'll love you *and* the kids forever. That I'm so
glad we took this vacation. That I'm grateful, for
everything. That I'm glad we're communicating,
even if I don't always like what you have to say.

NIKA
(frowning)

You mean like when I don't feel like having sex?

ETHAN
(laughing)
Yeah, and some other things.

NIKA
(smiling)
Would now be a good time to say I'm feeling like I
need a nap?

ETHAN
(eyes widening)
Is that a euphemism?

NIKA
Why don't we go find out?

THE END

author's note

I still remember the day my mom bled through her summer shorts onto the plastic outdoor chair while sitting at my friend's house. Mom was in her late forties then, most likely amid "the change," and instead of talking to her daughters about it, she went home, cleaned up, and didn't address the incident again. I don't fault her—especially after learning how Mom was raised—but the image of that crimson stain is what surfaced anytime I thought of menopause.

Now that "the change" is knocking on *my* door, I know better what it's about. That knowledge is mostly due to my education as a physiologist and my curiosity to know more about my own body. Society has made some progress in talking about menopause and what it means, but we still have a long way to go.

What I know is that while immense and irregular bleeding can occur (and they have to this author), those are the least of *my* worries. Like Nika, I've experienced slowed metabolism and bowels, tanked libido, vaginal dryness, mood changes, fatigue, dry skin, and loss of skin elasticity, just to name a few. That means my clothes fit differently, I go to bed earlier than normal, and I'm angry for no particular reason, not to mention that my sagging breasts have *literally* hit a new low. Recently, a man said to me that "men, too, deal with things like menopause." It took all my energy not to extend my hand to his face and slap it—and I'm not the violent type.

Many of us are going through "the change" every day, and just like it takes a village to write a book and raise children, I think it takes a village to help menstruating people traverse menopause. This novel is meant to educate and entertain, and even if Nika's entire experience doesn't resonate with the reader—that's okay. Perhaps it will help readers communicate more openly with people in their lives, and maybe it will help some find the courage to schedule that appointment with a therapist they've been putting off.

I also want readers to understand that sex *can* be fun, and it *can* be important to a relationship, but it doesn't have to be. Nika wanted to want intimacy, and that's *her* story. If that's not your story, don't sweat it. Relationships aren't one size fits all!

Finally, it's important to note that Nika is weighed down by more than just the everyday grind of life. She reacts to society's viewpoints and constructs regarding women and minorities, and she's frustrated by the patriarchal nature of those viewpoints and constructs. While she comes to understand her body and mind, she also finds her voice, and Nika in the here and now will speak up for what she believes in and for those who might not be able to.

The late—and great—Supreme Court Justice Ruth Bader Ginsburg once said, "Real change, enduring change, happens one step at a time." Nika takes that first step in *The Marriage Debt*. I consider writing and publishing this novel a step that I'm taking. Find the courage to take your own steps. We'll be here to support you.

acknowledgments

Taking anyone for granted is never my intention, so I apologize up front if I forget to thank someone who had even a pinky toe in this book. My plan is to spill the names of everyone who helped bring this book to life and pledge undying gratitude to them. So, here it goes.

The Plot Sisters—Cindy Cremeans, Jen Messaros, Ruthann Kain, Traci Ison Shafer, and Jude Walsh—read pages of the manuscript, gave unabashed feedback, and supported this endeavor wholeheartedly. The Cute City Bitches—Meredith Doench, Erin Flanagan, Katrina Kittle, and Sharon Short—provided forward momentum, encouragement and support, and numerous writing dates. Two super readers and talented creatives, Erin Flanagan and Ruthann Kain, helped me restructure the book (which it *so* needed) and provided a keen eye about too many things to mention, respectively.

Many folks talked to me about their experiences with perimenopause and menopause, both firsthand and secondhand, including many details my mother would have deemed "earthy" or "inappropriate," all of which helped shape Nika's experience and perspective.

My sisters, Gina Consolino-Barsotti and Tara Consolino, also shared their experiences with "the change" and genuinely support my writing. My aunts—Linda Serafini, Jean Conrad, and Sandy Mueller—provide more than they know with their enthusiasm for my writing. My dad, Anthony, despite being in the throes of vascular dementia, *always* remembers to ask about my projects and how they are going.

The idea for this book emerged long before Kirsten Miller's *The Change*—a phenomenal book about three menopausal women who come together and make a difference—but her (very different from mine) work prompted me to keep going with my drafts. I'd like to think that Nika would get along spectacularly with Harriet, Jo, and Nessa.

Almost five years ago now, I was lucky to be included in a virtual debut group, and there, I "met" numerous helpful, talented, and supportive people. There are too many to include here, but please know that every one of them is in my heart.

Kim Wilson of Kiwi Cover Design Co. and Sarah Kil of Sarah Kil Creative Studio knocked the cover out of the park, and Diane Windsor of Motina Books has shown interest and enthusiasm for this project from the start, which made all the difference!

In my dedication, I mention two librarian friends, Kelsey Madges and Jane Miller. They are strong, intelligent, thoughtful women I am so honored to know and learn from. Let me tell you—if you have a question about *anything*, go ask a librarian. The world is a better place with librarians in it, especially these two. A huge thanks to all librarians!

My children—Zoe, Talia, Aaron, and Melina—have more confidence in me than I do and more confidence in themselves than I ever had at their ages. Maybe I did something right! Much love and gratitude to these four who bring me so much joy!

I also dedicate this book to Timmy. Ethan is not Timmy, and Timmy is not Ethan, so readers, please do not look for him on the street and ask him about his chaps (though, he'd probably be up for wearing them if I asked). Choosing him decades ago was one of the best decisions I've ever made. I love you.

about the author

Christina Consolino is a scientist turned freelance editor and teacher who writes fiction about Midwest families like yours. She is coauthor of *Historic Photos of University of Michigan*, author of *Rewrite the Stars* and *The Weight We Carry*, and she writes romance under the pen name Keely Stephens. She's a big believer in perseverance and will be the first to say, "If I can do this, you can too."

Learn more at www.christinaconsolino.com.